STIX & STONE

ALPHA'S REJECTS - BOOK ONE

COURTNEY W. DIXON

This is a work of fiction. Names, characters, organizations, places, events, and incidents are either products of the author's imagination or are used fictitiously.

Published by Courtney W. Dixon

Book Cover Design by Courtney W. Dixon

Alpha Readers: Nicole Arbuckle

Beta Readers: Joelle Lynne, Kalie Gerwig, Nikki Johnson, Rosa Donahue, Lia McKnight

Proofreader: Anna Potter

Preface

Welcome to Stix & Stone, book one from Alpha's Rejects. My inspiration for my skater boys came from a Red Hot Chili Peppers' music video for Dark Necessities. The video featured skater girls, and at the time I was planning this series at the beginning of 2022, I was still writing MF romances. Initially, I intended this story to be about skater girls, but I'm so happy I switched to MM. I love Stix & Stone despite all the grief they gave me as I wrote this book.

We find our Rejects struggling to make ends meet and finding a sort of family among friends at Alpha's Rejects, a bar that supports the queer community. All these young adults had been rejected in one form or another and found their way to Kingston McLaren, or Alpha, as they call him.

The premise of this story completely changed from my original plan. Meaning, it did a one-eighty on me. I had to scratch everything I had planned and outline it all over again. The characters had refused to work out as intended. But I like the way they turned out so much more, and I hope you do, too. They're not always the smartest bunch and tend to do stupid things now and then, but I love them in all their glorious faults.

As you read this, I hope you don't go into this expecting typical enemies to lovers. This is mainly a one-sided hate. There is some bullying, but it's also not typical. And I do not address the reason for Stone's hatred toward Stix right off the bat. Sure, he complains and bitches about petty things, but it's much more deeply rooted than that. His reasons are addressed after several chapters. Also, do not expect hate sex. As much as I enjoy reading it, it won't work for Stix and Stone.

This is a slow burn only in the context that we don't see much happen sexually until about halfway. If that is something you don't like, you may find this book annoying, but I hope I have created enough sexual tension between the two before things get steamy. Stone is a demisexual, so I didn't want to rush the sex.

I've written a demisexual before writing A Home in You, but Stone is a bit different than Dillon, and you'll find out why as you read. I spent quite a bit of time reading about Demisexuals and their relationships, especially regarding sex, in their own words, from how aroused they can get or even kinky, as long as it's with that one special person in their lives. So, I hope I did them justice.

Thank you for taking the time to read Stix & Stone. I hope you enjoy it as much as they gave me grief, which is saying a lot.

Happy reading!
Courtney

Triggers

LISTED BELOW ARE THE trigger warnings for this book. Reading them may cause spoilers.

Abuse of a child (there is a graphic depiction in the form of a flashback), PTSD, internalized homophobia, prostitution, drug use, underage drinking, poverty, homophobia, physical assault, bullying, mental health issues, self-loathing, suicidal ideations, explicit language, and sex.

Due to the nature of these triggers, this book is not suitable for those under 18.

Also By Courtney W. Dixon

Kings of Boston

In Silence

In Retribution

In Strength

In Redemption

In Preservation

In Vindication

Ohana Surfing Club

Impact Zone

Pura Vida

Double Up

No Man's Land

Knights of Boston

The Healer

The Boxer

The District

His Death Bringer

Alpha's Rejects

Stix & Stone

Standalone Novels

A Home in You

Standalone Novelas

Trapped for the Holidays
The Candidate's Obsession

Anthologies/Collaborations

Once Upon a Halloween Night

Stix & Stone Playlist

https://sptfy.com/StixStone

CHAPTER 1
Stone

No one had ever accused me of being nice or kind. I wasn't a bad person per se, but I simply didn't have it in me to just be a regular guy who smiled easily or made friends with little effort. The couple of friends who put up with my ass didn't call me 'Stone' for nothing, though that wasn't what my parents had named me. The word played on my last name, or so my friends said, meaning it rhymed. It was a stupid fucking name, but I embraced it because it helped me forget where I came from and my life before this one, as if severing my name severed me from my family. *Family*. What a joke. My birth name was Damien Sloan, but

I'd just as soon forget I had ever been born to the monsters who called themselves my parents.

I used to be Damien, trailer trash and abused child. Now I was simply Stone. Introverted, self-reliant, and hardworking.

Abuse, drug addiction, and prison tend to leave you bitter and resentful. While you're a child with no way out, not knowing when you'll be fed, hit, loved, or hated is suffocating, leaving you confused about who you are or what you want out of life. Ambitions are snuffed out with a slap to the face. And you're afraid to ask for anything from that fear, surviving day to day, not knowing if tomorrow will be your last day on this sorry planet. Always wondering when that pivotal moment would happen that pushed your parents over the edge to finally kill you.

My only reprieve from pain was I finally got the balls to leave my mother behind after the police arrested my father. I moved as far away as the money I had saved allowed, which landed me in Baltimore, Maryland, from Fredericksburg, Virginia. I didn't run too far, but it was far enough away so my drugged-out parents wouldn't find me, not that they'd bother. It would take too much effort and money to leave their piece-of-shit trailer.

Baltimore was a cesspool, littered with crime, but it was a hundred fucking times better than where I came from. This grungy city became my salvation in a way. I left shortly after eighteen after my father got sent to prison for drug dealing fentanyl to a minor, a girl of seventeen, who nearly died after overdosing. He got ten years and has already served half of that. What mattered most was that I left them far behind. They became my past, while Baltimore became my future. Some future. It wasn't a future where you looked toward the horizon with hopes and dreams. Seeing the possibilities of where life took you. No, my future was just surviving. Nothing more. Nothing less.

Whatever. I didn't have time to be friendly and sit there with a smile on my face, fucking pretending all was right in this piece of shit world. Simply existing was already an exhaustive effort, but I kept doing it for some reason. Something kept pushing me forward to keep on breathing, even though I had nothing worthwhile to look forward to other than being away from pain. Sometimes that was enough. Sometimes I suffocated for more, knowing I'd never get it.

I sat on the fire escape outside my window from my dump of an apartment, smoking a cigarette before heading to work. The building stood alone, which was a perfect metaphor for my life. It had been a part of row houses once upon a time before the city had them condemned and demolished. Now, only concrete and weeds surrounded our lonely building that people use as a parking lot or the homeless used to camp out nearby. It was as abandoned as I was. I shared the place with the only two people I gave a shit about, and even that was questionable.

My tatted arm rested over my bent knee while I stretched out my other leg as I watched the bane of my existence do the same thing from two apartments over on the same floor.

It was early morning in late September, with a chill in the air as people woke up for the day, getting ready for work. You could almost smell fall approaching over the scents of the city. It was distinct as if you could actually smell cold. The sun had yet to rise, so I doubted the dude sitting across from me saw my glaring and loathing, but he sensed me there and understood enough about me that I'd never smile back at him. He saw me in the darkness the same way I saw him, mostly using our senses rather than our eyes.

Even if I couldn't pick out his features or see his facial expression, I felt him, always knowing when he was around or not, and I fucking hated it. My body thrummed with a strange sort of electricity whenever he was near. It made no sense, and I didn't understand it. Not one bit, making me twitchy as fuck whenever I was around him. I hated all this confusion. It disrupted my orderly life.

He knew damn well how I felt about him, too. I said nothing outright, but it was all in my reaction to his presence. Even worse, he always wore a smirk I wanted to punch off his face, which wasn't terrible to look at, making me hate him even more for even thinking about violent urges or pretty faces with soulful, dark eyes.

Those urges of violence reminded me I was my father's son. Both of my parents beat me, but I got it worse from Dad. I fought every day not to turn into him. No drugs. No violence. Even drinking alcohol, I kept to a minimum and never got drunk. But that was another reason to loathe the guy across from me. He brought out this anger in me that I struggled to explain. Things I desperately tried to keep under control. I fucking despised strong emotions. Strong emotions pulled out urges from me that scared me, especially when I didn't understand them. Typically, I was calm and cold. Cold as stone. But whenever he was near, I was the fire. A simmering volcano, ready to explode. Especially when he smirked my way like an asshole, intentionally pushing my buttons.

Both of us took a drag off our cigarettes, watching the ember glowing brightly, barely whispering the appearance on his darkened face. Our smoke mingled with the morning traffic and still air. The only thing that stood out about him was his bleached hair, shining like a neon sign in the morning darkness. I couldn't tell from here if he stared back at me, but I knew for a fact he wouldn't be filled with the same sort of animosity I stabbed his way. Or maybe he did and used his smart-ass taunts to hide his disdain. I wasn't a likable person. Not like him. Everyone fucking loved Nico 'Stix' Jamieson, from his family to his friends.

Not only was I forced to be his neighbor in this hellhole, but I recently took an extra job and now had to work with him in the evenings on the weekend as a bouncer at the bar known as Alpha's Rejects. Both of my jobs sucked, but beggars couldn't be choosers, especially for someone who barely graduated from high school with limited work experience other than working dead-end jobs for the past five years. Yet it was still a goddamn wonderland compared to my past home life.

Even worse than having to work with Stix was having to listen to him day in and day out with those fucking drumsticks of his, tapping and dinging on anything to make drumming sounds, giving me a goddamn headache. Hence, his stupid nickname. And he couldn't even spell it right. Or maybe he thought it was cool, being as ironic as his irritating graphic T-shirts.

As my cigarette burned down to the filter, I watched him flick his smoke down to the sidewalk below and stand on the precarious grate that was our shared fire escape and just stood there. I couldn't see his face, but he was staring directly at me, and, no doubt, wore a smug smirk as usual.

"Have a great day, Rolling Stone. See you tonight at work."

I flipped him off as he chuckled and climbed back into his apartment through the window. I swear to fucking god; he taunted me on purpose because no one was that fucking nice. No one. That had to be sarcasm that had rolled off his tongue. Not that I was any good at picking up on social cues.

To make my hatred for him grow, much of my animosity stemmed from jealousy. I was smart enough to admit that. He always had an easy smile on his face. How? Life fucking sucked. Admittedly, he seemed to have a good home life with a loving mother who wasn't a drugged-out loser and a little five-year-old sister who always tried talking to me whenever I saw her. He worked almost every night at the bar, and I heard sometimes he'd sit in for a band that was playing for the night and thump on the drums, but I'd yet to watch him play. I had my doubts about his abilities, being the annoying fuck he was.

Despite his family's struggles, they were happy and took care of each other. But if life taught me anything, it was that no one was that happy or that good. It was a statistical improbability. I didn't trust overly happy people as much as I didn't trust the hateful ones, but at least with hateful people, you knew exactly where you stood. And I'd never come across a kindness that hadn't been seeped in ulterior motives, like when my mother cried after one of her binges and woke up to me bruised and broken. She wept her lies about how horrible she felt, only to beat me again two nights later.

Fine, I was a bitter fuck, but why bother to change? Nothing good ever came out of my efforts to improve my life. I always fell back into struggles and hardships. For five years, I floated through life. Life was lonely as hell and all about putting one foot in front of the other and doing what I could to survive it. Then, one day, it would all finally be over. The only thing that gave me any sort of joy was getting a new tattoo whenever I had the money, or doing tricks on my skateboard.

I flicked my cigarette down the four-story drop onto the sidewalk and climbed through the living room window. My roommates, Blaze and Cueball, were still asleep, not having to work until later.

Inside, I pulled on my worn black Chucks and tossed on my black hoodie. After I shoved on my gray beanie, I grabbed my Powell-Peralta skateboard, my baby, which took me months to save for. It was my only mode of transportation besides the bus and subway, but I didn't live too far from Harborplace, where I worked as a fish cutter during the week. It was stinky work, but it paid eighteen bucks an hour, and I got basic health insurance and some sick days out of it, too.

Once I stepped outside, I dropped my board and took off down the street, weaving in and out of the growing morning traffic. I had to be at work in twenty minutes, so there was no time for tricks. I just pushed on my board to keep up the speed. With five minutes to spare, I reached Sal's Fish Market and rushed inside, hit with the scent of salt water, old fish, and bleach. I clocked in, threw my crap into my locker, and then tossed on a thick apron over my hoodie and went to my station, where I fileted assorted fish to be sold to local restaurants around the harbor and at the market for the general public.

I'd been doing this for eight months now, and it was the longest job I'd ever held. It was disgusting, and it smelled, but for some reason, quickly slicing through fish was mind-numbing work and precisely what I needed for my troubled thoughts. It was one of the few times throughout the day when I wasn't drowning in my past or pain.

Even better, it was a job that I didn't have to fucking chit-chat. Sure, the staff talked amongst themselves, but they knew I'd ignore them if they spoke to me. Small talk made my brain itch. They were mostly just focused on their fish, trying to produce as much as possible. If we reached a certain amount of fish to gut and cut per week, we got a bonus at the end of the month, so I learned quickly. That bonus allowed me to get my skateboard a couple of months ago. I guess I could've saved up for a car, but I never went anywhere, anyway, so anything extra went toward a tattoo once in a while.

I wrapped up my eight-hour shift by three o'clock, with a fifteen-minute break to eat my sandwich and smoke a cigarette. My lower back ached, and my hands were cold and raw, making me feel older than my twenty-three years. A couple of fingers were also bleeding from nicking them with the knife, but I was used to it.

After clocking out, I returned to an empty apartment with my roommates at work and took a long shower, washing off the stink from the day. The warmth from the cascading water blanketed me, soothing away the day's aches and pains. I quickly dried off and tossed on a pair of sweats without a shirt, and climbed into bed to sleep for the next five hours before I headed to my second job. Tucking my arm under my head, wishing I had a thicker pillow, I stared at the ugly popcorn ceiling and willed my mind to shut down through the yelling couple across the hall and a baby wailing from somewhere. But I was used to the urban din and the too-thin walls of apartment living.

I bolted upright with my heart pounding and my body covered in a sheen of sweat, trying to find my phone on my bed to shut off the blaring alarm clock, which mingled with the police sirens outside, driving through almost daily and sometimes more. I hadn't realized I'd fallen asleep earlier.

"Fuck," I growled, rubbing my tired face, not feeling refreshed at all. It was never enough sleep. Not on the weekends when I needed to work until two in the morning, but at least I had Saturday and Sunday off from the fish market. During the day, Sundays were reserved for skateboarding and hanging out with my bros. Then, on Monday mornings, I'd drag my carcass out of bed and straight to the fish market at the crack of dawn with only a few hours of sleep, taking me most of the day to recuperate before I had to do it all over again.

I threw off the worn blanket and shoved my hand down the back of my sweats to scratch my ass as I dug around a plastic container where I kept my T-shirts. I grabbed a black one to hide any drinks dumped on me for the night, then went to our shared bathroom, quickly brushed my

STIX & STONE PAPERBACK

teeth, and washed my face. When I came out, my numbnut roommates were bitching at each other while playing a video game on our
shared used PlayStation we all chipped in to buy. Well, Blaze did
most of the bitching.

"Fuck you, dickhead! You killed me!" Blaze groused. His name
was Aiden Reeves, but apparently, he proclaimed himself as 'Blaze'
because Aiden wasn't tough enough. I had a feeling it had to do
with his short stature. He was a dickhead, was what he was, but
still a friend. His smile could be downright scary, but I sometimes
wondered if it was just an act like he had some Napoleonic complex
to keep people from hurting him.

He grabbed the game controller from Cueball with ringed fingers covered in tattoos and holding a cigarette. "Now, I gotta get my
shit back, man." He shoved back his long dark bangs from his face
and tried to play before Marco, also known as 'Cueball,' reached for
the controller, but Blaze kept it away from him with one hand and
held Cueball back with the other.

"No smoking in the apartment, asswipe," I said. I enjoyed smoking, but this hellhole smelled bad enough without adding smoke into
the mix. "Take it outside."

"Whatever..." He didn't like it, but he dumped the cigarette into
his beer can as he continued to shove our friend back.

"Dude..." was all Cueball said, rarely one to talk much.

"It's my fucking turn, asshole. Now I gotta find my shit, and you
better hope some other online player didn't steal it."

My two roommates were polar opposites. Cueball was a massive
six-foot-five-inch behemoth with a shaved head, hence his nickname,
whereas Blaze was only five feet five inches, but that didn't stop him
from being a fucking alpha gremlin.

I'd met the two idiots at the skate park last year, and they insisted on being friends, if you could call us that. All we did was bitch at each other. And I never got in the middle of a video game fight. About three months ago, this place came up for rent, and we all moved in together. It had two bedrooms at least, while Cueball slept on the couch since he paid the least.

"Yo, I'm outta here," I said as I shrugged on my worn black bomber jacket and grabbed my board.

They both turned to look over the back of the beat-up sofa. "See ya tonight, right?" Blaze asked.

"Sure."

I locked the apartment behind me, and as soon as I stepped out into the dimly lit hallway, wouldn't you know it? Fucking Stix was coming out of our neighbor's apartment with a hand down the front of his jeans, adjusting his dick without a care in the world.

What the hell?

My own dick fluttered to life, watching him, and I shut that shit right off, cupping it to calm it the hell down. My dick had no business reacting to him. It wasn't the first time it had happened, making me resent him that much more. It should always be flaccid with thoughts of him. And not only because he was Stix, the one I loathed, but because he was a dude.

He fingered his bleached floppy hair away from his face, which fell longer in the back and front and short on the sides, looking choppy like he cut it himself. With the hair temporarily out of his face, it looked younger and smoother and... fuck. As he walked away, he didn't turn to look back at the man he'd just left.

Our neighbor, Brian Ledger, was a thirty-six-year-old gay man who flirted with everyone. He liked to call himself Brie as if he was a fucking piece of fancy cheese. He was a flashy gay, constantly fanning himself with a fancy fan like some lady from a hundred years ago.

I tucked myself against the wall in the shadows where a bulb had burned out, hoping neither of them would see me as I watched Brie lean against the doorway, fanning himself though it felt cool in here and wearing some silky robe over his boxer briefs. His eyes scanned every movement Stix made as he walked back into his apartment.

Now, knowing that Stix was probably gay or something did nothing to improve my view of him. If anything, it made it worse, which confused me even more because I should've known since Alpha's Rejects was staffed with mostly people from the LGBTQIA+ community. It wasn't quite a gay bar since they welcomed everyone, but it was a safe place for queers. I didn't know why learning this about Stix pissed me off so much. It wasn't like he did anything particular to me besides being a taunting dickhead. There was just something fucking about him that ticked off all the wrong boxes in my messed up head. It had to be messed up because no one made me react like I did when Stix was near.

Maybe it was that he'd probably just fucked Brie, which sent waves of rage through me, boiling my blood. Mr. Goody Good Boy, sleeping with the local flirt, had my hands fisted until my knuckles turned white, and my fingernails dug into my calloused palm. I relished in the stinging pain to pull me away from the scene.

I had to get out of there before I snapped my board in half in my other hand. That was when Brie saw me standing in the dark corner of the hall like a creepy stalker, but instead of going inside, he ignored the anger emitting from my body, which was my perpetual mask, and wiggled his fingers at me.

"Hello, cutie Stone. Off to work?"

I grunted and stormed down four flights of steps, ignoring his cackling.

Fucking asshole.

CHAPTER 2
Stix

"SEE YOU NEXT WEEK, same time?" Brie asked, fingering his thick, sandy brown hair away from his face, then tossing on a floral silk robe. He was a good-looking dude who could be sweet but was annoying sometimes. His screeches and moans as I screwed him grated on my ears and head, especially after listening to it for over a year. I only put up with it for the money, and he liked my work, which put food on the table. Maybe if I had someone special in my life, I'd actually enjoy those sounds, knowing how much pleasure I gave my partner. But Brie wasn't my partner. He was a paycheck.

"You got it," I said, trying to be more upbeat than I felt as I shoved my dick back into my underwear and pants before zipping up. It wasn't like I was some professional prostitute. I mostly did blow jobs on the side for fifty bucks a pop. But Brie paid a hundred and fifty for me to fuck him each week. The money helped a lot, while I made Mom believe I had a day job to contribute.

He shoved the cash into my hands and gave me two air kisses since I refused to kiss him outright—or anyone, for that matter. Way too fucking intimate, and I also didn't fuck facing him, only from behind. That was one of the rules. Watching someone's face in ecstasy because of me, someone I didn't care about, left me dead inside. I just couldn't do it.

I made a lot of rules because this job sucked, pun intended, and I didn't want to catch shit and get sick. I had enough health problems. The biggest rule was that condoms always needed to be used, even for blowjobs. I won't swallow your fucking cum, no matter how much you pay me.

I kind of fell into this job spontaneously. When I finally got the balls to come out as gay at nineteen, three years ago, despite me always knowing it, Dad walked fucking out, confirming my fears. God, his face when he looked at me was so full of disappointment. I'd never forget it.

He left Mom, my little sis, and me behind with absolutely nothing. And Mom hadn't seen a dime of child support for my sister. She didn't have the time or money to fight it, so she gave up and did the best she could. Eventually, she said it was easier just to simply forget he ever existed.

The guilt still sat heavily, perpetually weighing me down. We suffered because I had insisted on him accepting me the way I was. At least

Mom loved me, no matter what. Now, I did what I could to help with income and take care of my little sis.

My neighbor, Brian, or Brie, as he liked to be called, always flirted with me. To be fair, he flirted with everyone, so I didn't take it all that seriously or like I was anyone special. Whenever I saw him, he'd run his fingers through my bleached hair and tell me how pretty I was, then ask if I wanted to come up to his place for some fun. While that would've bothered most people, since it wasn't exactly appropriate, it had given me an idea. And just like that, my prostitution job was born when I told him on a whim that I only fucked for money. We'd been doing this weekly for over a year. I had no idea where he got the money to pay for it, and I didn't fucking ask or care.

Eventually, I branched out, trading favors for blow jobs when I was broke. Like if I needed some milk and bread, among other things, from the store, I'd suck the store manager's dick. I doubted they were all gay or bi, but I guess a mouth was a mouth. Word soon spread to where I had enough clients to keep a steady flow of cash coming in.

Mostly, I did this for my five-year-old sister, Nova. She didn't need to suffer because of me. Mom didn't make nearly enough money as a waitress at a 24/7 diner where she worked. And because I had an evening job, and sometimes she worked nights, we needed someone to watch Nova.

My little sister had been a complete surprise when Mom got pregnant with her. For seventeen years, it had only been me and my parents. Then came along little Nova. I fell in love with her on the day she was born and stepped in to be the best big bro possible.

But it wasn't only about her and the guilt. I'd been saving for medication for the autoimmune arthritic disease I was born with. While a careful diet and exercise helped, I still got flare-ups that left me incapacitated or nearly blinded by pain in my eyes. It didn't happen often, but it happened enough to affect my quality of life, especially since each flare-up left behind damage to my bones and vision. The injections were expensive as hell when you didn't have health insurance, but they'd really help with keeping the pain under control. Maybe one day.

Despite that, I probably would've left already to live on my own were it not for the guilt and the need to help out. I couldn't abandon them. So, we all crammed into the two-bedroom apartment, where I shared a room with my little sis. It wasn't exactly convenient if I wanted a boyfriend, but I dealt with it. Not that I had any boyfriends. If I did, though, they'd have to be *really* cool with what I did for a living.

But my biggest dream was signing on with a band as a drummer. I was self-taught, but I didn't think I was too bad. Sometimes, the bands at Alpha's Rejects, where I worked at night, would let me hit some beats. It was the only real practice I got since I didn't own a set of drums, using objects to make my music with my worn drumsticks. Another thing on my bucket list was a set of drums—too many dreams and not enough fucking green.

I readjusted my dick as I walked out of Brie's apartment, feeling his eyes burning on my back. He wanted more from me than a quick fuck, but I wasn't interested. He was my money-maker and fourteen years older. No thanks. Besides, he was too fem for me. Nothing was wrong with that, but it wasn't my type. I preferred a guy bigger than me who could toss me around like a rag doll and pound the hell out of me. I topped for money, but I'd bottom for love.

My apartment was empty with Mom working and Nova at the sitter's, so I stripped off my clothes and took a quick shower to wash off the Brie sex and get ready for work. As I put on my boxer briefs, Mom texted.

Mom: I'm running ten minutes late. Please get Nova from the sitter before you leave.

Me: yep.

I quickly ran my fingers through my floppy hair, which I bleached over my dark brown hair last year, and stuck with it. Then I put in several earrings and two bigger hoops. Next went the chain chokers around my neck. I tossed on one of my ironic T-shirts in black that I got at Goodwill that said, *'World's Okayist Dad.'* It was my thing.

With one more look in the bathroom mirror, I ran out of the apartment, locked it up, and headed to the first floor to grab the munchkin. As I walked down the stairs, I taped the metal railing with my drumsticks, forming a rhythm that played only in my head. The sound echoed through the stairwell as a real song evolved, and the beat made more sense.

Sounds of a cartoon echoed into the hall from the apartment as I knocked on Mrs. Gordon's door. An older woman of about seventy and five-foot-nothing answered. Her gray hair was cut into a pixie, and she was the nicest lady ever, watching over Nova whenever we needed her for cheap, using the babysitting money as supplemental income. It was even better that we trusted her.

"Well, hello, Nico. Come on in. We just finished a snack, and she's watching TV."

"Was she good today?"

"She's always good."

And she was. Nova was the sweetest kid I'd ever known. But I could be biased.

I pressed my finger to my mouth so Mrs. Gordon didn't let her know I was there yet, and I snuck into the living room, seeing Nova sitting cross-legged in front of the ancient television, watching a recording of Sesame Street.

Her brown hair was in long pigtails but was a mess, and the tails were lopsided. I squatted behind her and snuffled her neck, making her squeal and giggle. "Gotcha!" I said.

"Nicky!"

We both stood, and I lifted her in my arms.

"Were you a good girl for Mrs. Gordon?"

"Yes! I learned to make mac and cheese today. I got to stir in the cheese."

"You did? Well, aren't you a little chef?"

She nodded with a massive smile on her face, and her dark brown eyes that matched mine were wide as she played with one of my dangling earrings.

"You ready to go, munchkin?"

She nodded and suddenly yawned.

"Say goodbye to Mrs. Gordon."

"Bye, Mrs. Gordon."

"Bye-bye, dear. See you tomorrow."

I carried Nova on my hip up four flights of stairs, feeling a twinge in my back from her weight and walking up so many steps. By the time I got her settled, Mom walked in looking harried, carrying a bag of groceries, and still wearing her work uniform.

Her brown hair sat on top of her head in a messy bun. She had me at seventeen, so she was still young and pretty. I wish she'd find herself a boyfriend or something. She deserved some love and attention. But she'd always brush me off when I suggested it, saying no one wanted a waitress with two kids. What did I know? I had never had a boyfriend before. I've had guys who didn't have to pay me, but we never had anything genuine or lasting.

"Sorry, I'm late. I had a straggling customer and couldn't leave."

"It all worked out. Gotta go before I'm late, though."

She waved me bye as I kissed the top of Nova's head. I grabbed my worn skateboard, trying not to wish I could afford a better one. Well, I could, but I needed that money for more important things. I tossed on my army jacket I bought at a thrift store, and while it wasn't the warmest, it was enough until winter hit hard.

Alpha's Rejects was a bar owned by Kingston McLaren, who was only twenty-eight and fucking young to own a successful bar. But it had been going strong for two years, filling the house with good live rock music, supporting local bands, serving delicious beer, and having a welcoming environment.

He sort of adopted most of his staff before even opening the place, including me. Not in the legal sense, but he took us under his wing and helped us through hard times while giving us work, kind of like a mentor. It kept us off the streets with the goal of staying away from drugs and crime. That was the deal. If he found out you did drugs, you either went to rehab or were out of the group. And none of us wanted either.

Because he was a natural leader and charismatic, we called him Alpha, and that was how he came up with the name for the bar. And we became his rejects because we all had been rejected in some form.

There were seven of us in our crew, including Alpha and me, and we all skated. We lived and breathed skateboarding whenever we could. We had all met Alpha at the skatepark a few years ago. He was one of the best skaters around, even winning some competitions, and we stood in awe, instantly gravitating to him and getting guidance.

The day I met him had changed my life. I'd been drowning in guilt and alcohol after my father walked out on us, filled with disgust and self-loathing. I'd barely been able to skate, and I kept falling or crashing into other skaters, pissing them off because I drank more than half a bottle of whiskey Dad left behind. My last bail off the board had Alpha picking my sorry ass off the ground and taking me to get something to eat as he forced me to talk about what the fuck my deal was.

And I told him, despite vowing to myself that I'd never come back out of the closet again. It was like breathing again, sitting across from this tall, tattooed blond man with the kindest blue eyes. They were so blue they looked almost a turquoise color. After I told him my pathetic story, he opened up, telling me he was gay, too. His parents kicked him out of the house, and he lived on the streets for a while before getting his shit together. My story suddenly didn't seem so bad. At least I still had a mother who loved me.

Still, I missed my father, even to this day. We had been so close and talked about everything. I thought coming out would've been easy. But the hurt, disappointment, and anger in his eyes showed he put conditions on his love.

Soon, some other kids and I all grew to be friends. Whenever we weren't working, we spent it hanging out and skating, and we were all queer one way or another. We were like some motley crew queer skater gang. And they quickly became my second family. Who knew where I'd be without their support and love?

The bar hadn't opened yet when I walked in and waved to Alpha, who was drying glasses behind the bar, getting ready for the evening. The band was setting up on the small stage, and I pined at the drum set, wishing I could play tonight. My fingers tingled and itched to pull out my sticks poking out of my back jeans pocket, but I had to keep that shit under wraps while I worked. I knew the band members, so maybe I'd get lucky tonight.

Before I reached the backroom to dump my stuff, one of my friends, Jaxon Kean, hefted me out of nowhere and tossed me over his massive shoulder, laughing like a loon.

"Ajax! Put me the fuck down! Just because I'm smaller than you doesn't mean you get to manhandle me! And I don't even get sex out of it."

He snorted a laugh and dragged my struggling body around the bar, whooping and completely ignoring me. "Look at what I caught! A scrawny little chicken!"

My face burned, hating when he did this, and he knew it. "I'm not a fucking toddler!" I wasn't that short, but I wasn't all buff, either. There was plenty of muscle, but it was all lean. Fine, it was on the skinnier side.

"Put him down, Ajax, and let Stix get to work."

"You're no fun, Alpha," he grumbled, putting me down anyway.

I scowled at him and nearly punched him for it, but no one messed with Ajax like that. He wasn't all there sometimes, and it took little to set him off. His moods were always hot and cold. Despite that, Ajax was the closest to me between all seven of us. He was no one's best friend, but we got along pretty well until he did dumb shit like that.

His dark, floppy bangs fell in his face as he air-kissed me. I rolled my eyes and flipped him off as I walked back to shove my shit into a locker.

As soon as I walked into the small employee lounge, I stopped in my tracks, seeing fucking Stone with his back turned as he hung up his bomber jacket in one of the lockers.

He recently started working at Alpha's as a bouncer, but he wasn't family. Not yet, anyway. And how could he be when he hated my guts? I had no idea what the fuck I did to him to set him off, but he made it abundantly clear he didn't put up with my ass. And to deflect from the strange hurt over it, I made it my life's mission to goad him, itching to set off his cool vibe and break his carefully constructed walls, brick by brick. Though his aura color was rage, he held it all in check, never quite lashing out, but you could tell it was all held together by a single thread. That didn't stop him from being a dick to me sometimes, although I could admit a lot of it was my doing since I enjoyed pushing his buttons so much. It was either that or cower. And I never cowered to bullies. I couldn't help myself. It was like he begged me to do it, and I couldn't stop it if I tried, like those big, red, shiny buttons that just called you to push them.

He slammed the metal locker door too hard, making my heart jump, and rubbed a hand over his short-cropped dark brown hair. It wasn't quite buzzed, but it was close. His six-foot-two frame was broad, putting him four inches taller than me. And he was all fucking muscle. I tried not to be curious about his tats peeking out from his long T-shirt sleeves, which he had pulled up over his deliciously muscular forearms.

When he turned around, he also stopped in his tracks as his hazel eyes flecked with gold narrowed and bore into mine. His full lips sneered as he chewed on a toothpick, looking like he was ready to rumble. God, how could someone be so intense and scary, yet sexy at the same time? And while he had the prettiest eyes I'd ever seen with thick, black lashes under thick brows, the clef in his chin always sucked me in. I wanted to lick it. Don't ask. And, of course, he had the perfect amount of scruff over his chiseled fucking jaw. Why did he have to look so fucking perfect on the outside and be so rotten on the inside? Assholes like him had no right to look so hot. And he was exactly my type in the looks department.

"Hey! If it's not my little angry pet rock. Looking adorably scowly as always, Rolling Stone," I said, walking into the room and shoving my jacket and board into the locker with a nonchalance I didn't feel. Honestly, he scared me a little, but I couldn't let him see my weakness. The last thing I needed was to look like prey more than I already did. I wasn't nearly as tough as my friends. They'd been through a hell of a lot more than I had.

"Fuck off," he hissed.

I turned to face him and winked. "You know, I'd really love to, but you'd need to be into dudes. Although, you got the perfect amount of growl, so I might be willing to negotiate."

He rushed at me, and I may have seen my life flash before my eyes and stood toe-to-toe with me while my heart threatened to leap right out of my chest. I did everything not to show fear while also trying not to imagine his hand on my throat, squeezing tightly as he pounded into me. Yeah, I was fucked up. I shouldn't want this asshole to fuck me at all, but I couldn't help it. My body knew what it liked.

While I tried not to appear afraid, I also struggled not to reach for him and beg him to take me. Right here. Right now. I bet it'd be hot as hell. He could yank my pants down just enough to expose my ass, flip me around, and shove his cock... Okay, I needed to settle down with that visual before my body betrayed me.

Then again, maybe his type liked to be controlled and fucked. That would be something exciting to see. Bend him to my will. Have him whimper and beg for more of my cock. Only if he liked cock, which I highly doubted. But still, it would be fun. Honestly, I could go either way. I just didn't have a death wish. I liked living. Despite my fears, my dick wiggled, enjoying the idea entirely too much.

"You've got a big fucking mouth," he said, standing so close I could smell whatever body wash he used. It was woodsy but not overwhelming, unlike him. Everything about Stone exuded strength, power, and intensity.

"Some say it even looks nice."

Hey, at least I stayed away from a dick joke that I wanted to lob at him. Before I could give him my smuggest of smirks, I nearly died as my breath caught when he instantly glanced down at my lips. *Gotcha*. But I kept that little tidbit to myself.

When he looked up, I swore his eyes dilated into daggers.

I swallowed hard, and he watched that, too, instantly seeing my weakness. Or was he more interested in me than he let on?

Not good, Nico. You've got enough jacking off fodder from his face. You don't need to get any more ideas.

After staring at me for another couple of seconds to show who dominated here, he crowded into my space even more. Strength and danger exuded from every one of his pores and blanked over me. While I was slightly terrified, I lusted after him, too. It would only take a couple of inches to push forward and claim those full, cherry-red lips of his.

Shit, I really needed to get with the program Stone couldn't stand my guts, and there was no way we'd ever be a thing. Not that I really wanted us to be. He was just fun for the imagination whenever I got some privacy. And now I had more filed away.

CHAPTER 3
Stone

DESPITE STIX'S BIG MOUTH, his large, chocolate-brown eyes flashed in fear. So, he wasn't as immune to me as I first assumed, and I used it to my advantage by standing close enough to inhale him, which was a fucking mistake because he then swallowed. While it coincided with fear, my mind flashed for a quick second of him swallowing my dick. Fuck, that came out of nowhere, and I had to shut that shit down. I wasn't fucking into dudes, but it didn't stop me from scanning him from head to toe. His blond hair was a bit longer in the back and messy, like he intentionally did it that way. He wore too many damned earrings and chains around his neck. And what the fuck was up with that stupid

T-shirt? All his T-shirts were fucking stupid, like he was attempting dry humor and failing miserably. But I didn't terribly hate it either. It worked for him. He wore torn jeans, and I wasn't sure if it was intentional or not, and he had on worn black-and-white checkered Vans, which were probably used. But the whole thing looked good on him. And that right there was a problem. I shouldn't think anything looked good on Stix. The thought had my hands growing clammy and shaky. I folded my arms and tucked my hands under my pits, so he couldn't see my growing fear.

My reaction to him only served to piss me off more, but I kept it in check because I wasn't my fucking parents. He may have pissed me off, and I hated his goddamn guts, but I didn't hurt people. Not physically, anyway. But Stix didn't have to know that.

"What's your fucking problem, Jamieson?"

He schooled his features, then raised a brow. "You're kidding me right now, right? *My* problem? I'm just trying to make you fucking crack a smile through all that concrete in your thick skull, but you're drier than the Sahara."

"Knock it off, asshole."

Stix folded his arms, mimicking me, and smirked, which only had me seething. He did it with so little effort, and I couldn't even begin to explain how he easily triggered me like no one else could. He was a fucking pro at annoying me.

"Hmm, you know, I'd like to, but you make it so easy." I hated how he read me like a fucking book. But I hated it even more that I exposed myself so much to him. To everyone else, I was emotionless. Cold. A rock.

"I'm warning you... Shut the fuck up."

His dark brows slammed down his eyes, such a contrast to his bleached hair. "Or what? This isn't high school, dickhead. We are grown fucking men, so grow the fuck up." He turned his back to me and slammed his locker door, dismissing me.

Fuck that.

"Just leave me the fuck alone, Jamieson."

He turned around and tossed his arms in the air. "Gladly!" Then he stormed out, leaving behind a fresh scent like laundry detergent in his wake. I should've been glad he did as he was told, but I wasn't. Fuck, he confused the hell out of me.

I rubbed my hands over my face and growled. Why did I let him get to me like that? They called me Stone for a reason. Instead, he broke down all my carefully constructed walls just by being near me. All he had to do was utter one quip, and I wanted to throttle him, or... Ugh!

There were a lot of layers to this that I wasn't comfortable addressing, but I had to admit a lot stemmed from jealousy. Maybe I wasn't so smart, but I wasn't blind, either. Fuck it. I had to start work. No more focusing on Stix. He had nothing to do with me.

I headed toward the front door and grabbed a wooden stool to sit on by a podium with a light to check IDs as people came in. This place was always hopping on the weekends, so I'd be busy tonight. Hopefully, people would behave.

A dude of about nineteen or twenty walked up to me before I recognized him as one of the guys who had been working here. Kingston, the bar owner... or Alpha, as they called him, introduced me to everyone, but I kind of blanked out. I didn't remember most of their names except for Ajax because he was a bouncer here, too. His skin was dusty, and his curls were unruly. He was skinny, reminding me of Stix.

"What's up, Stone? Need anything before it gets busy? Water? Coke?" he asked.

"No, thanks... uhm..."

"They call me Nacho, remember?"

I didn't. "I'm good."

Just leave me alone now. I had to work, but I really hated to mingle, while I didn't mind bouncing. Most of the time, the crowd could be pretty chill, and I got to sit around checking IDs and listening to music while getting paid about five hundred bucks over the weekend, not including tips. Working seven days a week sucked, but it kept a roof over my head and me fed, and I could actually save a few bucks for a rainy day or another tattoo. It wasn't much, but better than what I'd expected when I first moved here, with nothing but a trash bag of clothes and a couple of personal items.

By eight o'clock, my shift had started, and I got ready to take IDs. It could be boring and monotonous, but after a couple of hours, when the place grew packed, the band started to set up. I scanned the crowd to make sure there was no trouble going on. They had another dude, Jaxon or Ajax or whatever his name was, prowling the crowd. He was a few inches taller than me, broader and crazier. When he smiled, it'd send chills down your spine. I didn't know if that was how he usually was or for show.

Soon, the door opened, letting in cooler air, and in walked Blaze and Cueball.

"Yo, brotha!" Blaze said with a smirk on his face.

He rummaged in his pockets for his smokes, pulling one out, but I yanked it from his mouth. "No smoking."

He scowled as he shoved the cigarette back into its pack. "Asshole," he muttered.

"I don't make the fucking rules."

Cueball ran a hand over his freshly shaved head as he scanned the crowd with his amber eyes. Then he looked at me and jutted his chin. "'Sup."

"Is the band gonna be good?" Blaze asked.

I shrugged. "It's some punk shit, I heard."

"We're gonna get some drinks." He grabbed Cueball by the arm as if my bigger roommate could be led, but he didn't protest. Then they were gone.

I followed them with my eyes to their destination at the wooden bar, only to catch a glimpse of Stix with a tray, tossing empty glasses into the large sink filled with water, and started washing them before setting them out to dry. He wore an easy smile as he chatted it up with Alpha, who served drinks with Pippin, the bartender.

Alpha was close to most of his employees. All except me. They'd apparently all been friends before he even opened up this place. Whatever, I didn't need any more friends. The two I had were complicated enough.

Alpha laughed at something Stix had said and slung a tattooed arm over Stix's shoulder. I tightened my fists at the scene with a surge of... I didn't fucking know, but it made my heart race. I just wanted them to stop it. No, for Alpha to stop touching Stix. It was irrational, but I couldn't control the surge of... whatever it was. As soon as Alpha moved away from him, I breathed easier, like a hand had let go of my throat.

When Stix finished with the glasses, he left from behind the bar and moved through the place gracefully, easing in and out of the crowd with little effort. He took drink orders from customers who managed to snag a table, keeping it clean and the tables clear of unused bottles, cans, and glasses.

It was hard to take my eyes off him. Whenever he was near, he was almost always my main focus. Why, dammit? He'd talk to customers, always wearing an easy smile for them, looking bright. Girls would flirt with him, but he brushed them all off with a kind laugh. I hadn't really thought of his sexuality before today when I saw him leave Brie's apartment. Now, it made sense that he never had a girl or showed any interest when they talked to him.

Then again, neither had I. I slept with a few over the years, but none of them interested me. The whole one-night-stand shit annoyed the piss out of me. It was fucking pointless. Why fuck someone I didn't know or care about when my hand was perfectly capable? Though, I did try because I was lonely sometimes. But I couldn't bring myself to be interested in more with them. There was something about them that had me losing interest. Maybe it was the shallowness of it all. Even worse, there were times I couldn't even get it up. It wasn't that I didn't find them pretty or attractive... I just couldn't put my finger on it, like something was missing from the equation.

A slap on my back snapped my eyes away from Stix and to the shot glass in front of me filled with amber liquid.

"Drink up, dickhead."

I took the small glass from Blaze, and the three of us clinked glasses before tipping it back in one gulp. I winced at the cheap whiskey as it burned going down, warming my body and flushing my face. Then Cueball handed me a beer. I took a sip to wash down the harsh whiskey. I wasn't much of a drinker, and I stayed the fuck away from drugs, not wanting to end up like my parents. What a fucked up shit show that had been. I was glad to be rid of them. Every day, I was grateful they weren't in my life any longer, no matter how shitty it currently was.

Blaze nudged me with his shoulder. "Who do you keep lookin' at? Is it that chick with the dark hair? Or maybe the blonde one, her friend."

I tensed at getting caught staring at Stix. "I'm not looking at anyone. It's my job to scan the crowd for trouble, like you two idiots." No one knew of my obsession with Stix except for Stix, and I planned on keeping it that way. My friends knew I couldn't stand him, but not how much or how I physically reacted to him sometimes. And no one would ever know that. The very thought had the liquor burning in my gut.

Then he elbowed Cueball, who glared at him. He tended to speak mostly with his eyes rather than his mouth, which conveyed two emotions—pissed off and nothingness if you could call that an emotion. The only ones he put up with were Blaze and me. More so with Blaze.

"Our Stone here is checking someone out, and he refuses to tell us. I'm hurt. Aren't you hurt, Cue?"

Cueball grunted, and I couldn't tell if he agreed or not.

I rolled my eyes as Blaze wrapped his tatted arm around me, still shorter than me, even when I sat down. "You see, your eyes and head weren't moving. As I grabbed us some drinks, thank you very much, you were staring at the bar the entire time and not at me."

I sipped my beer to hide my annoyance at his observation, needing to be more careful. "There looked like someone was about to stir shit up," I lied not so smoothly, but fuck him. Fucking nosy prick. I shoved him off me. "We aren't girlfriends, asshole."

He was undeterred as he chuckled. "How many chicks has our Stone brought home, Cue? One?"

"Two," he said.

"Two in nearly a year."

I pinched the bridge of my nose. It wasn't just me that Blaze needed to know everything about. He was pushy and nosy with everyone. Still, it pissed me off, which was why my mood turned more dickish than usual. I didn't owe him shit about my personal life, friends or not.

"Back off."

He smiled like a loon. Why did people love to get a rise out of me? "Touchy, touchy."

Whatever. It was our thing. All we ever did was needle each other and bicker. Well, Blaze did most of the needling. Still, it wasn't a good night to torment me.

Thank fuck, a group of girls came in, forcing me to work. "Go. I gotta work."

They finally walked off, leaving me to check IDs and watch Stix when I should've been fucking ignoring him.

There was a tap on the microphone, and I turned to see one of the band members playing tonight standing there in black torn jeans, a black torn T-shirt, and a neon pink mohawk.

"*What's up, Alphas! We havin' a good time tonight?*" he screamed into the microphone.

Everyone yelled, whistled, and clapped in response.

"*Yeah! Well, if you don't know us, we're the Flamin' Nutters! And I'm Alfie, the singer.*"

More hooting and whistling.

Their logo was a walnut on fire, which was as ridiculous as their name.

"*So, to start us off tonight, we're handing the drums over to our pal Stix Jamieson for the first song! Come on up, dude!*"

My heart rate kicked up a notch as I stood taller to look over the sea of heads at the raised stage.

I hadn't been working here long enough to see him play, but I heard he was pretty good, which was hard to tell with all that fucking tapping on anything he could get his sticks on, giving me a headache, especially when we shared the fire escape, constantly dinging on the metal. It took all my control not to take them and snap them in half.

His nearly white hair wasn't hard to miss as he gave a bro hug to Alfie and then sat behind a drum set with the flaming nut on the base. The rest of the band gathered their instruments and waited for Stix to give the cue. He twirled his sticks between his fingers, then pounded them together, counting to three, and it began.

The crowd moved up closer and started banging their heads to the beat. The guitar was screechy and heavy, and the base kept the tempo as Stix wailed on the drums, moving faster than I thought possible. I'd seen a few bands and amazing drummers, but honestly, I always figured him for a dumbass.

His long, thin arms flung over drums and cymbals as he smashed the bass drum. The song was hard and fast, and Alfie started to sing some guttural vocals, but I was only focused on Stix, who was lost in his movements and keeping up the beat and was stronger than he looked. His hair soon got soaked with sweat, and I wondered where drummers got their energy. The beat paused briefly as he twirled a stick between his fingers, then hit it again.

I got lost in his movements as he got lost in his own little world. It was quite something to watch. His energy, vibrancy, and excitement strangely moved me like I was right there with him in the zone with flashing colored lights that changed the color of his hair. He looked like a neon rocking angel.

The song abruptly stopped, and that was when I felt how hard my heart beat inside my chest. I rubbed it as I watched Stix hug his temporary bandmates, laughing and doing some weird handshake that spelled friendship and camaraderie, giving me this strange sort of ache in my chest.

Suddenly, his eyes met mine, and I held my breath. There could've been someone behind me, but I didn't think so because his smile dropped. We stared at each other for a beat before someone grabbed his attention, severing us like a snipped wire, allowing me to breathe again.

Then, the familiar anger hit again, simmering just below the surface. I didn't understand all these emotions and reactions to him, and it drove me fucking crazy. I just couldn't explain it. To share a connection with him more? No, I fucking hated him. That couldn't be it. But a part of me wished I had his life. He smiled easily, joked, made a lot of friends, and had not one but two families where I had none of those things. Nothing seemed to fucking bother him. Yeah, I was a tad envious. But even worse was that he drew me in like no other. Did it run deeper than that? Once in a while, when I'd come across people, I'd wish I was someone else or wanted the things they had, but I never felt this sort of animosity or magnetic pull.

I shook my head to snap myself out of it. I had to let this obsession over Stix go. It wasn't healthy. But I didn't stop watching him, unable to peel my eyes away, as he returned to work and the band resumed with their current drummer, who honestly wasn't nearly as good.

CHAPTER 4
Stix

AJAX AND PIPPIN HAD the day off from their day jobs, so I met them at the diner Mom worked at to grab some food; then, we planned to skate before heading to work at Alpha's tonight.

One of the benefits of living in the city was that you could go just about anywhere or get anything without having to go far. I'd have to have a car if we lived in the burbs. Sometimes, I'd have to take the bus or the Metro, but usually, my board was enough to get me where I needed to go.

The diner where Mom worked was close enough to ride my board to and have my friends meet me there. Sally's Diner was a decent place, not what you'd expect. Most diners tended to be holes in the wall or rundown. Dives that people still enjoyed going to. But Sally's was pretty swank with gleaming chrome, red vinyl seating, and black and white tiled flooring, made to look retro. It was a popular hotspot, so seating wasn't always easy to come by, but if I told Mom my friends and I were coming, she'd save us a table as long as we didn't take too long.

I met Ajax and Pippin outside of the diner. They were leaning against one of the large windows, smoking, when I arrived. Ajax wore his usual white T-shirt and ripped jeans with Vans. His dark hair needed a cut as the bangs fell in his face. Pippin looked like he always did, with a black T-shirt and an old Fedora covering his red hair.

Ajax bounced and lumbered over to me, putting me in a headlock, then rubbed his knuckles through my hair.

"Off, fucker!"

Sure, he treated me like I was his little brother, and brothers were fucking annoying sometimes.

He chuckled and let me up a little, but kept his arm slung around me as we made our way inside. The place smelled perpetually of coffee and breakfast, and while most people thought those scents smelled of home, it got nauseating after a while. I hated breakfast food because of it. Give me oatmeal or cereal any day. Bacon and eggs made me want to hurl, especially runny eggs. Sure, it made me weird, but my stomach didn't care.

When we walked in, Mom saw us and waved us over to a booth she'd been holding.

"Afternoon, boys."

"Hey, Mrs. J," Pippin said.

Then Ajax pulled Mom into a hug. "What's up, Stix's mom?" It was the only time I'd ever seen him be affectionate to anyone. Sure, he messed with me, but he was always sweet to my mom. And she loved my friends and was so good to them.

She dropped menus on the table. "What do you boys want to drink? I already know what you want, Nico."

Pippin smiled up at her as he sat down. "I'll have a root beer."

Ajax raised his hand. "A coke for me."

She left to get our drinks as we looked at the menu, even though I already knew what I wanted.

"So, how's Nacho?" I hedged toward Pippin. It was the closest thing I could give regarding hints. Nacho would kill me if I told Pippin he had a crush on him. But I wanted to see where his head was toward his best friend.

"Uh, fine. You just saw him the other day, dude."

Ajax and I looked at each other and rolled our eyes. Pippin missed it with his nose in the menu. I swear to god, he'd never figure it out unless Nacho wore a neon sign saying, 'I want you.'

"And what about you?" Ajax asked me, holding his menu in a death grip.

I raised my brow, wondering what the hell he was talking about and why he was so angry about it. "Uh..."

"Don't be a Pippin," he said.

Pippin raised his head and looked at us, confused. "Huh?"

Ajax aimed a thumb at him. "See what I mean?"

I was usually quicker than this and less dense than Pippin. "You've lost me, dude."

"What's his face... Stone? The new dude at Rejects."

I pinched my lips together and quirked my brows. "Can you be any less specific? Please feel free to add more vagueness."

He grabbed his paper napkin and began shredding it in his usual nervous way. Ajax tended to be bouncy with triggering moods, but today was one of his better days. "Why is he always looking at you like he wants to kill you and fuck you, and not necessarily in that order? He's always watching you."

Mom returned with our drinks, placing the large glass of orange juice in front of me. I tried to eat healthy and get vitamins whenever I could to help me.

"What would you boys like?"

"I'll have a steak salad with the vinaigrette on the side," I said.

Ajax ordered the bacon cheeseburger, while Pippin ordered the American breakfast. Gross.

"So?" Ajax aimed back at me. "What's with you two? And don't tell me you haven't noticed. I have to watch the bar, remember? I observe shit."

I shrugged and stole his straw, tapping out a beat onto the table using my straw and his. "I don't know what you mean." Honestly, I didn't want to tell Ajax that Stone hated my guts. He might beat the hell out of Stone in his need to always protect me. He protected all of us, which was in his nature, but especially me.

"You can't tell me you haven't noticed how he glares at you."

I shrugged again. "I dunno."

"You fucking suck at lying, Stix."

"What's this now?" Pippin finally chimed in.

Ajax nodded a head my way. "Stone... the new dude at Alpha's been watching our Stix a little too hard, and Stix is lying to us that he hasn't noticed."

"Dammit, Ajax. Just leave him alone. I'll deal with it. I didn't say anything because I know how you can get."

He huffed and resumed tearing up his napkin. "What's that supposed to fucking mean?"

"It means nothing. You just get a little... too protective sometimes. I can handle it."

He slouched in the booth as he pouted. "I just want to make sure no one bugs you."

"Thank you, but I can take care of myself. Please. I beg you. Leave him alone."

"Fine, but if he touches you, he's gonna have some random broken bones."

"Why does he hate Stix?" Pippin asked, a day late and a dollar short, as always.

Ajax and I rolled our eyes again. It wasn't that Pippin was slow, but I think he may have had ADHD or something, not that I was some doctor. His mind could be all over the place sometimes, and he struggled to focus unless he tended bar. He was a genius at mixing drinks, and smart as hell, yet he always seemed out of it.

Soon, Mom returned with our lunch and ruffled my hair like I was some fucking child, but I sucked it up for her. "Eat up, boys."

"Thanks, Mom."

After she left, I poured some dressing on my salad. I rarely got to eat as healthy as I'd like, since eating healthy was expensive. At the same time, I needed the fat and calories because I was kind of thin. It was a perpetual conundrum. Healthy foods helped with my arthritic disease, keeping me away from trigger foods, but organic fruits and vegetables were a luxury when you were always poor.

"Hey, after we eat, I want to show you something on our way to the skate park," I said.

Pippin looked at me with dripping egg over his chin.

I gagged. "Gross, dude."

"Where to?" Ajax asked.

"You'll see."

After lunch, we paid for our meal, and I kissed Mom on the cheek before heading out. We hopped on our boards and skated four blocks until we came to a small neighborhood of old, rundown townhomes. I must've passed by here a hundred times while skating by on my way to the skate park, but about three months ago, a house came up for sale.

These homes had a hard time selling since the neighborhoods weren't the safest, and the homes needed serious work. But our neighborhood and apartment weren't much better. A little TLC could make it look amazing. Well, at least livable.

I looked up the place online when it came up for sale, and it was only selling for a hundred thousand. There was probably no way I'd ever save up enough money, prostituting myself to buy the place. At least not before it was sold to someone else. I had over three thousand bucks saved that I refused to touch for this very purpose and to save for my meds. Being with Brie really helped with that.

It wasn't more than a pipe dream, but I couldn't help but dream for more in life. It was all I had. Those who had so little either had the biggest, unreachable dreams of getting out one day, or they gave up and just lived day to day. I didn't want that to be me. I wanted to achieve something, but I wasn't smart enough for college, especially since my high school grades and SATs scores weren't the best. Urban schools lacked the proper funding for good teachers and resources.

"Come on," I said when we got there. My friends took in the place. It was clearly in need of love. The concrete walkway was cracked, and the matchbook-sized yard was mostly dead weeds. "We can get in through the back. I found a window that wasn't locked."

We grabbed our boards and walked around to the back alley, looking behind us to make sure no one saw us. I then slipped in through the chain-link fence to the tiny backyard. I dropped my board, shimmied up toward the kitchen window, and shoved it open. Once I climbed inside, I opened the back door for my friends, who walked in, examining the place.

It wasn't much to look at inside either, with peeling paint and wallpaper. Trash also filled the house, and I was sure some animals scurried about in there. But it was two stories with original wood floors that only needed some sanding and new stain. The old, peeling wallpaper in the kitchen needed to be stripped. And with several coats of paint, this place could be decent. The kitchen and bathrooms were dated as hell, but the sinks and toilet functioned, so who cared? I didn't need fucking fancy.

"This place is cool, man," Pippin said, looking around and touching everything from the butcher block countertops to the wooden cabinets in the kitchen.

"Right? I imagine all the cool shit I can learn and do in here to make this place a home for Mom and Nova."

We made our way through the house and up the stairs.

"It has three bedrooms and two and a half bathrooms, which is totally awesome. God, it would be nice not to have to share a bathroom with two other people."

"And even your own room," Ajax said, bouncing around from room to room.

"That too."

Ajax popped his head out of one of the bedrooms with a crazed smile on his face. "You gonna get it?"

"God, I wish. I've been dying to, but I don't have enough money to put down, or credit, or anything really. It's mostly a dream, but fuck, I'd love to buy this place. The house even has a tiny garage where I can set up some drums to practice on. And a tiny study is downstairs that I could make into a playroom for Nova. Fuck, why do we need to have a gazillion jobs simply to make ends meet?"

It was a rhetorical question, but Pippin answered anyway. "Because no one cares about us, man. It's all about the wealthy and holding them up on pedestals to worship. We aren't worth noticing if we haven't succeeded like them. I tried to get into one dude who seemed to care but lost him. His name was Felix something. I had a dog named Felix once. He died when I was eight, after my birthday. I didn't have a lot of friends then, but... did I tell you what happened at my party?"

Ajax and I said nothing as he rambled. As oblivious as he could be, he was insightful sometimes, even if he struggled to stay focused.

I had no response to that, so I just said, "Truth."

"Well, this place is badass," Ajax said. "I hope you get it one day."

"I hope so, too." In reality, it'd be sold before I could ever afford it, but places like this gave me hope. I didn't need anything fancy or live in the burbs. This house or one like it would be good enough for the Jamiesons.

When we finished exploring, Ajax and Pippin left out the backdoor, and I locked it, then climbed out the window, closing it as much as I could. I dropped to the ground as we gathered our boards and skated off to the park.

CHAPTER 5
Stix

It was early in the morning when my phone pinged, waking me up. I scrambled to silence it, so my sis didn't wake up—the drawbacks of sharing a room, among other things.

I rubbed my eyes and yawned as I read the too-bright message that had come in. Who the fuck texted at seven in the morning? Shit, I did not get nearly enough sleep. I hadn't gotten into bed until after three in the morning after having to help close up the bar last night.

Fucking Joshua. I liked him well enough, but not at fucking seven in the morning. He worked the front desk at a luxury hotel and would send me periodic clients if he had someone who asked for discrete services.

We'd been friends back in high school. He was a cool dude, and he helped me find a few of my regulars. Even better was when a high-end customer came in, willing to pay a pretty penny for my services. That was one of the rare times I was willing to do more sexually. The money was just too good.

Me: Dude it's early.

Josh: I got someone for you. Don't you want $$

Me: Yeah hit me

Josh: A businessman came in last night asking if I knew anyone who could help him out. I told him yeah and to set him up for tonight.

Me: You tell him my rules?

Josh: Of course. He wants you at seven sharp. Can you get off work?

Me: I'm already off

Josh: Can I tell him yes?

Me: How much?

Josh: You decide. He said money wasn't a factor.

Shit, this could be good to add to my savings.

Me: Set it up.

I hung up, stretched, and then rubbed my face. It was time to get up since I wouldn't be able to get back to sleep. At least Nova was still out.

Two hours later, I fed my sister and went downstairs to Mrs. Gordon's place. Now, I could focus on tonight. I needed to plan and to prep. Ugh. Fucking tedious. I usually only did the fucking, but for a special price, I was willing to bottom. I hated it because I wanted to do that with someone special. Not a client. Who knew? Maybe he wanted me to fuck him. I hoped so. Still, I needed to get ready. Most of my clients just got blow jobs, so they didn't care how I looked. But a high-end customer would expect me to be properly shaved, clean, and looking nice.

I spent most of the late morning shaving my pubes, making sure I was smooth. The rest of my body didn't have much hair, but I shaved what little I had on my chest, too.

There would be no cleaning myself out and then showering until later, and my meals would be light. Ugh. I was going to fucking starve.

Think of the money, Nico.

It was five thirty in the evening as I put on my only suit. I got it last year when my grandfather died from colon cancer, and I needed to wear something presentable at his funeral. It was a cheap suit, but better than ironic T-shirts and ripped jeans.

I left off all my jewelry this time and didn't wear a tie, leaving my white button-up unbuttoned at the top. I couldn't do much about my hair being a mess. I mean, I liked it, but it wasn't exactly classy. I combed it as nicely as possible on the side. That was the best I could do.

Since I couldn't skate to the place, I had to leave earlier to take the Metro train, not wanting to ruin everything I had worked on. The last thing I needed was to fall off my board and tear up my only suit.

By six, I was ready. I left my apartment, locked the door, and headed downstairs, but I stopped in my tracks as soon as I saw Stone walking up the steps with his head down. He must have sensed my presence because he looked up to see me.

His hazel eyes went wide as they scanned me, but any other sort of reaction he had, he shut it down.

Oh, shit. My mouth wanted to start with him. It was an itch I couldn't reach. "I look hot, right?"

He grunted as he tried to pass me. Not to be daunted, I continued to needle him because I had a fucking death wish.

"Hmm, I think you're supposed to cut the fish, not wear it, Rolling Stone."

He turned with his free hand fisted while the other one tried to crush his board. "Stop calling me that."

"Why? It fits."

"It doesn't make any fucking sense."

I shrugged. "You roll on your board, and you're stone. Nope, it makes perfect sense."

He scoffed and rolled his eyes. "In your fucking demented head," he said before turning around and walking up the steps again. Then he turned back to face me. "Where are you going?"

"I knew you thought I looked hot!" His face flushed red, and I relished in it. I wanted to bathe in his discomfort. Not sure how that would be possible, but if it were a thing, I'd do it. "To answer your question, I... have a job interview. Sort of."

"What is a 'sort of job' interview?"

"Wouldn't you like to know?" I winked at him and skipped downstairs before he lost his cool and shoved me down the steps.

One point to Nico. Zero points to Stone.

Apparently, I was supposed to sit at the bar and wait for my gentleman of the night.

The hotel was pretty swank, situated in a really old building downtown. Inside was filled with chandeliers, navy blues, yellows and creams, and old wood. I rarely got a client from Josh, especially for a queer client, but when I did, I loved it here, pretending I could even afford such a place for the night.

I shoved my hands in the pockets of my slacks and walked past Josh, who was still working and gave him a nod before stepping into the bar, which was as extravagant as the rest of the place. I sat at the bar but didn't know what to order. They probably didn't even serve the cheap beer I usually drank.

"What can I get you?" asked the female bartender.

"Uh, I'm not sure."

"What are you in the mood for? Something sweet? Strong? Zesty? Refreshing?"

Ugh, so many choices. I didn't usually drink anything that required mixing. "Uhm, refreshing?"

"I know just the thing. But I need to see your ID first."

Shit, good thing my client wasn't here yet. I tried not to flush as I dug out my worn wallet, pulled out my ID, and handed it to her. I didn't have a driver's license since I didn't exactly have a car, making me feel way younger than I was. Well, I only recently turned twenty-two, so I guess I was still pretty young. Hey, at least I was legal.

She checked the date and handed it back. The bartender returned shortly with a tall glass full of some yellowish-green drink and a sprig of mint.

"Try that. It's a mint margarita and a favorite here."

"Thanks."

She stood in front of me, staring. Oh, I guess she wanted me to try it now. I took a sip from the glass and moaned. "Whoa, that's pretty good."

She smirked and walked away. "Told ya."

It was delicious, but I was afraid of how much it'd cost—probably a twenty-dollar drink.

Before I had my fourth sip, a gentleman sat next to me. This must've been my client for the evening because there were plenty of other seats instead of right next to me.

He was tall and broad. Yep, I'd probably be a bottom for the night, dammit. His nearly black hair was slicked back without a strand out of place, and he wore a crisp charcoal gray suit with a royal blue button-up. The scruff on his face was thick and intentional. He must've been at least forty, but he was handsome in an *I'm super wealthy and can afford the best* way. At least he smelled really good, with a clean, masculine cologne that wasn't overpowering.

The gentleman waved to the bartender and ordered a scotch on the rocks. Of course he did. Rich, businessman's drink of choice. Once he got his drink, he finally acknowledged me.

"You must be my date for the evening," his voice was deep, reminding me how much of a man he was compared to me.

"Yes, sir."

His lip twitched into a smile. "I like that." He took a sip of his drink and licked his full lips. "You're a little young."

I shrugged. "I have no control over my age, but I'm legal... sir."

"Indeed. You're good looking, at least."

There was no more talking as we quickly finished our drinks. He stood and waved at the bartender. "Charge the drinks to room 508." When she nodded, he faced me. "Ready?"

"Yes." Well, at least I didn't have to pay for my drink.

Once we got to his room, he removed his jacket and started to unbutton his shirt, exposing black chest hair on a fit, muscular frame. "Now that we're in private, how much?"

Three hundred slipped out of my mouth with ease. Twice as much as what I charged Brie. I probably could've gone higher, but I didn't want him pissed if I couldn't fulfill his needs.

He nodded, reached into his pants, grabbed a beautiful leather wallet, and pulled out three crisp one-hundred-dollar bills, setting them on the dresser. "What are your rules?"

"We always use condoms, even for blow jobs, and never kiss."

"Very well. Get fully undressed, then get into the bed on your hands and knees with your face down into the pillows and ass in the air."

"Yes, sir."

Good thing I cleaned up good today.

Three hours and a sore ass later, I waddled out of the hotel. Fuck, I was going to feel his dick in my ass for days and his hand *on* my ass. Those spankings hurt, along with the few bite marks, but he enjoyed it. I should've fucking charged him more for that. Stupid. At least I was three hundred dollars richer and had a promise that when he returned, he'd hire me again.

It was only after ten at night, so I took the bus instead of the train and made my way toward Alpha's for a couple of drinks before I made my way home. The evening was nice and not too hot, with a slight breeze, so I removed my jacket after stepping off the bus and walked the two blocks to the bar.

There was no line waiting to get in, which meant the crowd was mostly inside now. Stone sat on a stool outside since it was warm out, scrolling through his phone. The glow of the screen lit up his focused face, giving it a strange glow.

My stomach did one of those weird dips from seeing him. It was a rare moment I could observe him when he wasn't scowling at me. He had a cigarette dangling out of his mouth, looking weirdly cool and oblivious to my presence. He looked good, too, wearing a tight black Henley with the sleeves pulled up to expose his strong, tattooed forearms. His jeans were ripped in the knees, and he wore his Chucks, as always.

With a swallow and a deep breath, I made my way toward him with my suit jacket slung over my shoulder.

Sensing me, he looked up, and once he saw who I was, he pulled out his cigarette from his tight, full lips and narrowed his eyes. God, I really wish I knew what I'd done wrong toward him. We could've had a lot of fun together if he could just get his head out of his ass. And by fun,

I meant either sexually or as friends. But preferably sex. I still had my doubts he wasn't queer, but no one knew much about Stone. And in one of those rare moments, I imagined him like my client tonight, taking control, fucking me. I shuddered at the visual.

"How'd the interview go?" he asked.

My mind instantly shorted out at the non-threatening question. Stone had never simply talked to me or asked questions, so I had no idea what to make of it. In fact, it had me even more on guard and suspicious. We always had a strange rapport going on, and he suddenly changed the rules on me.

"It was... interesting."

"Get the job?"

"In a way."

He huffed a growl, which went straight to my nuts. "What the fuck does all that vague shit mean? Jesus."

As if I would tell him what I did for my day job. Well, sometimes in the evenings now. But I found myself getting defensive, being completely off-kilter by his questions. "What does it matter? Why do you even care?"

"I fucking don't."

"Right... sure you don't."

He went back to smoking and scrolling on his phone in dismissal. Because that shit pissed me off even more, I stood close to him. So close we almost touched, and I could smell his woodsy body wash, or whatever he used, mingled with cigarette smoke. "I think you want to know more about me, Rolling Stone. I think you care a lot."

While he continued to ignore me and scroll through his phone, his entire body tensed and vibrated with dangerous energy, yet that didn't stop me from pushing his buttons.

I touched his knee with my fingers, which he quickly snagged and twisted my hand in a tight grip. "Don't fucking touch me," he hissed.

I knew how to get out of it, so I wrenched my hand away, trying not to wince at the pain. "Just admit it. You want this." I waved a hand across my body.

His hazel eyes flashed with doubt and confusion, but only for a second. "In your fucking dreams. I hate you."

I stood straight and shrugged. "So you keep saying..." With that, I walked into the bar with a hammering heart, questioning my desire to poke the bear.

CHAPTER 6
Stix

MOM WAS IN THE kitchen, feeding Nova lunch while I downed some coffee, having woken up late when someone knocked on my apartment door. I smiled as I rushed to answer it. Today was my day to fuck around and not have to work. Well, not until tonight, anyway. My friends and I lived for Sundays, skateboarding, testing tricks, and mending cuts and bruises. It was a day that I could let go and not be fucking responsible for anything, allowing myself one day to let go of the guilt and the need to make money. To just live for myself and my closest friends. Sure, we skated sometimes during the week, but Sundays were the best when my friends and I could all be together since no one had to work, except for Alpha, who always fucking worked.

The twins were standing there with smirks on their faces and boards in their hands. Claire 'Jazz' Chapman rested her elbow on her brother's shoulder, wearing overalls under a white tank top and a zipped hoodie on top, with her baseball hat turned backward. She had bleached hair as I did, but it had stripes of teal in it and was cut into a pixie with long bangs. She had angel piercings on her upper lip and gauges through her ears. And her right arm had a vibrant tattoo sleeve, mostly in teal and red.

Jazz was the only girl in our crew and pretty tall at five-foot-nine. She was a badass and fun as hell.

Her twin Christopher, 'Blondie,' also had bleached hair. He wore a tawny sweater that fell off one shoulder, exposing a bit of his chest tattoo. He, too, had a smirk on his face. Though they clearly weren't identical, they looked alike and acted alike, even both wearing makeup. He liked to add lip gloss with glitter and some dark eyeshadow around his eyes. He was also a couple of inches taller than his sister.

They both came into our fold last year as runaways, leaving foster care. They kept getting separated through the system and got tired of it, figuring they were better off together. Once they turned eighteen this year, and thanks to Alpha, he helped them get their GEDs, so they could hold real jobs.

I stood aside to let them both in as I grabbed my things. Jazz and Blondie rushed to Mom and hugged her, and then they chatted a bit with Nova. All my friends thought of Mom as their second mother. And I didn't mind sharing her.

"You kids behaving?" Mom asked, winking at them.

Jazz grabbed a carrot stick Nova had handed her and munched on it. "Always, Mrs. J."

Mom scoffed and raised her brow at Jazz, who was always trouble.

I slipped on my old Vans and threw on my army jacket over my T-shirt of the day that read *'OFD: Obsessive Fishing Disorder,'* which was two sizes too big, before I stepped on the edge of my board to flip it up, grabbed the nose, and tucked it under my arm.

"Ready?" The twins nodded and met me at the door. "Later, Mom and Nova."

I shut the door behind me and stepped out into the hall just as Stone and his asshole friends came out of their apartment. Judging by their boards, I guessed they had the same plans, which wasn't surprising. Hopefully, they wouldn't be going to the same place we were today, but they probably would. They always seemed to be where I was with my friends. Fucking annoying.

I blew an air kiss at them. Cueball had no reaction. I swear, he was dead inside or something, but Blaze looked like a fucking serial killer ready to slice my throat with that crazy smile eerily similar to Ajax's. Meanwhile, Stone glared daggers at me. I smiled broader to piss him off more as I gave him a little finger wave.

Before they started anything, the three of us rushed down the stairs. I jumped the last four steps and smashed against the lobby door to let us out. Once we got hit with the cooler air, we dropped our boards and jumped on them before pushing off toward Old Town Mall. Traffic wasn't as busy on Sundays. While Baltimore was starting to boom again after the pandemic lockdowns, it was still struggling.

There were a few skate parks around, but they were constantly fucking crowded on the weekends, and everyone tripped over each other. So, some of us regulars headed over to Old Town Mall, the outdoor shopping area that had been built in the early 1800s. It struggled for a long time when suburbs grew outside of Baltimore, but by the 1980s, with poverty and unemployment, the place was left abandoned. It used to have shopping and restaurants, and there had been talks about restoring it, but with the current economy, it didn't look like it would happen anytime soon.

Skaters before us had broken into some buildings that had been gutted to skate inside. One building even had some ramps that they had built before we ever arrived.

Before we reached the Old Town Mall, the twins and I pulled up to an old brick building that had seen better days. Outside, Ajax bounced and paced while smoking a cigarette, waiting for us.

"Sup," he said.

We did an elaborate handshake before he slung a heavy arm around me and practically put me in a chokehold, as he was prone to do. It was Ajax's way of showing affection, even if it fucking hurt and annoyed the hell out of me. I twisted out of his hold and shoved him off, but he was too big, and I ended up bouncing off him. "Off, you fuck."

He smirked as he took a drag and said hi to the twins.

"Where's Pippin and Nacho?" Blondie asked.

"They'll meet us there. They're stopping by the liquor store. Alpha can't make it today. Inventory or some shit," Ajax said.

That was happening more and more. As his bar succeeded, it took away his time from skating and hanging around with us.

"The dude needs at least one day off," I said.

"Preach," Jazz said.

Ajax shrugged. "Alpha does what Alpha wants. You know how anal he is. Let's go and get some skating in. I've been itching all fucking week for this."

These days, we were all getting too busy to skate as much as we'd like, with all of us having day jobs as well as working at Alpha's at night.

We pushed off on our boards, banking, carving around block corners, doing ollies with our noses in the air, and riding on our back wheels. I did periodic board slides on the curb and flipped my board under my feet, warming up for the day.

Fifteen minutes later, we showed up at Old Town Mall. The place looked like it came right out of a dystopian movie, with run-down buildings and fallen storefront signs, and there were more weed vines and graffiti than stone or bricks. The brick sidewalk was too wonky to skate on, and it was also covered in weeds. Honestly, it amazed me how easily nature took back what was stolen by us humans. Plants pushed through brick and concrete to find light and water, slowly breaking down what we created. It was kind of awesome.

The old building we broke into was an old market or something that had smashed-out windows that someone had boarded up, which had been taken down for the day to let in light. The large metal grates covering the doors made it easy to break the locks off and roll them up, so we could get in. Inside, it had been cleaned of debris and completely gutted, with several ramps scattered throughout the concrete floors. Graffiti also covered the inside. The walls were so colorful they looked like murals.

Before we ever discovered the place, someone had decorated it with mannequins abandoned from the other shops and spray painted and dressed up like something out of a horror movie, like some deranged, giant Barbie.

The building held about twenty of us skaters, and while it was a lot, it was still better than those parks on Sundays. Someone had brought portable lights, so we didn't have to skate in complete darkness.

Pippin and Nacho were already waiting for us in a corner next to an ancient boombox playing some old grunge tunes from the nineties.

Pippin was so old school. As usual, he wore his fedora over his red, floppy hair and also had a perpetual smile on his face. While he struggled to remember shit and focus, he was one of the sweetest next to Nacho, who wore a black T-shirt over his skinny frame and a black beanie covering his unruly curls.

"Beer or a swig of whiskey?" Pippin asked us.

Ajax took a swig while the twins each grabbed a beer, while none of us gave a shit that Nacho and the twins were underage. We didn't fucking drive anywhere.

I grabbed my smokes, pulled a cig out, popped it in my mouth, and lit it. After I took a drag, I took the whiskey bottle from Ajax and chugged down a few sips. I coughed from both the smoke and the burn of the alcohol, making my eyes water, before wiping my mouth with the back of my hand and handing the bottle back to Pippin, who also took a sip.

We called Sampson Maguire 'Pippin' based on the character from Lord of the Rings. They had that same dumbass yet upbeat vibe. But we loved him all the same.

Nate Lamont was called 'Nacho' for obvious reasons. It was pretty much all he ate. In fact, he currently had a small paper plate of nachos with hardened cheese, since it was too cold outside to keep it melted. He was three inches shorter than my five-ten height, but just as skinny. Don't let his sweet shyness fool you. He'd just as soon gut you if anyone messed with his new family, especially if anyone messed with Pippin. Pippin was too fucking oblivious to notice Nacho's love for him. He'd figure it out one day, or so we hoped.

After a few more sips, I said, "I'm ready to take some air, dudes."

I jumped on my board and pushed off to one of the lesser-used ramps. It was smaller, but good for practicing my tricks.

Gaining momentum between the two ramps, I picked up speed until I could catch air at the lip. The higher I got, the more tricks I could do. Between drumming and skating, I was in my zone. This was life. This was my stress relief. Without them, I'd be a miserable piece of shit. And I hated to be miserable. All my guilt was enough to choke on, and I was allowed a few moments of happiness, dammit, which also kept me happy and pleasant toward others.

After a few minutes of skating, my nemesis showed up with his pals. Fuck. Well, he wasn't my personal nemesis, but apparently, I was his. I'd hoped they would've gone somewhere else today and left me the fuck alone for five minutes. It was bad enough that I had to live next door to them and work with Stone. And he looked fucking good today, too, wearing all black and a black beanie. It made his pale skin look like porcelain and his hazel eyes extra intense. Fuck, I really needed to stop thinking about this asshole being hot. There were plenty of good-looking men who weren't dickheads. Or so I assumed, not that I'd met any yet. See, if he weren't such a dick and was gay, we could've had something fun.

I tossed my jacket onto the ground as I continued to skate, trying to ignore that Stone was watching me. Always watching. What the fuck? Did he hate me so much that he had to glare at me while I tried to skate? Why couldn't he leave me alone? This was *my* thing. *My* day. And he was fucking ruining it by making me tense.

Stone had me so distracted that I took air too high and missed my handplant, trying to do a handstand while grabbing my board. I wasn't going to make it, so I had to bail by kicking my board out of the way—better that than landing on it. I came down on the wood hard, ripping my already ripped pants at the knees, tearing my skin along with it.

"Fuck!"

I clutched my knees as they bled all over my jeans. My face and ears burned at my fall right in front of the very person I was hot for and who hated me. "Fuck... Goddamn, that stings," I mumbled to myself. I held my breath and clenched my body to the pain, willing it to hurry up and pass.

Suddenly, I heard laughing and squinted over to see Blaze holding his stomach and laughing hysterically. Even Cueball was twitching a smile, while Stone gave nothing away. Not even his disdain. In fact, he walked away as if I had failed him somehow.

"Yeah... well fuck you, too!" I yelled at him as I got up, but Blaze thought it was for him. It wasn't like me to get pissy, but dammit, my knees fucking burned along with my humiliation.

"What'd you just say to me, bleach head?"

I glanced one more time at Stone, who had his back to us and grabbed one of his beers. Looking back at Blaze, I stood straighter, despite being five inches taller than him.

I clenched my teeth from the pain and winced a smile. "Oh, nothing. I was just saying I fucked your mama the other night. Made her feel so good. Didn't you hear her screaming out my name last night? *'Oh, Stix... you're so big!'*"

His crazy smile dropped as he stomped over to me, followed by Cueball, who could probably hammer me with his fists if I wasn't careful. But I stood taller and fisted my hands, ready to fight if I had to. I just preferred not to, wanting to be left the fuck alone to skate. God, and after getting hurt, I wasn't in the fucking mood to be snappy and make jokes.

"What did you say about her? You makin' mama jokes? To me? Do you have a fucking death wish?" He stood so close to my face I could smell cigarettes and some cheap-ass cologne. The combination made me gag. "You've got some balls on you."

"That's what she said." I tried not to wince again at the pain or look for my friends, who were either skating or drinking. "Besides, you're a ferret on steroids." *I'm so gonna die.* It was mean, but I couldn't afford to back down. Backing down in front of guys like him spelled weakness. That was a death sentence right there. Or at least landed you in the hospital.

Without gulping down my lack of spit, I shrugged and tried not to limp back to my board, dismissing him. It was dangerous to turn my back on someone like Blaze, but I had to maintain the upper hand. With a deep breath, and despite the need to sit to get off my knees, I resumed skating to show those asshats that they had no effect on me.

As I made the downturn, suddenly, something forced my board to stop and knocked me off. I fell onto my back, knocking the wind out of me. I was dazed that the laughter in the background sounded like it echoed around in my brain, and I felt a little dizzy. Then, the back pain started as clarity hit me. I fucking hoped this didn't flare me up again. Fuck, I couldn't afford to be laid up or go to the hospital. I rolled over on my side, clenching my core to help keep the pain in my lower back in check while struggling for breath as my friends rushed over to me to help me up, but all I saw was fighting. At first, I thought it was Ajax coming to my defense, but I did a double-take to see who it was.

No. That was impossible. My eyes were playing tricks on me.

CHAPTER 7
Stone

WHEN I SAW BLAZE chuck that full can of beer at Stix, I saw fucking red. Everyone in the building immediately vanished. All sounds, sights, and smells were gone, leaving me with just Blaze and my rage. I grabbed him by the back of his jacket and yanked him back as he was laughing before turning him around to face me. It took only a fraction of a second to completely lose my fucking control and punch him in the face. I ignored the pain in my hand as it met with bone before drawing back for another. I needed more blood, but my arm was stuck. I tried again, unable to hit the fucker over and over. He wasn't bleeding enough. No one fucked with my Stix.

My Stix?

Fuck me.

I was snapped back with clarity as I let go of Blaze. He dropped to the ground, bleeding from his mouth, and I shrugged off whoever was holding me back. Though I let go of Blaze, that rage wouldn't let go of me. I turned to see Cueball with a worried look on his face instead of the expected anger. When I looked back at Blaze, he stood back up and scowled as he wiped the blood from his mouth with the back of his hand.

"What the fuck, Stone?"

"I..."

"You hate that prick! It was funny. You... fucking hit me!"

"I..." I needed to think quickly, but nothing came to me other than the fucking truth. "He's mine to fuck with. Not yours. I may hate him, but I'd never physically hurt someone."

"You fucking physically hurt me, you liar."

I rubbed my head as I quickly glanced over at Stix, where he was currently sitting with his friends, being doted on, but watching my every move with wide, dark eyes. They must have helped him back to their little corner. Someone was pouring whiskey on his bleeding knees. He hissed and turned to look back at his injuries while Jazz had her head on his shoulder, which sent another wave of anger through me that I couldn't fucking explain. All his friends were talking to him simultaneously while sending Blaze and me death glares. And Ajax looked ready to kill, and he probably would've if not for Pippin and Nacho holding him back.

"You shouldn't have hurt him. He's mine to hate." I said to Blaze. I refused to back down from that.

He's mine. He's mine. He's mine.

That mantra kept running around in my head as soon as I saw him get hurt by one of my fucking supposed friends. Then the guilt slammed into me. I lashed out without a thought. I hurt someone like my parents used to hurt me with absolutely no remorse. After swearing I'd be more under control, I wasn't. All because of fucking Stix.

A surprisingly gentle hand landed on my shoulder, and I turned to see Cueball. "Dude, do you have any idea how fucked up that sounds? He's yours to hate?" He rarely said more than one or two words, so hearing him say full-on sentences told me this was serious. That I'd really fucked up this time. "What Blaze did was an asshole thing to do—"

"Hey!" Blaze snapped.

"Yeah, you're being a fucking prick right now. Sure, we don't like those assholes, but you went against the code, man. You don't mess up the tricks. I love you, man, but stop being a dick for five minutes."

Blaze's eyes widened, then his brows slammed down angrily as he flipped Cueball off. When in the hell did Cue get so smart... and talkative?

"As for you, Stone... this isn't like you. You're calm as fuck, dude." He had no fucking idea. Calmness did not exist in me. I was constantly in turmoil, deep inside, fighting the rage, depression, and uselessness of life. I had no goals, wants, needs... I simply existed to exist. No, I was never calm. My outward calmness was a complete facade.

Cueball stared at me for a moment with narrowed amber eyes, then they widened. "You like him. That's not hate. People don't beat up friends over someone they hate."

I scoffed. "No. I don't like him. I fucking hate him. In fact, I'm pissed off that I reacted like this *because* of him. Fuck him."

But Cueball wasn't buying it, shaking his head. "No, you like him, and that's why you're so pissed and why you've always hated him. Are you... gay or bi, man? I mean, we've only seen you with a couple of girls, so we just assumed you were straight."

Blaze gave a derisive snort. "You can't tell me Stone is fucking gay. No way. Especially not with Mr. Fuck Mouth Stix."

I snapped my eyes at him, ready to hit him again, and this was a fucking problem. Fears of turning into my parents filled me, while flashes of being beaten and put into the hospital at thirteen for... No, I couldn't go there. I wasn't fucking gay, bi, or anything. There was no interest in Stix other than loathing. Right?

Right.

Still, what Cueball had said resounded in my ears, making me question fucking everything, right along with my reaction to Blaze. I shouldn't have cared what Blaze did, but I wanted to crush his thick skull over it. I still did.

"Stone?" Cueball asked.

I growled and shoved away from them, mumbling an apology to Blaze for beating him, though I didn't really mean it. Suddenly, I was unable to breathe. The pressure squeezed like a vise around my chest as the panic descended on me. I couldn't become like my parents. I just couldn't. I didn't fucking escape my personal hell only to turn out like them.

After grabbing my board, I left the building with my eyes never leaving Stix, who also watched me with a mixture of curiosity and disappointment until I was outside.

So much for a fucking relaxing day skating, though I knew it was going to be shit the moment I walked out my apartment door and saw Stix there with his friends, being a smug asshole as always, constantly goading me.

I didn't even feel like skating at all now, so I put my board under my pit and shoved my hands into my jacket as I walked home. But after about a mile, I stopped at the liquor store and bought a bottle of vodka and a new pack of smokes, then continued on my way home. It took me a good thirty minutes by the time I got my keys in the door.

I dropped my shit on the floor and made my way onto my fire escape as if I could literally escape my current hell. After chugging several sips of vodka, I wiped my mouth with my hand and lit a cig. Resting my head back on the bricks, I struggled not to think about my strange obsession with Stix and my need to break Blaze's face for hurting him.

"Fuck!" I ran a hand through my cropped hair as I ran over Cueball's words over and over. I couldn't just brush them aside because he rarely talked, so it had to mean something for him to say so much. Was he right? Was I attracted to Stix?

I couldn't be. I couldn't allow it, even if I were. But it explained my hatred for him, especially learning that he slept with men, recalling my rage and jealousy at seeing him come out of Brie's place. Don't even get me started on the fact that I liked his face. I tried to ignore it, but Cueball forced it to the front of my mind. What was once hatred for Stix suddenly morphed into internalized anger and frustration.

And I sure as fuck didn't know what to do about it.

It was Sunday, and I still had to work at Alpha's tonight. I'd be tired as fuck tomorrow at the fish market, but then I could go to bed early tomorrow night.

Once I started to feel a buzz, I put the cap back on the cheap liquor and shoved the bottle into the freezer for later. I didn't want to be drunk at work. Or at any time, really. It was a perpetual struggle not to turn into my parents, so I vowed to never get married or have kids. I didn't trust myself. Today proved I was correct.

Was that why I didn't bother to find relationships? Or was it something more? Hell, I was barely even interested in sex, which was why my dick coming to life seeing Stix adjust himself yesterday sent confused signals to my brain. It wasn't like it was even that hot. Fine, the one thing I didn't hate him for was how he looked.

I shoved Stix out of my mind with difficulty and took a quick shower before I headed to work.

That night, when I stepped into the employee lounge at Alpha's, my heart and brain stopped at seeing Stix there. I had no idea what to do. Did I ignore him as always until he made some snappy comment? Should I check to see if he was okay? Fuck. Why did I care?

I didn't.

When I opened my locker, I quickly glanced over to find him scowling at me, but he also had confusion in his eyes. But even worse, he had no quick barb or snarky comment at my expense. Only anger as he slammed his locker door. *Even worse?* I hated his snark. I should've been fucking relieved he kept his mouth shut.

Seeing him limp away made me wish I had hurt Blaze even more. God, what was wrong with me? I was all over the fucking place. I should've been grateful he wasn't being a smartass, since it annoyed the fuck out of me. Usually, I was clear-headed with one foot in front of the other, just trying to eke by in this life. And Stix turned my head into a scrambled mess. I shut my eyes to calm the growing panic again. Every time I wasn't sure what to do or where to go, I grew overwhelmed.

Apparently, I went brain-dead when I stepped out in front of him to block his path out the door.

His dark brows slammed down, his mouth twisted as his hands fisted, and his dark eyes dilated in anger. I wasn't used to this side of him, who was usually all smiles and sarcasm. Even his fucking T-shirt was plain and bland, sending more waves of anger at Blaze. Plain T-shirts didn't belong on Stix.

"What?" he snapped. "Isn't it enough that your fucking asshole friend tried to kill me and I got injured? Isn't it enough you hate my guts for no apparent reason? So what now? You here to remind me that you can't stand my presence while being in my presence? As if my simple existence annoys you? Fuck!"

"No."

That only seemed to piss him off more. He fisted my T-shirt and shoved me against the lockers. My body loudly slammed against the metal, rattling the metal, sounding worse than it was. "What the fuck is your problem, *Damien*? I'm sick of this. It's one thing to deal with your shit, but now your shit has rubbed off on your friend. I've been fucking putting up with your attitude, making light of it, but now I got physically hurt, and I've got enough health problems without you all making things worse for me. This shit just got serious. It fucking ends now!"

Health problems? "I didn't know, okay? He just reacted."

He sneered and got in my face so closely that I could smell his spearmint gum on his breath. "Didn't know? Of course, you knew. You mouth off to your friends about me, and then they take it out on me. What did you fucking expect with your little hate game?"

"I punched him for it. He won't touch you again."

He shoved me hard on my chest, but I was bigger, so it didn't hurt, which pissed him off even more.

"I don't get it! What the fuck did I ever do to you? I've been racking my brain, trying to figure it out."

I couldn't turn off the anger if I tried. Angry at Blaze. Angry at Stix for calling me out on my shit. Angry at myself for this fucking mess and not making any sense of it. But the word vomit came tumbling out as soon as I fisted his shirt and swapped places, shoving *him* against the metal this time, pushing out an 'oof' from his lungs.

"You think you're so perfect with your perfect little family, all smug and self-righteous, always pushing my fucking buttons. The constant banging with those fucking sticks day in and fucking day out is driving me goddamn insane! No one is that fucking happy all the time."

He scoffed as he tried to pry my hands off him, but I was immovable. "You're pissed because I'm happy? Look, dude, I'm sorry you had a shitty life, and you have no idea about mine—"

"And you came out of Brie's place," I blurted, and wished I could suddenly take it all back and bury myself under a mountain of rock for the rest of my life. Even worse, I burned from my throat straight up to my ears.

Stix raised his brows, showing how wide and dark and... pretty his eyes were. How thick his lashes were. I physically shook those thoughts out of my head.

"So?"

"You and he have a thing?" I asked, despite my humiliation. I could stop the question as much as I could stop the wind or the sun from rising.

Now his brow was cocked. "A thing? Are you pissed that I'm gay, or are you jealous?"

Fucking both.

He slammed his hands back at my chest again. "Get the fuck off! You better not be some fucking homophobe because I can tell you right now that you don't belong in this job, nor do you deserve it. Alpha's is a safe place. Homophobes aren't fucking welcome. So which is it?"

My breathing picked up as my lungs constricted, and the palpitations in my heart were nearly painful, feeling cornered with no answers to give. It slammed into me like a ton of bricks dropping on my head that it wasn't about Stix being gay, but fear that I was. And I was a whole lot of jealous.

Cueball was right.

Fuck. It wasn't that I was necessarily clueless, but in fucking denial. It all became clear right then, seeing him so angry and slightly afraid. He licked his plump lips, and I internally groaned, just like what happened yesterday, right in this very spot we were in. I couldn't want him. Only pain came from wanting a man. My parents made sure I always understood that. I'd forgotten about it in between all the other abuse and drugged-hazed rants over the years. They all mingled together into a life of horror, but one specific day stood out to me suddenly.

I panted and started to sweat as he waited for my answer, consumed with too many emotions to pinpoint—a tornado of thoughts that made no sense as I spiraled out of control.

Instead of saying anything, I grabbed his face with sweaty and shaking hands and slammed my lips against his. Then, I was suddenly hit with a sense of home for the second time in my life.

Home. I am home.

CHAPTER 8
Stone

I fucking hated P.E. Each time I had to strip down to put on my gym clothes, everyone stared at my body. Not because they wanted to tease me about it. Most kids left me alone since I was bigger than a lot of the boys. It was my scars and bruises, wearing them like a second skin because they'd been a part of me for the past eight years. I couldn't remember what my body looked like without them. It had been a long time since my skin was pristine.

While I'd grown used to how I looked, what made it worse was the silence from others. Maybe there'd be some whispers. Everyone figured I *was being beaten by my parents, but no one did shit. Maybe they cared. Maybe they didn't. But I'd lie every single time I'd been asked by some adult, knowing that if my parents learned I'd told anyone about what had happened, they'd put me in the hospital worse than the last time. I'd tell whoever pretended to care that I was in a fight or that I fell off my bike. I was sure I reused stories. There were only so many lies I could keep up with.*

The only one who knew and cared was my best friend, Alec. He was my only friend. He didn't know the full truth, but I couldn't hide it from him, no matter how many lies I spun.

I removed my shirt, and gentle fingers instantly touched my tender skin. It should've hurt, but all it did was send a wave of chills throughout my body. I hated to be touched, but I loved it when Alec did. I struggled to explain it because I didn't understand my feelings for him.

"Fuck, man. What did you do to piss them off this time?" he whispered, so the other boys didn't hear. His blue eyes dilated to deep ocean black in his anger. His dark brown waves fell in his face as he bent down, inspecting me, making me itch to comb them back to show off those eyes I'd grown obsessed with.

"Nothing. I was skateboarding, and when I tipped off the lip of the ramp, I crashed hard, man."

"Whatever, Damien. You realize your lies don't work on me."

"What do you want me to say?"

He stood straight and looked right at me, forcing me to glance away from his intense stare that always penetrated into my soul. "What I want is for you to turn their drugged-out asses in. Get them arrested so you can escape them."

I slammed my locker too hard after getting on my ugly high school gym shirt in yellow and black. "Then what? Get sent to foster care? Be subjected to other forms of abuse? And who would want a fucking sixteen-year-old?

Everyone wants babies. All I'd be doing is trading one horrible life for another. At least..."

He aimed his head to force me to look at him when I glanced away. "At least what?"

At least I have you.

If they took me away, they'd take me away from Alec. I couldn't do it. I didn't understand it, really. He was beyond my best friend. At some point, I fell hard for him. I liked girls well enough, but I wasn't really interested in kissing them or anything and hadn't been interested in boys at all before until Alec. My parents could never know, though. They'd kill me. They hated anything remotely gay. But a small part of me didn't care. If I ever got a chance to kiss Alec, death would be worth it. I could die happy, as morbid as it sounded. That was how far gone I was for him.

Alec and I did everything together. He moved into our trailer park last year, and we'd been inseparable since. We rode bikes, skateboarded, hiked, swam in the lake nearby, and fucking talked about everything under the sun. No, he was way more than a best friend. I was obsessed with him. I'd never had anyone I'd bonded with before, like the world made Alec just for me. He was my sun.

"Damien..."

"It doesn't fucking matter," I said and walked off toward the gym for P.E.

Alec and I skateboarded home, back to our trailer park and my personal hell. We worked on our tricks, flipping our boards around, trying to land without crashing on our asses. I always had fun around Alec. He was the light, the sun, the moon, and the stars, as far as I was concerned.

"*You want to come over?*" *I asked.* "*Mom and Dad are at work today.*"

"*Cool.*"

"*Cool,*" *I agreed.*

Maybe today was the day. The day I got the balls to claim what I wanted. It wasn't without a fuck ton of fear, but Alec was worth it. If I could have him in my life, all my pain would be forgotten. He made everything right in my world. I stopped questioning why months ago.

We dumped our boards outside of my trailer and walked inside. Despite Mom and Dad being drunk or drugged out half the time, she kept the place pretty clean. Mom worked as a nurse during the day, and I had no fucking idea what Dad did to make a living.

Alec followed me back to my room as I wiped my clammy hands on my jeans. I had a little TV back there. Sometimes he'd come over, and we'd watch a movie, or we'd do homework together. Alec was way smarter than me. Maybe I was smart, but I didn't bother to try all that hard. What was the point? Mom and Dad made sure I had nothing to look forward to in life, reminding me of how worthless I was.

We dropped our backpacks on the floor and plopped on my bed before turning on the TV. I popped on a movie in the DVD player that was older than I was. As it started, Alec climbed into my bed next to me and lay on his side.

I turned to face him because now was the time. I just hoped I didn't ruin our friendship, but I needed more of him. To explore my new found sexuality. Was I gay? Bi? I had no idea since he was the first person I was ever remotely into sexually. I may have jacked off to fantasies of kissing him a few times.

I sat up and crossed my legs, and he sat up to face me. With strength I had no idea I had, I took his hand in mine and played with his fingers, unable to look at him. He didn't freak out or pull away, so I took that as a win. *When I finally got the guts to look at his pretty blue eyes, they were soft, and he wore a little smirk. My body instantly relaxed because I understood right then that I had a chance to be with him the way I wanted.*

"I like you," I blurted. My face burned on fire, but instead of getting freaked out or pissed, he smiled broadly.

"I like you, too."

My eyes rolled, feeling more at ease. "No, I mean... more than a friend."

"So do I. It's about time you told me."

My eyes bugged out of my head. "You knew?"

He nodded as his waves fell in his face again. I finally got to brush them back, feeling comfortable enough to do so. "I'm gay and haven't told you because I know how your parents feel about it. And while I trust you, I was still a little scared. I had a feeling you felt the same, just from the little things you do. Some touches here and there, catching you staring. Things like that."

"Now I feel stupid."

He huffed a laugh before he leaned in and pressed his soft lips against mine.

Home. I am home.

CHAPTER 9
Stix

FOR A COUPLE OF seconds there, I was in meltdown mode, which wasn't the first time when it came to Stone. My body and brain completely shorted out, especially when Stone shoved his tongue into my mouth before I came to my fucking senses. I didn't know where I got my strength from when I pushed Stone off me. He had a good several inches in height on me and was broad and muscular. But fuck him. I was already madder than hell, and for him to kiss me like that? Who the fuck did he think he was? Of course, I chose to ignore how much my dick liked it. Fucking traitor. This was the problem with having the hots for my damn enemy.

At least he quickly backed off. In fact, he looked downright confused, mingled with shock, in his wide hazel eyes. And before I told him
off or... fucking kissed him back, he stormed off and took all the oxygen
with him as I bent over and panted for a moment, trying to clear my
head.

Well, that was different. And unexpected.

My anger quickly deflated as I shook my head, confused as hell.
Perhaps it wasn't so confusing and actually made more sense now.
Admittedly, when I saw Stone punching his own friend when I got hurt
today, I didn't know what that meant or why he would do such a thing.
He hated me, right? So why did he get so pissed at his friend? Pissed
enough to hit him. But this confusing hatred of me grew clearer by the
minute. Maybe it *was* jealousy over my life. I had no idea what Stone had
been through, but I could understand the envy if it had been so terrible.

While I tried to be empathetic, my life wasn't great, either. I sucked
cock for money, for fuck's sake. Then, there was his resentment of me
being gay. Or was it? He never answered, but the kiss was an answer in
itself, wasn't it? Especially after his initial shock, right? If I took a guess,
I'd assume he had some internalized homophobia. Was he gay and in
denial? Or did he recently realize he was and hated himself for it and
hated me for being part of that discovery?

Too many damn questions. Too much confusion.

Or I could just not fucking give a shit. Stone had been a dick to me
for far too long. He couldn't just come up and kiss me like that. Fine, I
didn't hate it, but still. That shit wasn't going to fly with me.

If he wanted me, he'd have to get cool real fast and do some serious
groveling. Shit, I guess I should, too, since I enjoyed tormenting him so
much. Not that he'd even try again. Judging by the look on his face, he
freaked himself out. Would I even really want him, anyway? Oh, well.

I needed to stop thinking about fucking Stone and get ready for work. He'd already taken up entirely too much time and space in my brain.

As I cleared away beer bottles and glasses throughout the evening, I kept glancing over at Stone. He'd been monitoring the floor tonight while Ajax took IDs. Not once did Stone glance over at me or acknowledge what had happened in the employee lounge. Honestly, it was kind of getting on my nerves. I mean, come on. We kissed! Yeah, I shoved him away, and it probably pissed him off even more, but still... Ugh, why did I even want his attention, anyway? I mean, my back killed me, thanks to his asshole friend. And Stone had always hated me, and he wasn't even that fucking cool. *Fine*, he was really cool and really hot, but those things weren't justification enough to get me to like him or care how he felt about me.

God, I was being weird tonight, and it was all his fault, dammit.

If he wanted to ignore me, two could play that game.

By Friday, it had been almost a week since Stone tried to kiss me. And all that time, he'd avoided me like the plague. If he came out onto the fire escape to smoke, and I was out there, he'd go right back inside until I finished. We hadn't stumbled into each other or met each other accidentally in the hall of the apartments as if he was looking out his peephole to make sure we didn't see each other.

What a dickhead.

Whatever. I had more important things to deal with than some asshole with internalized homophobia. Life was complicated enough, and I was too busy trying to earn money to pay bills and figure out my own life.

I tossed the used condom in the trash and washed my hands as Brie stood in the bathroom doorway, watching me as he always did with that disappointed look on his face. The feeling was mutual, although his disappointment differed from mine. He wanted more from me, and not simply to save money. He wanted all of me, whereas I grew tired of this arrangement and wanted to stop fucking and sucking. I stuck with it because there was no other job out there that paid me what I made per week or gave me this sort of flexibility. I only answered to myself, so if I wanted to take a sick day, I didn't have to ask for fucking permission. But, god, if Mom ever found out, she'd kill me, even if I was a grown-ass adult. Alpha would probably wring my neck, too. He'd been trying to get us to shoot straight instead of zigzagged through life.

"I want more, Nico," he said boldly.

And there it was. He finally got the guts to vocalize his wants. If I said no, there was a good chance that our arrangement would come to an end, then I'd have to kiss a hundred and fifty bucks a week goodbye. I didn't want to have to find a replacement. It took me forever to cultivate my client list—men who became regulars and wouldn't turn me into the cops, and who trusted me in return.

I fixed my hair and glanced back at him in the mirror. He leaned against the door jamb, still naked. His light brown hair was still damp, making it curl on the ends, but the sheen of sweat over his body had dried. Brie was a good-looking guy, but I just couldn't be with him. Honestly, the only one who'd been plaguing my sexual thoughts lately was Stone, no matter how hard I tried to shove him out of my brain.

"I can't, Brie. You understand this."

"You realize I wouldn't be bothered with you doing this with other men, right?"

And he probably wouldn't. While he made a valid point, it didn't change the fact that I wasn't attracted to him that way. I was attracted enough to my clients to get my dick up because sex was sex, but nothing deeper than that.

I sighed. "I know you wouldn't, for now. Eventually, you would."

He stood taller with widening blue eyes as if I gave him some hope. "I won't... I swear."

"Brie—"

"God, Nico... I just want to fucking kiss you. To have sex with you facing me."

"I'm a whore, Brie. Nothing more. Nothing less. I'm not equipped to have a relationship right now, and I need the money. But if... you can't do this anymore; I understand."

He looked down, picking at his cuticles while I splashed warm water on my face so I didn't have to see his hurt. I felt terrible for the guy. He was lonely. Hell, so was I. We were on the same page in that department. Being with men for money didn't make one feel less lonely. In fact, all this sex made it worse sometimes. The feeling left me a little dead inside when I sucked the dick of someone I didn't care about. It had all become a chore at some point. And I really wanted someone to hold sometimes or to be held back and loved on.

I really needed to end this with him, no matter the money. He was getting too attached and wanting too much, and we'd been doing this for too long, which was the problem. It would only hurt him more in the long run.

After drying my face, I turned to look at him and bit the bullet. "Maybe it's time for us to make... new arrangements. To move on."

His eyes grew wide again as he looked at me. "No... I'm sorry I brought this up. Really. Ugh, can I just take everything back? This arrangement is fine. It's good. I love having you here and getting what I can get."

I stood closer to him with folded arms. "Wouldn't you rather not have to settle? Don't you feel you deserve more than that? You're a great man, Brie. You're attractive, fun, and smart. But if I'm being honest, I have my eyes on someone else."

He looked down again at his feet and nodded. "I see. Shit, I wish I hadn't said anything."

I grabbed his shoulders and shook him gently to look at me. "I'm glad you did. You deserve better than this."

His blue eyes glistened with unspilled tears. "I'm going to miss this."

"I will, too." And that wasn't a lie. I'd gotten used to this arrangement and the money. And he *was* a cool dude.

To ease him into our new dynamic, I cupped his face and pulled him into a kiss. He whimpered against my lips to hold back a sob and tentatively rested his hands on my naked hips. My tongue slipped into his mouth, and our kiss deepened before I pulled away, not wanting to give him the wrong impression. I just felt I owed him a kiss after all our time together.

"That was the saddest and most beautiful thing, Nico. Thank you for that."

Tears finally let go, and I wiped them away from his cheeks with my thumbs. "You'll find your man. I promise. And someone a hell of a lot better than me. Someone who can meet all your needs. You deserve more than a fuck, Brie."

My hand cupped the nape of his neck and pulled his head down to kiss his forehead.

"Can we still be friends?" he asked.

I smiled and nodded. "Definitely. We're neighbors, after all, right? And we've been through a lot together."

He gave me a wet smile before I moved into his room and gathered my clothes to get dressed quickly. I needed to hurry and get ready for work.

When I stepped out of Brie's apartment, there he was. The stone man himself. Mr. Granite. My heart and breathing stopped for a second before going into hypersonic overdrive.

I would've found a way to tease him if it weren't for his tight fists that looked ready to crush the nearest person and his narrowed eyes of death, looking between me and Brie's door.

Right. Stone had no idea what I did for a living, probably assuming Brie and I were a thing, which he intimated about the other day. If Stone's jealousy were real, he'd be fucking pissed right about now, and he looked the part.

Instead of being afraid or getting defensive, I waved and winked at him. "See you at work, Rolling Stone." Fine, I had to tease him just a little bit.

His growl went straight to my nuts, which also pissed me off. God, he was so fucking confusing; even my body couldn't figure him out.

Before I could say anything else, he took off quickly down the stairs. Asshole.

I didn't know the band tonight, so no drumming for me. That didn't stop me from tapping on the bar, stools, and tables whenever I had downtime. I also practiced my spins, twirling the sticks between my fingers, trying not to drop them. I really needed to save some money for a drum set. Then I could get some pads to muffle the noise and not drive Mom and the neighbors crazy. Although, driving Stone crazy seemed like my goal lately. But, at this rate, I doubted I'd ever find a band to play with. I sighed and cleared off the bar after some patrons left.

"What's going on with you?" Alpha asked, elbowing me. "You're awfully pensive today. And that's a lot of sighing you've been doing all night."

"I'm not sighing," I huffed, proving him right.

"Sure you're not. So, what gives?"

"Nothing."

He folded his bulky inked arms and leaned against the bar. "You're much more chipper than this. Out with it."

Well, I lost my best client today, but I wasn't about to tell him that. Alpha would kill me along with my mother. "It's just... someone's bugging the hell out of me. I can't tell if I want to kiss him or fucking punch him. Honestly, I'd be content with either."

His smile was broad as he chuckled. "Ah, love. Who is it? Someone I know?"

I bit my bottom lip for a second, debating on telling him. "Maybe."

He raised a brow and wore a crooked smirk. "It's got to be someone already here to get you this riled up. A customer? An employee?" Then he looked around his bar for a while before his eyes landed directly on Stone. I knew he did because Stone was looking directly at us, wearing a scowl that could peel paint. "Found him."

"Goddammit. You're an intuitive dickhead."

"Ha! I *love* being right!"

"Stop looking at him. He's going to know you're talking about him."

Alpha turned to face me. "So, what are you going to do about it?"

"Absolutely nothing."

He frowned. "Why? He's an attractive guy, if not a bit broody."

"He's an asshole who hates me."

"How could anyone possibly hate you?"

I tossed my arms up in the air. "Fuck if I know. I'm pretty fucking awesome. But don't say shit to him. I mean it, Alpha."

He threw a wet rag in my face, laughing. "As you wish."

"Gross!" I snapped and threw it back, completely missing him as he walked off. I ignored his cackle before I grabbed my tray and started to clean off the tables and take orders.

Not a few minutes later, as I watched the band for a moment, someone came up from behind me and grabbed my shoulder. My stomach flipped around, thinking it was Stone, but then it dropped when I turned to face Tony Solomon. I sighed in disappointment, not in the mood to deal with one of my clients, especially after today.

Tony parted his cropped brown hair on the side and kept it neat, and his brown eyes were soft with thick lashes. He was an okay-looking dude. But damn, he was built and bulky as hell, who stood at six feet even. Apparently, he'd been some linebacker in college until he had a nasty concussion.

"What's up, Tony?" I said as chipper as I could, regardless of my annoyance, not wanting to piss off a client.

He was the store manager at the grocery store down the street from my apartment. He had been another accident. Someone I stumbled into for making some quick cash. I had been with Brie for a month when I came into the store to find Tony in a foul mood, snapping at a poor old lady for breaking a jar of pickles on the floor, which wasn't like him. He was usually a chill dude.

I'd asked him what had happened when we were alone, and he'd finally admitted that he and his wife hadn't been intimate in nearly six months. It was stressing him out, and it wasn't like he could force her or beg her. So, it left him frustrated as hell. That was when I offered to get him off for fifty bucks, telling him to pretend I was his wife. Was it cheating if it was with a dude, and you weren't romantically into them? Maybe. He agreed to it, which surprised the shit out of me, considering he was not only married, but straight. I really didn't think he'd go for it. Since then, I'd hit the store on his break two to three times a week to suck him off. He was a needy dude. No wonder she frequently turned him down.

"Hey... Ah, I haven't seen you in like two weeks, Nico."

Usually, I stopped by the store, and I'd just give him a blow job, so he rarely called, but I hadn't stopped by, being distracted and all. It had just slipped my mind.

"Did you just come here to hunt me down for a blowie?" Yeah, I didn't mask my annoyance. "I do have a fucking phone."

He looked at the band while he rubbed the back of his neck. At least he had the decency to look guilty.

"My bad. But I'm desperate, man, and I can't find your damn number. Look, it's been a while, and you know how much I need it. Your mouth is like crack."

I couldn't help but snort a laugh, but I also gave him an eye roll. So, I grabbed his hand and pulled him toward the back storage room. No one went back there until the bar closed to restock, so we'd be safe. The problem was it didn't have a door, needing to do it behind a shelf or something. And we'd have to be quick because I was on the clock.

"You're the best, man," he said, unbuckling and unzipping his jeans and pulling them down around his ankles with his underwear.

"I know."

After slipping me fifty bucks, he stroked himself as I pulled out a condom from my wallet. I opened the wrapper and rolled it over his now-swollen cock.

"Thanks for this, Nico."

As soon as my mouth wrapped around him, he groaned, and his knees nearly buckled. "God, you give the best head."

I couldn't believe I agreed to this, but whatever. I lost a client today, so I could use the cash.

Once I got serious about sucking him off, I happened to glance up to find the last person I expected to see.

CHAPTER 10
Stone

WHY THE FUCK DID I kiss Stix? I berated myself for a week after I stormed out of the employee lounge. It just happened. Like my body needed him. But Stix, stopping me, had me coming to my senses. He was seeing another man and didn't need me messing with that, no matter how much I hated him dating our neighbor, despite Brie being too fucking old for him.

Of course, work had been a pain in the ass and awkward as hell with him running around, distracting me with being unable to take my eyes off him. That was when I noticed Tony. I knew him from the grocery store since I'd shopped there often enough. So, him knowing Stix didn't surprise me. But the sexual vibration emitting from Tony toward Stix *was* a surprise. What was going on here? Who were they to each other? And wasn't Stix already with Brie? That shit already pissed me off, but seeing Stix grab Tony's hand and pull him to the back of the bar had me seeing red, which became a common theme when it came to Stix. He always had my blood boiling.

I walked up to Ajax and tapped his arm. "Keep an eye out here for me."

Ajax narrowed his eyes, still pissed about what had happened while skating the other day. The only thing that kept me from getting pummeled was punching Blaze in retaliation. And there was a possibility Ajax could beat me. I was only a couple of inches shorter, but he had a lot more crazy on him.

"Where are you going?"

"Do you need to hold my hand while I take a piss, too?" I snapped.

He sneered at me but moved toward the front door to check IDs while keeping an eye on the floor.

I didn't know what possessed me to follow them, or what my intentions even were. I just had this instinctual drive to find out what was going on. I *needed* to know if they slept together, too. Stix and two men? What an asshole.

I rushed toward the back and couldn't find Stix and Tony until I stumbled upon them in the storage room, with fucking Stix on his knees and Tony's cock in his mouth. My breath caught, and my heart pounded, watching him. But I wasn't sure if it was out of anger or arousal. No, it was fucking both.

Tony had a fucking big dick, which stretched Stix's lips wide as he fisted the rest of Tony's shaft. He pulled Tony out of his mouth and licked from base to tip before slipping his condom-covered cock back into his mouth.

"God, you give the best head," Tony breathed, making my dick pulse and twitch to life.

I fisted my hands as I swelled in my jeans. I needed to leave.

Turn around. Leave now.

Then suddenly, Stix met my eyes, and I leaked inside my underwear. His eyes were darker than usual as he pushed Tony as deep as he would go down his throat. He wasn't shocked. He didn't stop sucking Tony's dick. Nor did he explain himself. Stix just kept on going.

I needed to go. To run. But I stood there, transfixed, and held captive with Stix not taking his eyes off me and putting on a show. I had no doubt he could see how hard I was, and I didn't hide it, afraid the spell would be broken if I dared move.

This was the first time I'd ever seen a man giving another man head before. My mind kept screaming at me to leave. Red flags waved, telling me this was vile and disgusting, just as my parents had beaten into me. The words rattled there in my brain, but my body said otherwise. I was glued to the floor, completely turned on, and it pissed me the fuck off because wanting Stix was dangerous.

My body trembled from a combination of fear and need as the voices kept telling me to stop watching because it was disgusting. But it wasn't disgusting. Not really.

Stix's hand twisted around Tony's shaft while the tip of his tongue darted out, swiping under the sensitive ridge and digging into his tip. Tony groaned as he forked his fingers through Stix's bleached-blond strands, then fisted handfuls of hair. I imagined they were my hands, controlling him as I pumped into him and fucked his mouth, making him gag on my cock.

He knew exactly what he was doing to me as he sucked down Tony again, almost to the root. And I knew he did it on purpose. That knowledge didn't stop my cock from throbbing, and it jumped in my pants when he gagged, making his eyes water and saliva spill out of his mouth. *Jesusfuckinggoddammit.*

"God, Nico... you feel so good. Don't stop. Don't ever stop."

Tony stood there, completely oblivious to my presence, lost in his own arousal, not even noticing that Stix hadn't once looked up at him. Stix's chocolate eyes stayed on mine the entire time. While I was way too aroused, watching my bane and my lust sucking someone else off, I fucking hated it, too. Hated that it was Tony. Hated that Stix had fucked Brie today. But the only thing that truly disturbed me more was that it wasn't me instead of Tony. Staring at Stix and his expert mouth made me wish I was the one lost in his wet heat. I'd never let a man touch me before, but I couldn't stop thinking about it now. Shit, if I were being honest, not even a woman had turned me on like Stix did right now. And he wasn't even touching me. How?

I should've ripped Tony away from Stix. The irrational jealousy floated about like an ominous thunderstorm, but my connection to Stix couldn't be severed, no matter how hard I tried. That connection had been a fucking problem since we first met.

I nearly blew right then when Stix undid his jeans and pulled out his cock, stroking it to the rhythm of his sucks. He had a long and smooth cock, which wasn't overly thick, and... Fucking hell. His eyes rolled back into his head, leaving my face for the first time since I'd found the two men.

"I'm going to come... So close," Tony groaned. "Fuck..."

Stix sucked harder and faster, hollowing out his cheeks and literally sucking the cum out of Tony's dick as he pumped his hand faster around

his own cock, which was swelling and turning red. Despite the muf-
fled music from the bar, the sucking sounds, slapping of cocks,
moaning, and gagging filled the air and clanged in my ears. I'd never
been so turned on before. Not even with the women I'd been with.
And the fact that I wasn't even being touched sent an odd wave of
pleasure rippling through me. If Stix could do that to me without
touching me, imagine what it would be like if he had. I shouldn't have
had these thoughts, but Stix owned me in that heated moment. He
held me captive. Right then, I'd give him the world for him to touch
me.

I fucking silenced my parents' hateful voices as I cupped myself to
stem the inevitable orgasm, which wouldn't happen because no way
could it without me touching it, right?

Suddenly, Tony's body froze. His orgasmic groan was so guttural,
like it came from the depths of his soul. Stix popped off as he stroked
Tony through his shudders and moans while stroking himself. His
eyes darted back to me before shuttering, and then his glistening lips
parted when he came, spilling all over his hand and onto the floor. His
own groan was almost as deep, while mumbling, *'fuck'* over and over.

The two men stood stock still, no doubt trying to calm their
hearts, while mine threatened to beat right out of my chest.

Tony looked down to see Stix's hand covered in cum and still
holding his softening dick. "Fuck, Nico... you never came with me
before. That's so... sexy. I shouldn't like that, but I do. Like a lot."

Stix's eyes opened straight into me again. I nearly felt his arousal,
and his silence was clear. That little show was definitely for me. I had
no idea what to make of it or why he did it. Hell, why did I even stay
and watch? Whatever the reasons, I needed to get off. There was no way
I could return to work on the floor with a hard-on that wouldn't quit,

and my balls ached from their heaviness. And it sat painfully hard inside my jeans, making it too uncomfortable.

I turned on my heels, rushed to the employee's bathroom, and stepped into the nearest two stalls. After quickly undoing my pants, dropping them along with my underwear around my knees, and pulling out my dick, I tried to shut the stall door behind me but couldn't. I turned to find Stix standing there, looking straight at my dick.

"Go the fuck away."

"Not a fucking chance."

"You did that on purpose."

"Of course, I did it on purpose. I can help you with that, you know."

"Fuck you."

I turned, trying to ignore Stix standing behind me because I was desperate. Short of a nuclear blast, nothing would stop me from coming. Not even him. My mind was like a drunk person, unable to think clearly, and all rationality flew out the window, leaving behind only impulsiveness.

I stroked fast and hard. The calloused skin on my hands was harsh against my sensitive cock, but eventually, I worked it enough to use my pre-cum. Soon the world vanished, leaving behind my grunts and skin slapping. But then surprisingly gentle caresses with fingers slid between my ass cheeks. I quickly turned to face him, continuing to stroke myself, wanting to... stop him? Beg for more? I didn't fucking know! But I kept at it as he moved closer, watching me. He was so close; I felt the heat from his skin and smelled the arousal of his previous orgasm. I drowned in his scent, willing to die surrounded by it by that point.

Instinct forced my forehead to rest against his, and I quietly whimpered at the contact.

"God, you have a pretty cock," he whispered. Stix reached around me and touched my ass again, and that was it. I just came over and over. It was fucking relentless, shooting my cum into my hand as much as possible, but some leaked onto the floor.

"Fuuuck!"

Stix's fingers quickly left me, leaving me aching for more, but grateful he stopped touching me. God, he turned me into a confused fucking mess.

When I finally calmed the hell down, I pulled up my pants and underwear as everything came back to me in a rush. That fucking bastard pulled that shit out of me without even trying. It was like his goddamn superpower.

I looked up to find him still standing there with wide, dark eyes and cupping his dick, which was clearly swollen again.

"That was so fucking hot, Rolling Stone," he rasped.

I growled and shoved my way past him, uncaring that I slammed him against the bathroom wall. Once my clarity returned, so did the disgust. Disgust with myself and my reaction to a fucking blow job between two other men. My parent's hatred and anger rang in my ears, and memories of fists against my small body slammed into me.

I gripped the sink in fists so tight my knuckles turned white, and my head hung low, gasping for breath. I needed to get back out there but couldn't move yet, desperate to find my lungs. Everything my parents did to me hung over my head like a hurricane, threatening to destroy my careful control. Fuck, my control fled as soon as I followed Stix and Tony to the back room. Everything I buried deep within myself came back with so little effort because of Stix. That was why he was a fucking problem. Now that he unlocked secrets not even known to me, I wasn't sure I could put them back, or if I even wanted to.

"Stone, I'm... sorry. That was—"

"Forget it." I took a shuddered breath and lifted my head to look at him in the mirror. His dark eyes were wide, and he was gnawing on his still-swollen bottom lip while he wrapped his arms protectively around himself, looking remorseful. But instead of getting angry as I had expected, I deflated like my muscles melted off me. We'd both gotten carried away. If it was his fault, it was mine, too. I didn't have to follow him and Tony. I didn't have to stay and watch. And I certainly didn't have to stroke myself to oblivion. But fuck, when Stix taunted, I reacted. Every. Single. Time.

I grabbed paper towels and wiped my cum off the floor before quickly washing my hands. Ignoring him and the pleading look in his pretty eyes, I headed back to my job and continued to ignore him for the rest of the night, despite his best efforts to burn a hole in me with his stares. Even though he never touched me again tonight, I felt him fucking everywhere. He was all over my skin and deep inside my soul.

When the bar shut down, and we were ready to leave, I shrugged on my jacket and suddenly felt a hand on my shoulder. I closed my eyes and held my breath, knowing instantly who it was. Goddamn Stix and our irritating connection.

"Will you please let me apologize now?"

I whirled on him, but glanced around to make sure there were no ears to hear us. "I said, forget it," I hissed.

"It was really stupid of me. I just saw you there, and... I don't know what came over me."

Same thing happened to me.

I had to know, since I had him here, forcing me to talk to him. "You a cheater? First, you're with Brie, then Tony. I thought Tony was fucking married."

He bit his bottom lip again, constantly forcing me to look at it, and then he rubbed the back of his neck. "I need a smoke, and... shit. I'll tell you. You can walk me home." He winked, and I scowled, but it was only half-hearted on both our parts.

There was something about kissing him tonight and seeing him giving a blow job while I let off steam that changed something in me. My gears wound a little smoother, so I wasn't so fucking agitated.

We headed outside with our boards tucked under our arms, but didn't skate, so he could talk and tell me what the fuck was going on. But judging by what he'd been doing with the two men, something told me he wasn't dating them as I'd first assumed. And I wasn't sure if that made me feel better or not.

The night was cooler than usual for late September, as Stix pulled out a pack of cigs and offered me one. I took it despite having my own. He lit his as I lit mine, then we started walking. This was the first time I'd ever put up being near him without being in some irrational rage. I really needed to keep that in check. My temper was too much sometimes, which scared me.

"So?"

He fiddled with one of his hoop earrings with his cigarette hand and glanced up at me. "Well, you know I have no dad around, right?"

"Yeah."

"I came out as gay three years ago, and he pretty much abandoned us. My fucking sister was only two. He couldn't take having a gay son, willing to give up his entire family, especially after Mom protected me. Anyway, I blamed myself for years. Hell, I still do. Maybe he'd still be around if I had just kept my yap shut."

"He would've left, anyway." It sounded blunt and cruel, but it was the truth. His father would've found an excuse to leave, eventually.

Stix shrugged, playing off the hurt. "Maybe."

"What does that have to do with sleeping with Brie and Tony?"

He sighed and ran a hand through his mussed hair, making it stick up more. I quickly glanced away because I liked it too much, imagining him looking like that right after getting fucked. God, what was wrong with me? I'd never thought of anyone this sexually before—man or woman.

"Well, it's not like Mom makes tons as a waitress at the diner. And my job at Alpha's helps, but it's not enough. Mom was going to get a second job, but I told her fuck that. I'd just get another one. I found one, but... it was by accident. Well, not really an accident. I saw an opportunity, and I jumped on it."

I shook my head and took a drag from my cigarette. "I'm confused..." I paused and stopped walking when it dawned on me. "Wait, are you saying—"

"That I sleep with men for money? Yep. God, please don't say anything to anyone. I honestly have no reason to trust you, but you've apparently caught me twice. Not even Alpha knows, okay? He'd fucking kill me. Anyway, I don't really have sex except with Brie, and only because he paid me pretty good to fuck him. None of them fuck me. Well, except one. Usually, I only give them blow jobs for some quick cash."

All this time, I thought life was good for him. He went to work, his family life was happy, and that was it. Fine, his family life was still happy, but he was missing his father from it. But was that why I really hated him? I think it was mostly directed at myself for being interested in him, and I had been in denial for a long time, so I projected my internalized anger onto him. Things were strangely clearer now. Was one strong orgasm all it took to make me see the truth?

"Why are you telling me this?"

"Dude, you caught me. You need to understand that no one can know. It's just a secret I'd like to keep, and I don't need you blabbing it to people. If you understood, maybe you'll be a little less of an asshole. Sorry, not sorry."

I stopped and faced him. "Is that why you apologized earlier? Because you got caught?"

"What? No! Okay, yeah, I'm a little worried, but I shouldn't have played with you like that or... touched you. Dude, I don't know what it is about you, but I toy with you like no one's business. I don't mess with anyone else, but you make me itch to do it. You're such a fucking dickhead, and you make it so easy. And you get so riled up."

"You're a fucking dickhead, too."

He snorted a laugh and took a drag of his cig before we walked on. "Fair. By the way, I've stopped things with Brie today."

"Why?" I swear to fucking god, my heart just bloomed at the news.

"He wanted something I couldn't give him."

"I saw the way he looked at you once." The same way I looked at him before I even recognized what I was doing.

He shrugged, changing the subject. "So... thanks for... defending me against your friend."

"He shouldn't have hurt you like that. That's my job."

"Dude! Did you just make a joke?"

I glared at him. "I don't joke."

He swallowed, looking unsure. I was only half-joking. If anyone was going to mess with him, it was going to be me. I still wouldn't have hurt him like that. At least, I hoped not.

When I finished my cig, I dropped it on the ground and put it out with my Chucks before shoving my hands in my jeans pockets.

"Does this mean we're friends now?" he asked, smirking at me.

"No." The flash of disappointment made me almost feel bad. "But...
maybe I don't hate you so much."

CHAPTER 11
Stone

I COULDN'T GET MY jacking off in front of Stix the other night out of my mind, or how he grazed my ass with his finger. Or how I faced him after he touched me as if we became fucking lovers or something. I hadn't come that hard in a while, and if I were being honest, it was the first time I had come that hard. Women never made me come like that, if at all. Fucking them turned into a chore sometimes, like it was something I had to do rather than wanted to do. I didn't know if it was my partner or simply a 'me problem.' There'd been times when I'd gone down on them just to get it over with, and they wouldn't question my lack of enthusiasm. I also really didn't want to admit what it all meant. That didn't stop me from jacking three more times since, with visions of Stix sucking dick... *my* dick. Jesus.

I'd also had to apologize to Blaze several more times, despite not giving a shit that I punched him in his smug mug. I didn't feel bad, but I also knew it was wrong. We were roommates and supposed friends, so it wasn't cool to punch your friends. Plus, Cueball pressured me to do it so we would all get along again. Blaze finally forgave me after stewing and giving me the silent treatment for a week when I bought him a bottle of cheap tequila and a pack of smokes.

My work day was nearly over, and I had been plagued with thoughts of Stix the entire time. I struggled to get him out of my fucking mind. If he had consumed me before, now he just owned every nook and cranny of my brain. Knowing he was some prostitute and thoughts of him fucking me for cash wouldn't leave me. And seeing him on his knees was a vision I couldn't pluck out of my thoughts, no matter how hard I tried.

The monotony of gutting and cutting fish guaranteed to clear my head, but not even that was my salvation. At the end of my shift, I headed home and jacked off one more time in the shower. There was no fucking relief in sight. No fucking getting Stix out of my brain. He lived there, rent-free. And I was damn near tired of being aroused all the time. Some men would love it, but I wasn't used to it at all.

When I came out dressed and headed to the kitchen, I found Blaze and Cueball in there making dinner. There must have been something on my face because they both looked at me with raised brows.

"What?" I asked.

"Something die up your ass, Stone? You're looking more scowlier than normal."

Cueball just nodded in agreement.

"Nothing's wrong. I'm fine."

"Sure you are, but you're Stone, man. Normally, you don't wear your emotions on your face."

I glanced over at Cueball, who was nodding again.

Whatever. I didn't owe them an explanation. I bypassed them, headed straight to the cabinet, and pulled out a bowl. Then, in another cabinet, I grabbed my box of cereal. Once I poured the cereal into the bowl, I put away the box and grabbed some milk, opening it and taking a sniff to make sure it was still good. While I made my meager dinner, I felt their eyes burning a hole into my back.

I leaned against the counter, with my back to them, hating that they read me so well, and took a large bite of my cereal. Milk dribbled down my chin, and I wiped it off with a paper towel.

"Spit it out," Cueball said.

I didn't look back at him. I couldn't. He'd be able to see right through me. Like somehow they'd know I'd been jacking off to Stix, the one man they knew I couldn't stand. Already, Cueball figured out my interest in him more than simple loathing. He turned out to be more intuitive than I gave him credit for.

"There's nothing to spit out," I said finally.

Once I finished my cereal, I washed the bowl and put it away. Then I headed back to my room, closing the door behind me. I grabbed my jacket, tossed it on, and grabbed my smokes and lighter sitting on my rickety nightstand. I hadn't been out to smoke on the fire escape very much, afraid I'd run into Stix. I didn't want to talk to him again. At least not yet.

Going back into the living room, I opened the window and peeked out to make sure Stix wasn't out there. When the coast was clear, I climbed out into the chilly night.

I lit my cig, took a long drag from it, and exhaled as I leaned my head back against the bricks, scrubbing my cropped hair with my hand. Fuck, why was I so obsessed with him? Whether it was from anger or... reluctant lust, he fucking owned me, and I didn't know how to get it to stop. No one had ever consumed me like he did. Why? It wasn't like he was some supermodel, perfectly fit, or someone who just stood out from the crowd. That was a lie. He stood out. He was Mr. Nice Guy, yet he stood up to me and always seemed fearless and... happy. Regardless, people were drawn to him, as I was, apparently.

If I really wanted to dig in deep, I'd discover that I was connected to him somehow. Well, I knew we were, but I'd been in fucking denial over it. He just drew me in, and I resented him for it. The truth was more complex than that. I was afraid of what I wanted. So much so that even jacking off to fantasies of him left my hands shaking. Those were residual fears left over from my parents. It had to be like some PTSD or some shit.

I closed my eyes and tried to focus on the traffic sounds as people drove home from work or to bars to drink away their pain. Sirens played in the distance, and everyone was fucking impatient around here, honking their horns when drivers didn't move fast enough. White noise usually helped calm me, but now, the din did nothing to distract me. And above all that noise was Stix, opening a window and stepping out onto the fire escape. I sensed him even before he showed his face.

Goddammit.

My heart beat a little too fast, and my free hand clenched on my legs that I had stretched out on the metal grate.

"Hey," he said, sounding tentative and unsure, probably because he confessed all that shit to me, then I completely ghosted him.

I couldn't speak to him. If I did, I'd say something I'd regret. Something like I hated him. I desperately wanted him. Fuck these confused thoughts. They drove me fucking crazy.

I pretended to ignore him and tossed my cig down to the ground below, climbed back inside, and headed to my bedroom, only to find Cueball sitting on my bed, waiting for me.

"What do you want?"

"Go to him."

"Fuck you."

"You can be pissy all you want. I realize you don't want to admit shit in front of Blaze, but you're safe with me."

"Safe? Why would I need safety?"

"You tell me."

"Get out," I growled, but I was the one who left my room, not wanting to talk this fucking shit out. Since when had Cueball been so insightful or... interesting? I struggled to figure him out. What was new? Apparently, I was incapable of figuring anything out.

I kept on walking, and before I realized it, I stood out in the hall and knocked on Stix's door, but I didn't turn away and go back. My brain told me to leave, while my body insisted I stay.

His mother opened it with a smile on her face. "Hello, Damien. What can I do for you?"

She knew who I was? Sure, I was her neighbor, but it wasn't like I ever introduced myself to her before. Stix probably fucking told her all about me. God, what if he told her how much of a dick I had been to her son? Then the guilt hit. If I cared about that, then it showed how wrong I'd been. What a piece of shit I was.

"Hi, ah... Ms. Jamieson."

"It's Grace. Please. I'm not that old yet."

I gave her a quick nod. "Is... Nico around?" *Yes, nimrod. He's outside smoking.*

She stood aside to let me in. "Sure, he's smoking, much to my dismay. He never listens."

I stepped inside to scents of garlic and tomato sauce and a sense of home I'd never had. Stix's little sister, Nova, sat at the table chowing down on spaghetti noodles with a big, messy smile on her face as she waved to me.

"Hi!"

I gave her an awkward wave. "Hey."

She was about to climb down from her chair to greet me before her mother stopped her. "Nope, finish your dinner. He's here to see your brother, not you, Missy."

I swallowed hard, with memories of my own mother smacking me across the face when I wouldn't finish my microwaved chicken nuggets that tasted like freezer burn and cardboard. Stix's mother was patient and kind.

"Nico, you have a visitor, she called out."

A bright blond head popped up through the window, and he looked directly at me, not hiding his surprise, probably because I'd been ignoring his ass as of two minutes ago.

He climbed through the window and walked over to me. Before I could process what he was doing and protest, he grabbed my hand, threaded our fingers together, which felt entirely too natural and comfortable, and pulled me toward his room.

There were two beds in there. Little girl stuff and too much pink covered one side of the room, and his side of the room was covered in band, skating posters, and other memorabilia.

He led me to his full-sized bed and pointed at it. "Sit."

I did as I was told, sitting on his thick, black comforter.

He sat beside me, leaning against the scarred headboard, and curled a leg underneath him. "So, this is a first. Welcome to my abode. What can I do for you, Stone? You've been intentionally avoiding me since our little discussion the other night. I have to admit; I thought maybe things had changed between us. Was I wrong?"

I rested my arms on my thighs and leaned over, shaking my head. "No."

"Why are you here, Rolling Stone?" he sighed.

"I... don't know."

"I think you do."

He wasn't wrong, but I fucking fought it. Hard.

We were quiet for so long that I worried I wouldn't get the balls to ask, but he waited me out, giving me more patience than I deserved.

"I want to... hire you." I winced at my words, but they needed to be said. Yes, I needed to try it. To test out if it was just him, or because I was into dudes, or that my obsession with him was some sort of weird fluke.

"Hire me?"

I finally glanced over at him, watching me, but I couldn't read his face. "Yes."

"To be clear, you want the services I provide for men like Brie and Tony."

All I could do was nod. Thank fuck, he didn't ask why. I'd never been so confused over a person in my fucking life.

"Can't," he admitted.

I deflated in disappointment, and at the same time, the rage grew again. My hands fisted, and I scowled at him. "Why not me, too? Why them? My money is as good as theirs." Not that I could afford much.

"You and I kissed," he said, shrugging as if that was all the answer I needed.

"So?"

"I don't kiss clients. Ever."

I sagged. That was the one thing I wanted the most.

He scooted close enough to me that we touched thighs and shoulders. At least he wasn't making fun of me or tormenting me about it. He grabbed my hand and threaded our fingers together again. The surge of electricity hit me as I tried not to let the disappointment consume me while it mingled with need and arousal. Who got aroused over being next to a person holding hands? Apparently, I did.

"Dude, part of me doesn't understand why I'm saying this, but if you want me, then you can have me." My heart surged to life again, and my hands grew clammy. What was he saying? If I could have him, why did he just turn me down? "I'm strangely attracted to you, despite you always being an absolute dickhead to me. But something's there. Some weird connection between us, and I think you like me, too, but it seems you're in some weird form of denial about your sexuality or interest in me." Before I protested, he raised a hand. "Hey, I'm not saying there's anything wrong with that. Lots of people are confused. I was, too, once upon a time. I don't mind being your experiment if you need me to help you discover what you like or don't like. So, come see me when you're ready. For free, man. But I don't think you are. Ready, that is. The only way you'll be ready is if you admit you're gay or bi or whatever. You don't have to come out to anyone but yourself. Just come to terms with it within yourself; otherwise, you'll only continue to be tormented about it. You'll never feel... whole if that makes any sense."

"Right, like it's easy for you. My life isn't like that."

"Dude, my father fucking left me because of coming out, and you know it."

"I know, but... Forget it..."

How did I figure things out or admit to myself if I didn't try with him first?

He gripped my hand as I tried to stand and leave. "I won't forget it. Talk to me. I understand you don't like to share shit, but as someone who's gay and came out, I'd be a good person to talk to. I won't make fun of you or make you feel bad about it."

I looked at his earnest, dark, and soulful eyes. "Why? I've been nothing but an asshole to you."

"True, but we're starting on a new path now. And I'm a forgiving guy. So, tell me why it's so hard for you."

I sighed heavily and glanced down at our hands, still entwined. I'd told no one about my parents before. No one knew my story. That wasn't something I was ready for. "I... can't."

He squeezed my hand in a silent acknowledgment. "No rush, Rolling Stone."

I rolled my eyes at his stupid nickname, making him smile. And that right there reminded me why I hated it when he smiled. Because it lit up his entire face, taking my breath away when it shouldn't. Like his smile was filled with sunshine. While it should've put me at ease, it only served to piss me off, which I now recognized as jealousy. Jealous that I'd never had that in my life. I'd never been able to smile like that.

Stix slowly leaned in close to me, and his eyes dropped to my mouth. "I'm going to kiss you, and the only reason I'm telling you is because I don't want you freaking out," he said. "Take it as my interest in you. But the main reason I won't let you pay me is because it gives you a shield and will keep you in denial. I want you free."

My heart pounded as a surge of emotion hit me. No one ever wanted what was best for me before. Ever.

"Yes or no, Rolling Stone."

"Yes," I breathed quickly.

Soft and warm lips landed on mine, and my eyes fluttered closed. The light scruff on his face was different, but I didn't hate it. When his hand gently slid up the nape of my neck and into my hair, our kiss deepened and sent waves of chills through my body. I shivered with need, feeling like... how could I put it? Like we fit. I had been bashing myself to fit into a shape that worked in this world with others. But with Stix, I didn't have to reshape myself. We just... fit.

Stix pulled away too soon as my eyes slowly opened to his hooded eyes and a small smirk on his mouth. "I knew it'd be hot kissing you. Imagine what it's going to be like once you let everything all go. You're going to feel so good."

It was the shortest kiss I'd ever done. There had been no tongue, lustful nipping, or using our entire bodies for the kiss. It was simple, yet perfect. No kiss from any woman had given me such a strong reaction, only confirming my worries and fears.

No, I needed to accept this. I wanted to stop being afraid.

CHAPTER 12
Stix

FUCK, THOSE HAZEL EYES. They turned nearly black when he opened them after I pulled away for that way too short of a kiss. I only meant to give him a taste, but I'd given myself a taste, too, and I wanted so much more. Those eyes of his told me he wanted this. He'd been either in denial or so deep in the closet that he didn't even know who he was. Who was I to say if he wanted to remain in there? Weirdly, I felt compelled to protect him from others because I was the first to get a glimpse of this side of him. Although he seemed eager to test this thing out between us, he had a lot of fear, too. As we kissed, I felt his trembling and stiff body, despite giving in to the kiss.

God, seeing him right then, said so much more than his wants. It explained his behavior for all these past months. His fear and need for this confused him and made him angry, taking it out on others, specifically me. Deep down, I knew he'd feel so much better if he accepted his true self. I understood him because I had been that person once. I hadn't taken it out on others, but fuck, if I wasn't hard on myself, taking me nearly seven years to admit it and to finally come clean to my family. And even then, I lost one parent because of it. I understood his fears more than he realized. But he was angry and afraid for a reason.

Regardless, I put the ball in his court. As much as I wanted to give in to him, and I so wanted to give in to him because shit, he was hot, even if he was an asshole, but he needed to stew over things for a while. I now understood him a bit more, which helped me shift some resentment away to give him a chance. Despite that, being hot wasn't enough. Not for me. Tony was hot. Brie was hot. But Stone? He was an entirely different beast. Underneath all that asshole demeanor was someone begging to be seen, and I found myself fucking relating to him.

Don't even get me started on watching him jack off after I put on my little show just for Stone with Tony and then touching him. I couldn't control myself. His pants had sat around his thighs, exposing the most gorgeous ass I'd ever seen, which was smooth, muscular, and round. But when he boldly turned around and finished his own show? Fuck, that had been fun. But soon, the guilt hit. Since he didn't break my arm for touching him, I'd been using that as jacking off fodder ever since. His noises and desperation to relieve himself... yeah, fucking sexy as hell. But fuck, when he rested his head against mine? He belonged there.

Mr. Stone. Mr. Unmovable jacked off and lost his cool because of me. Admittedly, it was a little ego-boosting.

I stretched to the early light streaming through the old mini blinds the following day. Nova was still sleeping, hugging her cheap stuffed monkey that I'd won her at the arcade using the claw machine. She was adorable and sweet, and I loved her, but I didn't love sharing a room with my little sister as a grown-ass man.

I yanked on my sweats and woke her up for breakfast. "Come on, munchkin. Time for breakfast and to take you to Mrs. Gordon's."

Nova was easy. She just woke up, rubbed her eyes with her little fists, and then padded to the bathroom to go potty and brush her teeth as I made her some cereal. Mom had to work early this morning, so getting my sister up and moving was up to me. Once she was at the sitter's, I'd do what I could to earn some money.

I tapped on the counter with my drumsticks as she sat and ate her Fruit Loops. "Do you want to go to the park and learn some more skating on Saturday?" I asked. I'd been teaching her whenever I could.

She looked up with bright eyes and a big smile. "Yes! Can we bring your new friend Stone?"

That was Nova. She liked everyone she met. I wished she could hold on to her innocence, but life was too hard for that. "I don't think so, munchkin, and I'm sure he's got other things to do."

"But you could ask."

As much as I wanted to say yes, he needed to come to me. He came to me last night, but he hadn't been ready. Hopefully, next time he would be.

"We'll see," I said to appease her. She'd forget by Saturday, anyway.

After eating breakfast and cleaning up, I carried her downstairs and knocked on Mrs. Gordon's door. She opened it to the smell of cinnamon and coffee. My mouth watered from the scents of sugar and caffeine.

"Good morning, dears."

I set Nova on the ground and walked her inside the comfortable apartment. "Morning," I said.

Once I hugged my sister goodbye, she ran off to the living room, pulling out some coloring books and crayons from a bin. I handed her an envelope with two hundred bucks. It wasn't nearly enough for the week for the amount of time she spent watching Nova, but I wasn't about to complain.

"Thanks, Mrs. Gordon."

"You're welcome, dear. Stay put before you run off."

She headed to the kitchen, then returned shortly after with a cinnamon roll in a paper towel. I took it from her and sunk my teeth into the soft, doughy goodness, groaning. "God, these are so good. Thank you."

At least there were a few people in the world who stayed kind and good.

After I left, I headed toward my first appointment. If anyone wanted my services, they'd text me. Last night, I'd already received three, but I got two more this morning, so that should make up for what I'd given Mrs. Gordon today.

I skated my way toward Harvey's Hardware, practicing my tricks. There was a younger guy who worked at the store, who was about twenty, named Mike. He'd learned about my services by word of mouth from another employee there and requested me because while he was gay, he'd never had a guy before and wanted to know what it was like to be sucked off. While I'd done that for him a couple of times in as many months, this time, he'd asked if he could blow me to learn how to do it. It wasn't something I usually did, but he was willing to pay seventy-five for my services. Not bad for thirty minutes.

At first, I got pissed off because no one was supposed to be talking about me. They could refer me to other people, but they shouldn't be talking about what I did for others to hear. The last thing I needed was for Alpha or my mom to learn about my extra job. But at the end of the day, it was more money in my pocket, and I'd need the cash now after losing six hundred a month with the loss of Brie.

Fortunately, Mom wouldn't notice the loss, since most of the money I earned from Brie personally went straight into a box I kept hidden in my bedroom to save.

I skidded to a stop in front of the mom-and-pop hardware store and walked inside, carrying my board and pretending to shop around, until Mike saw me. He jutted his chin toward the restroom, where we'd do our business. Not the most sanitary, but there was nowhere else. At least it was a single stall, and we could lock the door. Although, I wasn't sure why we couldn't do this at his place. In fact, I asked him that very question.

"Why does it have to be here?"

"Because I still live with my parents. They don't... know I'm gay."

"Fair enough."

Once inside the small space, I set down my board and removed my jacket, hanging it up on the back of the door. Mike watched with dark eyes and dark hair falling in his face as I unbuttoned and unzipped my jeans. He licked his lips as I pulled out my cock and stroked it to get hard. Typically, I wasn't sexually into what I was doing. I rarely got hard from this. It was just a job. So, I worried a little about getting it up. But I grew rock hard when Stone's bubble butt and his jacking off hit my vision. Shit. That was what he did to me.

Mike dropped to his knees and watched me stroke, looking like he was practically drooling. "God, you have a really pretty dick," he breathed. "Can I touch it?"

"Payment first." I let go of myself as my cock flopped hard against me.

As he dug in his pocket and pulled out a fist full of cash, I pulled out a condom and wrapped my dick. Then he handed me the money. I quickly counted it and nodded. He took my cock in his calloused hand and explored, looking at it, touching it everywhere, and ran his thumb over my slit. But as he played with it, it started to fail me, softening under his touch. And I knew why, which was a big fucking problem.

I leaned against the cold tiles and closed my eyes, searching for his face. Soon, I had Stone on his knees before me, discovering that he liked dick as much as Mike did. Stone stroked me with an unsure tentativeness, discovering every wrinkle, every vein, and every hair. He pressed his nose between the base of my cock and my thigh, inhaling deeply.

"I like how you smell," Mike said, yanking me out of my fantasy. Dammit! I grunted in response and forced Stone back into my thoughts.

Now Stone, finally giving in to who he was and accepting that he liked men, swiped a tongue over the head of my cock, licking up my pre-come, even though Mike couldn't do that with me wearing a condom. "Yes," I breathed.

But this wasn't about me or Stone. I was here to teach Mike how to blow a dick. "Wrap your hands like this." With my hand on top of his, I showed him how much pressure to use. "Treat my dick like yours."

Soon, I showed him how to lick, suck, and stroke until I finally blew into the condom. I managed it without letting Stone in too much. When we finished, we washed up at the sink.

"Thanks, man," he said

"I hope you enjoyed it and learned something."

He nodded and bit his bottom lip. "Yeah, I did. Now, I just need to find a boyfriend."

His big, dark eyes met mine. Yeah... nope. That was my cue to leave. "See ya, Mike. Text me when you want more."

"I will."

As the day went on, it slowly progressed worse and worse. It wasn't that I had bad clients or some couldn't pay or failed to show. They all paid and were eager. But for the first time ever, the guilt gnawed at me. It wasn't that familiar guilt of breaking up my family, but shame about Stone, which was absolutely ridiculous. He wasn't mine, and I wasn't his. Yet, I made a promise to him that I'd be there when he was ready. It almost felt like I was cheating, even though this was just a job.

When I first thought about having a boyfriend, I wanted someone who would be cool with what I did for a living despite it not being entirely realistic. Now, I was having second thoughts about doing it at all. Shit, but I needed the money. Well, if these feelings kept happening to where I couldn't provide my services, I'd have to think about getting an actual second job with real hours. But I loved the flexibility and being able to take Nova to the sitter and care for her when Mom couldn't.

I needed to talk to someone about all this. Not about the job, since no one knew, but about Stone. All my friends would probably torment me about it if I told them my interest in him, but there was one who wouldn't besides Alpha.

I put in a quick call to Nacho.

"Yo, what's up, Stix?"

"You busy?"

"I'm just getting off work in about ten."

"Cool. I'll meet you there. Need to talk."

We hung up, and I skated toward the pharmacy where he worked the register during the week. I propped myself up against the building outside and lit a smoke while I waited for him.

A few minutes later, he came out, and I offered him a cig. He took it and lit it up. His tawny skin on his face was smooth and blemish-free, and his dark curls fell into his face, covering his dark eyes and making him look shier than he was. While he was shy, he was a beast and loyal as hell.

"Walk me home, and we can talk on the way," he said.

We tucked our boards under our arms and slowly walked while puffing on our smokes. "What's bothering you?" he asked.

Everyone knew about his love interest in Pippin, other than dumb-ass Pippin. Still, I was the only one who had confronted Nacho about it, giving him someone he could openly talk about it with if he needed to without judgment. Now I needed him.

Rip off the bandaid, Stix. "So, yeah, I think I have a thing for Stone."

He raised a brow but didn't berate me as my other friends would've. "I guess you don't care if he hates you?"

"He doesn't really hate me. It's not my story to tell, but he's angry and just took it out on me."

"What do you need help with?"

"I don't know, man. Maybe simply to have someone to talk to about this." This was a mistake. If I told Nacho that Stone was interested in me, too, that would essentially out him, and I couldn't do that to him, no matter how much of a dick he was.

"Does he like you back?"

I shrugged and chose my words carefully. "I'm not sure if he even likes dudes." There. I could play dumb about his sexuality.

"Well, I gotta admit, it's not always easy to like someone from afar when they don't know. It can be frustrating. I'm hooked on Pippin, and I don't understand why. He's an amazing person and fun, but damn, he's clueless most of the time. He sucks at taking cues."

Stone liked me. At least, he seemed to want to try something. More likely use me for an experiment to test the waters, which was fine because I wasn't entirely invested in Stone yet, despite having the hots for him. It just made things easier.

"Have you tried talking to Pip?" I asked.

I already knew the answer, but Nacho had to get past his shyness first and finally approach Pippin. Pippin needed directness, not hints.

As suspected, Nacho shook his head.

"I think we both need to approach our guys," I said.

"Yeah, I'm just scared he'll say no. Like terrified, scared. What if he doesn't like me back, and it ruins our friendship?"

"You'll get there, hopefully. You two would be great together. I can't see Pippin turning his back on you, whether he likes you that way or not. You're already best friends."

"Yeah, and that's part of the problem."

As I talked to Nacho, an idea came to me. Instead of waiting for Stone, I planned to nudge him in my direction because I was already getting impatient to drag him into my life. To see if he'd be willing to hang out more and get to know each other. Maybe he'd realize I was worth getting past those fears of his. And perhaps I would feel more invested in him.

We stopped in front of Nacho's apartment building and slapped our hands together before parting ways.

"Thanks for the talk, man," I said.

"I'm not sure how helpful I was, but any time."

"Oh, you definitely helped."

CHAPTER 13
Stix

I KNEELED AT EYE level with Nova at our front door. It was after lunch when I set my plan in motion. Now, I simply had to hope that Stone was home.

"Remember, give him your cutest face and biggest eyes. You know, the one where you ask for a new toy." She covered her mouth and giggled, nodding, making her pigtails bounce everywhere. "So, just go over to his door and knock. If Blaze or Cueball answer the door, ask for Stone politely."

"Okay!"

God, I really shouldn't be teaching my sister how to manipulate more than she already did, but I knew no one could say no to her when she was at her cutest. She stood more of a chance than I did at asking him to the kiddie park.

Nova ran off two doors down and rapped on the door with her little fist. Then she stood back and waited, looking up at the door. Soon, Cueball opened the door. Relief washed over me that it wasn't Blaze. He may have been a dick to me and tried to hurt me, and surely he wouldn't hurt Nova, but I still didn't trust him.

"Hello," he said, running an uncomfortable hand over his shaved head.

"Hi! Is Mr. Stone home?"

Cueball's mouth twitched into a near smile. "He might be."

"I'm Nova!" she yelled. She tended to do that to tall people, as if they couldn't hear all the way up there.

"I'm Cueball."

She giggled. "That's a funny name."

He almost smiled again. "You can call me Marco if you want."

"Nah, I like your name."

He nodded. "I'll go get Stone for you, Nova."

She waited at the threshold patiently, then looked back at me with a big smile and wiggled her fingers.

As soon as Stone came to the door, instead of towering above her, he squatted to her eye level, which weirdly made my heart beat a little faster. It was thoughtful on his part and a little unexpected.

"Hi, Nova," he said in that deep, sexy voice of his.

"Hi, Stone. Can you come out to the park and play with us? Nico's been teaching me to skate."

"He has?"

"Yes, can you come with us?"

When Stone looked up over at my door, I ducked behind it like a coward.

"Uncool, Stix, using your cute little sister to draw me in."

"Did it work?" she asked.

Ugh. My face turned to fire. Little traitor. I peeked around the door and shrugged. I may as well own it. "Well, you've seen how cute she is. How can you say no to that face?"

Stone scoffed, but as much as he fought it, he still smiled, even if it was a small one.

Please say yes.

"I'll get my jacket and board."

"Yay!" Nova yelled and clapped.

When Stone went back inside, she turned to me, giving me a thumbs up. Little punk. But I gave her a thumbs up back.

I grabbed Nova's gear, our jackets, and our boards. As we waited for Stone, I put on her helmet, elbow pads, and knee pads. Then I put on her jacket and zipped it up.

Stone stepped out, looking fucking good in his ripped jeans, black hoodie, and Chucks. Always wearing black, but he looked so cool.

"Look at my new helmet," Nova squealed at Stone.

"Purple and glitter is your color, Nova."

She beamed up at him and nodded. I was so grateful he was sweet to her. For a hard minute, I had my doubts he could ever be kind.

"Thanks," I said, though I wasn't sure what I was thanking him for. For coming? For being sweet to Nova? For not being an asshole to me? All the above?

His hard hazel gaze met my eyes, and he gave me a curt nod. "Teaching a future skater? Sounds fun."

We made our way down the four flights of stairs. "I've taught her a few things. She's making good progress on popping her board. She's going to be natural."

"Cool."

Once outside, I double-checked her gear and put her board on the ground. "Hop on, munchkin." I made sure she was steady on the board, then held her hand as I pulled her onto the sidewalk. To my surprise, Stone took her other hand, and we both tugged her toward the park. My heart melted a little. I knew he wasn't as much of a prick as I initially believed, but this told me he was kinder than I thought.

The playground wasn't very far. I liked it because once she got bored with skating, she could run off and play on the swings or the slides. They had a small skateboard ramp for little kids, which was perfect for her.

"Show Stone how you pop off your board," I said once we got there. She'd been practicing hard at it, so I knew she'd love to show it off.

Nova stood on her board and pressed her left foot down on the back of the board, but not hard enough to press it to the ground before she jumped and landed back on her board. I caught her as she started to fall. She didn't catch much air, but she was only five.

Nova beamed at Stone's clapping. "Impressive," he said.

"Do you want to see it again?" she asked.

He nodded. "I'd love to."

She did it again, but this time, she landed smoothly and didn't fall.

Once she got bored with popping, I let her run off and skate on the ramp, back and forth. It was really small, and she was protected, so I just let her skate around without worrying about her. Besides, she needed to learn to fall and not get upset if she got hurt. But she was pretty good about just going back and forth.

Stone and I sat on an old wooden bench, watching her as we lit up a couple of smokes.

"Why am I here, man?" he asked.

"Why not? We've come to some sort of truce, and I'd like to see if we could try to be friends."

"Again, why? I've been nothing but a dick or a... confused nut job."

"It's cool, Rolling Stone. I get it."

We hadn't talked about what he'd requested since last week, so I had no idea where he currently stood on that. If he just wanted to be friends, I was cool with that, too.

He took a long drag from his cig and blew it out as he watched Nova skating her heart out. "Okay."

"Okay...?"

"Let's get to know each other."

It was a start, but I was itching for more. It'd have to be enough. "Cool."

"Cool."

Nova ran up to us and dumped her board. "Take these off. I wanna swing."

I helped her remove her gear and dug in my backpack for a juice box, handing it to her. She chugged it down and ran off.

"Where'd you grow up?" he asked, initiating the *'get to know you phase'* of my plan.

"Born and raised here in Baltimore. You?"

"I grew up in Fredericksburg, Virginia."

"Never been, but I've seen pictures of it. Seems nice."

"If you say so."

"Why Baltimore? This city's kind of an armpit."

He took another drag, finishing his smoke before dropping it on the ground and grinding it into the grass and weeds, still not looking at me. "Anything was better than where I came from."

"And where did you come from?" He knew I didn't mean the town.

He finally pinned his hazel stare at me. "I want to kiss you again," he said, completely deflecting my question.

My heart suddenly hammered. I'd love nothing better than to kiss him again. "Here? In public? You sure?"

Stone scanned the playground, then shrugged. "There's no one we know here."

This was a big step for him. It had to be, despite not knowing anyone here, so I wasn't about to deny him a kiss. I leaned in close to him, feeling the warmth from his skin on this cold afternoon. But I didn't push forward into the kiss. He asked me, so I wanted him to take that plunge.

Our mouths hovered as our eyes met for a moment before he moved in those last few inches. My eyes slid closed when his full lips hit mine. He was soft and tentative at first, while my body zinged with electricity straight to my nuts. There was just something sexy and hot about witnessing Stone open up more and more, and that I was the cause of it.

His kiss tasted like cigarettes and fear. He was still nervous, but I pushed our kiss deeper, and he relaxed more. I swiped my tongue across his lips, and he opened for me, allowing my tongue inside his hot mouth. My body burned for him. What was it about this guy that got me all hot and bothered? I burned so hot that I wanted to take off my jacket, and my dick grew alive, but I couldn't be bothered to care. My jeans were baggy enough so that no one could tell.

I tilted my head for more, and he finally touched me, running his hand along the nape of my neck and through my hair.

Yes! I loved kissing because they happened so rarely for me, but with Stone, it was a whole other level. This boldness from him was a fucking turn-on.

When we finally came up for air, his eyes were pinned on me, and I just stared at his swollen and glistening lips, dying to nibble on them, but I held back. This was his show.

"Yay!" Nova screeched. Stone quickly pulled away, and I nearly laughed as his face turned bright red, straight to his cute ears.

"Are you two boyfriends now?" she asked.

"No," he said at the same time I said yes, only to mess with him.

"Asshole," he muttered under his breath, which only made me smile bigger.

"I know you want it."

"You're fu... You're impossible."

"I'm easy... to please, that is."

Stone rolled his eyes at me, trying desperately not to smile at our banter.

Come on. Lighten up, Rolling Stone.

At least I managed to squeeze out a small smile.

We finally packed up everything, and I melted a little more when Stone gave Nova a piggyback while riding his board. I knew there was a good person somewhere inside of him. And Nova loved it. I rode behind them, carrying all her gear, just falling a little bit more for the man made of granite. Maybe settling for his experiment wasn't the best idea now that I started to get the first tingling of the feels.

Stone set Nova down when we arrived back at our apartments. I wasn't ready to let him go just yet. This was the longest we'd ever hung out together where we didn't want to kill each other. It was fucking nice.

We both stood there awkwardly by the main doors. God, I wasn't shy at all, so this was weird, but with a deep breath, I asked him. "So, Mom's working tonight for a double shift. We're having Stouffer's lasagna for dinner and some broccoli on the side. Nova needs her vitamins. Wanna join us?"

I tried not to show my disappointment when his face shuttered. There was a *'no'* coming any second now.

"I... gotta go."

Before I could respond or Nova could beg, he stormed inside and ran up the stairs. Fuck. We'd made such good progress, too. I had to remind myself I had to take baby steps when it came to Stone.

CHAPTER 14
Stone

SEVEN YEARS AGO

"What the fuck is going on?!"

Alec and I quickly pulled away from each other. No, I was severed by pain from the most perfect kiss ever. My first kiss. Alec's kiss. Mom's shock ruined it. She fucking ruined everything!

"I come home early from work to find you... kissing a fucking boy?"

Her eyes were bloodshot, with dilated pupils, and covered in a sheen of sweat. She was fucking high or drunk or both, and that was bad news for me.

As much as I wanted to lie and tell her she had made a mistake, I owned it. Alec was more important than my coming punishment. "But I like him."

He looked at me wide-eyed and shook his head, clearly terrified for me. I was a little disappointed that he didn't stand with me, but I knew he was worried about my safety and not his.

"Go home, Alec," she ordered.

"Yes, ma'am."

He grazed my hand with his as he climbed off my bed and grabbed his bag. Before he left, he turned to me. "Talk to me later." He meant to let him know if I was okay after dealing with my mother.

I said nothing as he walked out, taking my heart with him.

Fuck, this was going to hurt, but I went into this with open eyes.

Mom said nothing else before she reached out and grabbed a fistful of my hair, pulling me off the bed. My hands grabbed her wrists, and my feet tried to find purchase as she dragged my body down the hall. I had no idea how she was so strong. Maybe from handling patients all day, transferring them to beds, or something. It could've been the drugs.

The fear suddenly consumed me, and regret filled me over my actions. In place of a sixteen-year-old was a small child no older than nine, wanting to please his parents. To never get them angry. Their anger always hurt.

"Please, Mom... I'm so sorry. So sorry. Please don't hurt me."

"You'll be sorry, alright. I didn't raise a fucking fag. You know damn well I don't put up with this shit, and neither does your father. And how dare you do it in my house! You have no respect, you dirty boy."

"You're right. You're right. I'm sorry. It was a mistake. I didn't mean to," I sobbed. My eyes grew blurry from the tears and fear.

When she finally let go of me in the kitchen, my head was on fire as she ripped out a clump of hair. I grasped my head and curled on the floor, no bigger than a tiny boy who couldn't fight back. My body shook uncontrollably as my heart threatened to tear out of my chest.

Don't fight. Don't fight. It will only be worse for you.

She rummaged through drawers before she found what she wanted. I couldn't see because I cowered before her. My head bled, but I tried to ignore it as I bowed in front of her feet. "Please... I'll be good. I swear."

"You always say that, but you're always a bad boy. You defy me and your father at every turn. When are you going to learn? How much do we need to punish you before you finally get it? You're all that's wrong, you piece of shit."

"You're right. You're right. I'm a piece of shit."

I said anything to get out of this. It never worked before, but each time I begged, I hoped it would work this one time.

"Take off your shirt?"

I shook my head as my stomach turned, threatening to vomit my lunch from school today. It was instinct because I knew what was coming. If I gave in, I would be in a world of pain. If I didn't, I would be in a world of pain. My choices were always pain or pain. Nothing ever in between.

The metal spatula hit me on my head, right where she tore out a chunk of my hair. The pain sent shockwaves through my body, and I cried out. She was only getting started, but it was enough to do as I was told.

I yanked off my T-shirt with trembling hands, tossed it to the floor, and bent over to let her beat me with it on my bare back.

The last thing I remembered was waking up in my dark bedroom, covered in dried blood, lying on the floor. My back felt like my flesh had been burned off. I rolled onto my stomach and whimpered, and my tears spilled before I passed out again.

The slamming of my door against the wall startled me awake. I could barely move from the pain, but I forced myself to sit up and sit on my knees on the floor in front of my father. He was an imposing man, even when not being an abusive asshole. If I thought my mother was bad, Dad was three times worse.

"You fucking faggot. You will learn soon enough," he said as he punched me in the face. I nearly blacked out as I fell onto my back. The second hit did knock me out.

Apparently, I woke up in the hospital two days later with a broken nose, three cracked ribs, a sprained wrist, a concussion, and over thirty stitches in my back, along with other injuries and abrasions.

Mom was there as she rushed to my side, crying like she actually cared about my well-being. It was times like these when I wanted to believe her. That she really did love me and didn't want to hurt me anymore.

While she held my hand, the tears spilled as I thought about my Alec, needing him right now, wishing he'd barge in and save me. To take me away from all this suffering. But he never came. Not that day. Not any day. I saw him in school after I recovered from my injuries, but every time he came near me, I cowered. Seeing him was a reminder of all that I had suffered. There was no light left. No stars. No love. Only pain. I could never let anyone get close to me again. Loving people hurt too much.

Six months later, he moved away, and I never saw him again.

CHAPTER 15
Stone

I STARED INTO THE foggy mirror after my shower and touched my lips. Kissing Stix again had been even better the second time around. I didn't count the first time I had tried at Alpha's the other night. That wasn't a kiss. That was me being a dumpster fire. A nutjob. And fuck, could he kiss. My entire body reacted to him, and my dick got hard today from it. The only time I got hard with a girl was if she stroked or sucked me, but never from just a kiss. Shit, I was getting hard now just thinking about it.

Stix was the second guy I'd ever kissed. The first time had been so traumatizing afterward that I'd shoved it so deep into my mind, that I'd nearly forgotten Alec. But Stix not only opened my wounds but my eyes and soul. After my wounds opened, he started to heal them.

Now, I needed to accept the truth and stop being fucking afraid. My parents weren't in my life anymore. They couldn't find me or hurt me. But I still felt their beatings even after all these years. Every hit, slap, punch, bruise, and cut. I escaped them for a reason, dammit! To live my life as *I* wanted. It hadn't really been great so far, but my parents couldn't touch me any longer, and I needed to remember that.

I swiped my hand over the mirror as it fogged up and stared hard at myself, willing my brain to get with the program to work together with my body. The same familiar fear had me running tonight after Stix asked me to stay for dinner. Enough. No more fear. Accepting that I wasn't as straight as I thought needed to be done. I needed to be okay with that if I wanted Stix in my life. But a new feeling emerged as I looked at my hazel eyes. Guilt. I'd treated Stix like shit because of my jealousy and fears. He did nothing wrong other than be someone I was attracted to, which cranked up my fears about a hundred notches. No, it was more than that. His gravitational pull was fucking strong, like I couldn't avoid it if I tried. But I'd been so deep in denial and internalized hatred that I took it out on him. Fuck, I had been such an asshole.

I was done. No more. I fucking deserved to be happy for a change. My current path just wasn't taking me there. Tonight at work, I'd talk to Stix and apologize to him. To see if he'd be willing to explore this thing between us. He said he was open to the idea, but I didn't feel right about it until I came clean. I owed him that much.

Stix explained that I should accept myself, but what was I? Gay? Bisexual? I didn't have any fucking clue, since I had so little context and a shit ton of denial. All I knew was Stix drew me in from the day I'd met him, and my fears clouded over my want for him. I hadn't recognized it at the time.

Hell, maybe it didn't even matter, and why should it? Did I really need a label? Because my fucking asshole parents made it seem like it was the worst possible thing I could've done. But look at their fucking lives. My mother was a drunk and an addict. My father was a drug addict and seller and sitting in prison. What the fuck did they know? Not a goddamn thing. The sad part about them was that they hadn't always been like that. I remembered them being gentle and loving me once when I was little. Hell, maybe it was just the wishful thinking of a child constantly in pain.

Pounding on the bathroom door snapped me out of my thoughts.

"Hey, how long you gonna be in there, fuckhead? I need to take a piss and get ready to go out tonight," Blaze said through the door.

"Sorry, I'm done."

I opened the door and left as Blaze rushed in, cupping his junk, looking like he was about to piss himself before he stopped.

"What's wrong?" he asked.

Taken aback, I raised my brows. "Uhm, nothing."

"No. You just said, 'sorry.'"

"I've said sorry before. Where are you going with this?"

"Yeah, when you wrongfully beat me up. Not for holding up the bathroom."

"I didn't beat you up, drama queen." I pinched the bridge of my nose. Why was I friends with him again? "Anyway, there's nothing wrong."

"If you say so." He shut the door behind him as I went to my room to get ready for work.

I didn't have many nice things to wear. Well, none, really. But I pulled on a Henley in olive green that I knew brought out my hazel eyes. Then I put on a pair of dark-wash jeans, and the only pair without holes. I didn't understand why I had this need to look nice, or at least not look as much like a slob.

Once ready, I shrugged on my jacket, put on my Converse, and tugged on a beanie. It was getting colder out there now that October was almost here. Then, I headed into the living room and saw Cueball watching TV and eating a sandwich.

"Later," I said as I grabbed my board.

He grunted at me and resumed watching his show.

That was another thing I needed to do. I needed to be better towards my friends. Blaze was a dickhead, but he had his moments where he was cool sometimes. And Cueball proved to be strangely helpful.

For the first time in years, I felt better about life, or at least the promise of a better one. I finally had something to look forward to. The weird weight that had always pressed down on me slowly lifted and allowed my lungs to open up and breathe again.

As soon as I walked into Alpha's, I quickly scanned the place for Stix. I saw him laughing with Pippin behind the bar as he tapped on the counter with his drumsticks. Normally, that would've annoyed me to no end, but seeing him looking happy and not pissed eased something inside me.

Sensing me, Stix's dark eyes met mine, and he stopped laughing. I couldn't read his face, but at least it wasn't filled with disappointment like it had been earlier tonight when I turned him down for dinner after our great day with his little sister. God, I was such a coward, but no more.

I walked right up to Stix, who shoved his drumsticks into his back pocket as I got closer. He looked good as always with all his earrings and these chain-like choker necklaces. Tonight, his baggy gray T-shirt read 'Dad Jokes Are How Eye Roll.' Those things used to annoy me, but did they really? Now, I liked everything about him. Did he have tattoos, too? I shook the completely irrelevant thought out of my head.

His friends kept their eyes on me, unsure what to make of my approaching Stix when I usually avoided him like the plague.

I stopped on the other side of the bar. "Can we talk?" I asked, not daring to look at his friends and willing Stix to say yes, though he had no reason to, after my behavior today after the park. The biggest thing that had my gut really twisting tight was there was no typical Stix smirk on his face. I fucking hope I hadn't ruined this before it barely began.

"Sure," he said, dropping off the counter he had been perched on. He slipped out from behind the bar, and I followed him into the back. Instead of leading me to the employee lounge, he guided me straight out the back exit into the alley.

"There's more privacy here."

Stix leaned against the brick facade, resting one foot against the wall, and lit a smoke. He looked so cool and at ease with so little effort. "What do you want?" he said after he exhaled some smoke.

My mind went nearly blank as I rushed at him, grabbed his face, and pulled him into a kiss. Instead of kissing me back, he shoved me off of him. Shit. No, I was finally getting shit figured out. I couldn't have him mad at me.

"Dammit, Stone. You're fucking hot and cold, with a hefty dose of cold. We had a great time today, and you shut it all down. I'm trying to get to—"

"I know..." I ran a hand through my hair, trying not to feel like an idiot while attempting to be open and honest. Honesty wasn't a problem for me per se, but sharing emotions and shit was. "I'm... here to say I'm sorry."

He raised a brow and took another drag, looking way too relaxed as I slowly tore up inside. "For what?"

"You're going to be a pain in my ass, aren't you?"

He lowered his head and looked up with a smirk before he took another drag. "Maybe."

"Little fucker," I whispered as I stared up at the sky, missing all the night stars from the bright lights of the city. "I'm sorry I ran off tonight when you... invited me to dinner. Clearly, I got scared, but I should've stayed."

"Man, I don't care if you wanted to join us or not. That's your choice. I only hate that you feel you need to keep running from yourself. You can't outrun yourself. You understand that, right?"

I scuffed my shoe over the road and nodded. "Yeah, I know that. That's why I'm here now, talking to you. I don't want to run anymore. God, when I walked away earlier, it... almost hurt. So, I'm sorry, and I want to see where this goes between us. I remember you telling me to admit something to myself, and I have, I think, but I'm not sure what I'm admitting. That I'm not so straight? Yeah, but... do I have to figure this out? God, I'm not so good at this."

I was so focused on avoiding his face as I word vomited, staring at the ground; I hadn't noticed Stix coming up to me and lifting my head by my chin to look at him. "Dude, you don't have to figure out shit or even put a label on it. It would just be nice to see you stop hurting. To admit to yourself of all the possibilities."

"And, you'll be okay with that?"

"Yeah, man. When you're happy, you're not treating me like shit."

My face burned straight to my ears. "I'm sorry..."

"I'm joking; not joking."

My shoulders sagged as I exhaled. "I'm not only sorry for tonight but for everything. I took out all my issues on you. Just so you know, it was never you... Well, it was in part. I realize that now. Fuck, when I saw you coming out of Brie's place the first time, I wanted to fucking stab something. I really didn't understand how much of it was jealousy. God, this emotional truth shit hurts."

"Forgiven," he said as his hand slid up my neck and pulled me down towards his plump lips, waiting to meet mine.

"That easy?" My lips breathed the words over his.

"Yep."

Our mouths finally met, but it was too fucking short. Just a peck, really.

"Why?" I asked.

"Why that easy?"

I nodded. "I'm not sure if I'd be so forgiving."

"Because I was you once. Not like in the self-loathing part, but the confusion and fear. This need to be me, but not sure who 'me' was. I mean, there's still fear, especially after how my dad reacted, because if I want to be me and open as a gay man, I need to fucking come out every single damn time I meet new people. And it's also stupid. Why should I have to 'come out?' Why can't I just be me? Or why do I sometimes fear for my safety because of who I am? Why does this define me? Sorry, I'm rambling."

Shit, I hadn't even gotten that far with questions like that. The fear knotted in my stomach as my mouth grew dry. His hand cupped my face. "Hey, you don't have to be open about shit. I mean, you want to experiment with me? That's cool. Take all the time you need to figure shit out. I'm not going to rush you. No fears, okay?"

I scrunched my brows and nodded. "Yeah, okay. Thanks. How'd you get so smart about this shit?"

"Mom. She's fucking amazing. She lets me rant and rave whenever I'm upset or afraid. Then we talk it out. Honestly, I'm not sure where I'd be without her."

I had nothing like that in my life.

Wrong, dickhead. You have Stix now. He's letting you in.

"It's hard not to be afraid," I finally said.

"I get that, but as I said, there's no rush to come out."

"It's not that. Not about our friends anyway, though I'm not ready. My problem runs deeper than that."

Before we could finish our conversation, Alpha stormed out into the back. "Jesus! I've been fucking looking for you two. Get your asses inside. We've opened, and I've gotta go."

"What's happened," Stix asked.

"My foster brother... he's been in a wreck down in D.C. I'm headed to the hospital. You get to close up the bar since you two numbnuts are yammering back here instead of working."

Stix dropped his cig on the ground and crushed it with his Vans. "Text me to tell me if he's okay or not."

Alpha nodded. "I will."

He walked back inside while Stix and I stared at each other briefly before heading back to work. Then he twisted around, forcing me to stumble into him, and gave me a small kiss. "We're good," he said.

I smiled at his retreating back, feeling really alive for the first time since I could ever fucking remember. Like I was living for the first time instead of surviving.

Ajax wasn't around tonight, taking the night off, so it was only me left to handle the crowd. It was hard to watch everyone by myself and check IDs. Most of the staff, like Blondie, Jazz, and Nacho, were too young to card or serve drinks. Nacho would be twenty-one soon, but the twins still had three more years. Pippin was the bartender and too busy to help. I could've asked Stix, but he was currently serving drinks tonight for anyone who managed to snag a table.

Despite needing to focus on my job, I struggled to take my eyes off him as he moved about the bar, smiling, chatting, and, every once in a while, nodding his head to the beat of the music as the local band played. What a weird turn of events. First, I'd been full of unexplained rage when I looked at him. Now, longing and want filled me, feelings I'd never had or understood before.

Suddenly, my body turned cold when some fuckhat grabbed Stix by the arm, and I saw from here that it was too tight because Stix winced and shook the man off. Everything in my body told me to go over there and clock the prickhead for daring to touch Stix. That same rage I'd felt when Blaze hurt Stix at the skatepark. Being at work was the only thing holding me back and keeping me under control.

Stix walked off with an empty tray to the bar and gathered several beer glasses. I tensed again as he headed back to that same table. He set down the tray, putting everyone's beer glasses on the table. I saw they said shit to him again from here, and it couldn't have been good, since Stix wasn't his usual smiley self.

When that prickhead grabbed Stix again, my feet moved toward him before my mind registered what it was doing. I plowed through people, uncaring if I pissed them off. Stix tried to yank away, but the asshole's grip was too tight, while the rest of the douchebags laughed at him.

The word 'faggot' had me grabbing the asshole, holding onto Stix. The word had me yanking the prick from behind and lifting him off his seat. That word was enough for me to act. Years of being bullied by my own parents for their homophobia, among other things, made me want to hurt something or someone. All I felt at that moment was their inflicted pain. My fist raised, ready to beat the shit out of the homophobe, but a hand gripped me and kept me from lashing out.

"He's not worth it, Rolling Stone," Stix said behind me. "Don't."

I looked around and saw Pippin, Nacho, and the twins surrounding us, waiting on my call on what to do with these assholes. As much as I wanted to punch his lights out, I needed to be professional and remind myself I wasn't my father.

I fisted the guy's shirt and pulled him to me face-to-face. He tried to fight me off, but I was stronger. "Guess what, dick head? This isn't a safe space for homophobes. This is a queer-friendly bar, and you're not welcome here."

I turned my head back to his friends. "You're out of here. All of you."

"We paid to get in," said the dick I was currently gripping.

"If you don't leave willingly, I'll be happy to remove you all physically."

He looked over at his friends, completely undaunted by my barely holding on calmness. "Let's go, guys. If we'd known this was a faggot bar, we would've avoided it like a disease." Please, as if they didn't recognize the pride flags hanging over the bar and in the window. They came here with one intention only. To harass.

I ignored his taunts and let him go with the strongest control I'd ever had. Folding my arms with the rest of the staff behind me, I watched the six other men walk out of the bar, flipping us off.

A hand landed on my shoulder, and there were pats on my back. "Nice work," Pippin said and left.

I turned to face Stix. "You okay?"

He wore a crooked grin. "I am now. My hero."

The tension washed off me like dirt in a shower, and I laughed. It was an odd sound I wasn't used to. "I'm glad you're okay."

"I really want to kiss you right now."

My smile dropped, and the tension returned. A different sort of tension involving clammy hands. "I... I..."

He smiled up at me. "It's cool, Rolling Stone. Next time."

"I want to, but..."

"You take all the time you need," he said, giving me a reassuring smile and walking off to clear the table.

CHAPTER 16
Stix

GOD, THAT SMILE. WHO knew he had such high fucking cheek-bones and a dimple on one cheek. He was already hot as fuck, but his smiling made him stunning, especially with those couple of crooked bottom teeth. I quickly decided I'd make it my life's mission to keep that smile on his face. I needed it as much as I needed to skate. Mix that in with his growly protectiveness, and I was literally a puddle of goo.

As the night wore on, the band was about to wrap up before the singer called for me to come up on stage.

"Grab your sticks, Stix," he said, making the crowd laugh.

My gut twisted in a good way. I'd been making sure to get to know the bands when they came to play at the bar to put in a good word and sell myself. I'd ask them if they ever minded if I played with them for at least one song, always paying close attention to their rhythm and harmony to get a feel of their style. Though I had no drums to practice on, I had a pretty good ear for the beat and could pick it up even from a song I wasn't always familiar with, but they were also cool, allowing me to add my own style and flair.

Maybe one day, one of the bands would be short a drummer and ask me to be a part of their band. Honestly, I had no idea how to be a drummer beyond that. I couldn't afford to attend music school, nor did I know anyone who could play music or sing. Shit, I didn't have any idea how to write sheet music, though I could create it by sound and feel. It was wishful thinking but a dream that was hard to let go of.

I knew this particular band and was familiar with their songs, so I had an idea of what I'd be playing with them tonight.

I put down my serving tray, grabbed my sticks from my back pocket, and rushed to the stage. The singer and I did a weird handshake involving slapping hands and cupping fingers. I fist-bumped the rest of the band members before sitting behind the drums.

This was fucking home to me. I belonged behind a set of drums. The only way I learned all about them was on the internet and watching videos.

One day, Stix. One day. Sure, that was as likely as my dad coming back to us.

I started the song by banging my sticks and counting to three before pounding on the drums. The song was fast but uncomplicated, with a simple rift and beat. My arms and feet knew what to do as I let the music flow through me. To feel it rather than analyze it. Sure, I messed up a couple of times. But we kept going, and the crowd never seemed to notice.

My arms flailed in rapid beats, my sticks twirled in my hands, and my foot hammered the pedal on the base in perfect unison with the rest of the band as the singer's deep and guttural voice filled the bar.

It was hot under the lights, and I quickly grew sweaty from using my entire body to create music. After about three minutes, it was over, and way too quickly. But such was my life. My bits of happiness were summed up in a few minutes of musical notes here and there that I cherished and put into my little happy box. They would have to do until I reached my dreams. If I reached them. I was also a realist, so I knew that my life may never be much more than it currently was.

I shook hands with the band members before jumping off the stage and making my way through the crowd. Customers patted my back and shook my hand, and I glowed from the attention. The rush, as short as it was, was amazing.

I looked around and met those eyes that stared back at me. Eyes that I had already grown to love looking at, especially when they were no longer filled with anger and hatred. Stone gave me a quick smile and went back to carding people. That smile was an achievement in itself.

The end of the night was finally here, and everyone had gone home, leaving only Stone and me with the place to ourselves. I put on some radio station that played a mixture of rock on the speakers as we cleaned up the place and counted the money from the till before we dropped it into the safe. Alpha would take it to the bank later. Then, I handed Stone his tips for the night, which he shoved into his wallet before resuming his cleanup duties.

'Layla' from Derek and the Dominos came on, and while I wasn't a fan of classic rock all that much, preferring the punk and grunge styles, I loved this song. Especially the acoustic melody part toward the end.

"Do you dance?" I asked Stone as he wiped down the tables from all the sticky alcohol.

"Uh, I've never danced before."

I was about to grab the mop to clean the floor when I stopped and reached for the remote control to pause the music. "Come again? Never?"

He didn't look at me as he resumed cleaning the table. "Never had a chance or the time or the... person."

"Wanna learn?"

Stone raised a brow at me. "Now? It's past two in the morning."

I shrugged. "So? We have nothing to do tomorrow other than skate."

"I don't know..."

"It's just you and me here. And I wouldn't mind shuffling around next to you."

Fuck, his smile was so sweet and almost shy. Who was this person? This was definitely not the Stone I had come to know over the past few months.

"Okay."

"Really?" I had to admit, I was a little surprised he gave in without a fight, but Stone had been full of surprises recently.

"Yeah."

"Yes!" I turned the music back on, skipped over to him, and grabbed his hands. We slowly swayed to the piano and soulful guitar, pressed against each other, but I needed to be closer, so I wrapped my arms around his muscular back and rested my head on his very hard shoulder.

Shit, he was a rock. We were all pretty fit from working the bar and skating all the time, but Stone was steel.

I nearly melted again when he finally wrapped his arms around me and rested his head on top of mine as we swayed to a new song.

"Dancing's pretty nice," he said.

I lifted my head and smiled up at him. "Right?" I reached for his mouth and gave him a quick kiss. We needed to work on longer, hotter kisses, but this would have to do for now since we needed to wrap things up and head home.

"As much as I'd like to stay like this forever, we should finish."

He nodded as we reluctantly let each other go.

After we finished cleaning, Stone grabbed the garbage bags and headed out into the alley to toss them in the dumpster as I turned off the lights and the music. I walked into the employee lounge to grab my jacket and board, grabbed Stone's things, too, so he didn't have to, and made my way back into the quiet, dark bar. I'd expected Stone to be back already. It wasn't like throwing away trash took a long time.

I headed to the restrooms and opened the door. "Stone?"

He wasn't in there, so I dropped our things and headed to the back. Before I opened the door, I knew there was something wrong, hearing some yelling out there. I pressed my ear to the door, and I could hear the sounds of grunting and laughing. Fuck.

I quietly cracked the door open to find several guys hovering over Stone on the ground. My stomach instantly knotted up, and chills ran up my spine. I wasn't much of a fighter. I could hold my own, but not against that many dudes. Dudes I recognized from earlier tonight. Were they waiting for us outside?

After one kicked Stone in the stomach, I rushed back to the bar, quickly grabbed my phone, and dialed 9-1-1. I gave the operator our address and a simple rundown of what was happening. Then I informed her I would have a gun on me. I hung up before she could protest, opened the safe for emergencies, and pulled out a loaded gun Alpha had stashed there in case of an emergency, or we got robbed. I checked to make sure the safety was on first, as Alpha had shown me, then ran back out toward the alley, hoping Stone wasn't too injured.

Fuck, fuck, fuck.

I threw the back door open and aimed the gun with trembling hands at the men who were punching and kicking Stone. He was bleeding everywhere. Seeing him beaten down sent a wave of anger through me. I still shook, but that fear was overwhelmed by rage. He was fucking mine, and no one hurt what was mine.

"Freeze, fuckheads! Unless you want to die, of course."

They all stopped what they were doing, and I tried not to focus on Stone, who wasn't moving at all. Not even a groan. A few of the assholes were bleeding, so at least Stone got in some hits.

"Whatcha gonna do with that gun, little faggot?" one of them said as they made their way toward me, clearly drunk and pissed.

I removed the safety and put a bullet in the chamber. "Shoot you."

That stopped them. But before any of us could do anything, we could already hear sirens in the distance. Mention a gun, and the police come. Hopefully, they'd bring EMS with them.

"I've already called the police. That's them now. Think before you do anything stupid. But clearly, you all are idiots."

They cursed and took off. I breathed out a sigh. "Assholes." One guy left his credit card for their tab at the bar, so I was confident the cops would find them. Not only did we have plenty of witnesses earlier tonight, but the assholes had no idea we had a camera out here for this very reason. Baltimore wasn't exactly the safest city.

Before I rushed to Stone, I emptied the gun completely of bullets and turned on the safety before dropping it to the ground. The last thing I needed was to die by cop tonight. Then I ran to Stone and dropped to my knees.

"Stone! Talk to me." His face was a bloody pulp, and I barely recognized him. My hand hovered over his face, afraid to touch him. But I lifted him a little and put his head on my lap, so it wasn't sitting in filth.

"They're almost here, Rolling Stone. You're going to be okay."

I ran a still shaking hand through his thick, cropped hair, careful not to touch him where he was wounded. Then I cursed myself for not checking as I pressed my fingers to his throat to look for a pulse. I mean, those assholes could've killed him for all I knew. But he had a beat. I wasn't sure if it was steady or irregular. All that mattered to me was that he was alive.

"You're going to be okay," I said again.

It was four in the morning, and Stone was still in the hospital. I should've been home by now, and while Mom never waited up for me anymore, and I had no idea what time I'd be home, I called her anyway, so she wouldn't worry when I wasn't there when she woke up.

"Nico... you okay, baby?" she said in a sleepy voice.

"Uhm, I'm at the hospital... I'm fine before you panic. We had an incident at work, and Stone got hurt. I'm going to stay here to see how he is, and then I'll head home. I just wanted you to know so you didn't worry."

"You okay? Are you sure? No one hurt you?" She sounded clearer-headed now.

"I'm fine. Really."

"Okay, call me if you need me. I love you."

"I love you, too."

I hung up and texted Alpha what had happened. Knowing him, he'd call back immediately, so I turned off my phone, not wanting to disturb him while he was with his foster brother, allowing him to focus on his family.

A female doctor headed my way before I could relax in the waiting room again.

"I'm Doctor Cooper. Are you Mr. Sloan's family?"

I didn't know shit about his family or how to reach them. "I'm Damien's husband, Nico." Shit, he was going to kill me. "Is he okay?"

She shook the hand I had offered. I couldn't believe that worked since I didn't exactly look like husband material. "He'll be fine. He's suffered blunt trauma to the head, giving him a concussion. They broke his nose and three ribs. And his face has suffered minor abrasions that didn't require stitches. Most of the blood was from his head and nose. And it's his head we're worried about, mostly."

"What do I need to do?"

"Damien needs to rest for at least three weeks. Nothing strenuous. If you can, please make sure he stays in bed as much as possible and stays away from anything overstimulating."

Shit. How the hell was I going to do that? Stone did what Stone wanted.

"I'll do what I can."

"Good, and you'll need to keep his ribs bound. Other than that, there isn't much you can do about his ribs. They need to heal on their own. When he's ready to go home, we'll send him off with pain meds and antibiotics that he'll need to take."

"Okay. When can I see him?"

"Now, if you'd like. He's asleep, but you're more than welcome to stay. I'd like to keep him here under observation for twenty-four hours to monitor his head, but he can go home if all is well after that. I'll take you to him."

The doctor opened the door to his room, and my heart and stomach sank at his appearance. He was so bruised and swollen. "God, Stone," I murmured. He looked even worse in the light and with all his bandages and wires. That's when the guilt slammed into me. All this happened because of me. Those assholes targeted me, and Stone had to come to my defense, and then they took it out on him. I was a master at guilt, but I wasn't stupid. I knew those assholes were itching for a fight, too. Even so, he shouldn't have had to suffer like this because of me.

"I'll leave you to it," she said.

"Thank you, doctor."

I pulled a chair close to his bed and sat down. Then took his hand in mine. We weren't an item or anything. At least not yet. Tonight was the first time he'd come clean with what he wanted, which was me. But fuck, it hurt me to see him like this.

Now, to figure out how to make sure he took care of himself.

CHAPTER 17
Stone

MY BURNING EYES BLINKED open to the dimly lit room, beeping sounds, and wires, instantly recognizing the hospital, a place I'd been to countless times over the years. The pain coursing through my body was a cruel old friend. I was so familiar with it that I figured out, to the day, when I'd start recovering and feeling better.

Glancing around as my eyes grew focused, I couldn't describe the surprise at seeing Stix sleeping in an uncomfortable chair. He draped his legs over the armrests, and his head was craned, resting on the back of the chair. I wasn't sure how that made me feel. My parents stayed as I recovered in the hospital, pretending to care about my well-being and putting on a show for the nurses and doctors. Sometimes the fake love was worse, reminding me of all that I had never received from them. I needed to remember that Stix wouldn't hurt me. He would never pretend he cared. He was here because of the kind of person he was, a person who had empathy for others and a father figure in his little sister's life. Then my heart crumbled a bit, seeing him there, completely uncomfortable as he slept just for me.

My body tensed, and I winced from the pain as I tried to sit up, desperate for some water. Yep, I had some cracked ribs. The pain there would make it hard to breathe for a while. Fucking assholes.

What happened anyway? All that I remembered was tossing the garbage into the dumpster and turning around to find the same assholes from the bar surrounding me, and they were pissed, drunk, and filled with bigoted comments. I had swung at several, managing to hurt a couple of them, but they quickly overwhelmed me since it was six against one. Cowards. But once they had me on the ground, one kick to my head knocked me out.

While I knew I'd recover, losing out on work and pay would seriously put a damper on my finances. I'd have to take fucking time off. I saved up some sick days from the fish market, which was one of their benefits, but they wouldn't be enough to cover me as I recovered from my head trauma. Judging by the dizziness and pain, I could tell I had a concussion, which would take around three weeks to heal. I knew this from experience.

I reached for some water, but the pain was too much. My grunt must've been loud because it woke up Stix, who sat up and rubbed his tired, red eyes.

"Hey," he mumbled and scooted the chair closer to me. His voice was hoarse, and he stifled a yawn but tried to give me a smile. "How are you feeling? I bet you fucking hurt, man."

"Yeah, it's not exactly comfortable."

"Can I get you anything?"

I nodded my head at the side table. "Some water... if you wouldn't mind."

He snorted a laugh as he poured water into a plastic cup from the water pitcher. "Don't start getting all polite and formal on me now."

Stix handed me the cup, and our fingers touched when I took it. That now familiar electricity hit me, masking my pain for a second before it was gone.

He combed my hair with his fingers as I sipped the much-needed water. His touch was so gentle and tender, filling me with a strange emotion that I couldn't figure out. No one had ever been this kind to me. It was why I didn't trust it, but despite everything and my earlier resentment, I trusted Stix.

I wasn't very affectionate, but he seemed to be. I should've known that after seeing him interact with his sister. Suddenly, I didn't feel really all that worthy of him. I'd been nothing but a dick to him for so long, and he forgave me with so little effort, giving me a chance to redeem myself. Even so, I wasn't sure how much I could give to him emotionally. I had absolutely nothing to offer.

While I wasn't that affectionate, his caress pulled out an ache in me. Tender touches I'd starved for as a kid, and eventually got used to living without them for years and years. There were no relationships with others who offered me such kindness. I hadn't realized how hungry it made me for touch now that Stix was doing it without asking for anything in return. He was doing it because he was a great fucking guy.

But what surprised me even more was my leaning into his touch when his hand landed gently on my battered cheek. My reaction was completely automatic because even my skin craved gentleness. It all made my eyes water and my lips tremble, but fear told me to hold it all in. The pain of going through life without loving touches, along with the pain throughout my body and feeling unworthy, was enough to do me in. I wasn't quite crying, but my eyes were definitely trying to leak. When was the last time I'd reacted like this? I hadn't shed a tear in years.

"Hey, what's wrong? Ugh, stupid... You're in pain. Sorry."

I shook my head. "I'm used to pain. It's not that."

His eyes held remorse with a face so full of empathy, and so like Stix as I'd gotten to know him. "How can you be used to this sort of pain?" he asked.

"It's a long story. But... I'm not used to this, not with the hospital or the beating. I'm just not used to someone being gentle or... kind. Yeah, we kissed and held hands and all, but this is different. Intimate. So, I guess, along with what's going on with me, it's hitting sort of hard right now. God, I'm not even used to talking like this, but you fucking pull this shit out of me with so little effort. I'm honestly not sure how much I like it."

"I get it, Rolling Stone. I couldn't imagine not having someone to care about me. Do you have anyone to watch over you? The doctor said you can't do anything strenuous for three weeks while your head recovers."

Not one fucking person. Could you see Blaze helping out? Cueball? Me neither. I shook my head.

"What about your parents?"

"No!" I winced from my outburst as my ribs felt like they were crushing my lungs. "They... can't find out where I am."

His dark eyes grew wide, but his expression was full of understanding. "You got it. They won't know."

"Thanks."

There was a knock on my room door, but they didn't wait for me to give permission to come in. I expected the doctor or a nurse; instead, it was my boss, Kingston.

"Hey, Alpha. I thought you were with your brother," Stix said as he pulled him into a hug.

"I was, but I rushed back when you texted me about our Stone here."

Our Stone? He made it sound like I belonged to them. Like I was a part of their little family.

"Is your foster bro okay?"

"He'll be fine. He's a little banged up and has a broken leg, but he'll live." Kingston sat on the edge of my bed and patted my leg. "Damn, dude. You look like shit."

I scoffed and choked back my growing emotion. "Yeah, I'll live, too."

"Well, I just don't want you to worry about a thing as you recover, okay? Take all the time you need off. Alpha's has covered all your medical expenses since you got hurt on the job."

"What... no, that's okay." I didn't really mean those words because there was no way I'd be able to afford all this despite having health insurance. My deductible was pretty high. But I didn't want to owe anyone, either, let alone my boss.

"Uh, it's already done. I've got insurance for this sort of thing, so don't you worry about it. Just worry about you getting better. Do you have any sick days from your day job?"

I shrugged. "A few."

"Talk to your boss, and let him know what's going on. If I need to cover some of your expenses, then I will."

"I don't mean to sound ungrateful, but... why?"

Kingston scoffed and pointed his thumb at me while looking at Stix. "Can you believe this guy?"

Stix smiled and patted my shoulder. "You're family, dude. Everyone who works at Alpha's is fam. I didn't think you were at first, but I was wrong."

These two were going to fucking annihilate me with kindness. Fuck, I was so undeserving. "Thanks," I muttered.

"You're welcome. Anyway, I'm also here for when you get checked out. I'll drive you both home."

A couple of hours later, I was checked out of the hospital with a massive bill Kingston swore he'd pay. I tried not to worry or feel guilty and just let him do it.

Soon, he dropped us off at our apartment building, and he and Stix helped me walk up four grueling flights of stairs that took forever between the dizziness and the broken ribs. Fuck, I felt eighty years old instead of twenty-three. We reached our floor, and before I could dig out my keys, Stix steered me toward his apartment.

"What are you doing?" I asked.

"You're staying with me for a few days."

I didn't need to be a burden any more than I already had. "My apartment is right there. I'll be fine."

"My mom knows you're coming. We have a pullout sofa, and she's already made the bed. With us, you don't have to worry about getting up all the time and doing things you don't need to be doing."

I didn't deserve this. It was too much. For so long, I was horrible to him. "I... can't." It was my only answer.

"I think you should take up what Stix is offering, Stone. You need to rest, and Stix's mom is pretty much everyone's mom."

"It's just for a few days until you're feeling a little better."

"No." I needed to be firm on this.

Stix grasped my shoulders and made sure I looked at him. "Do you really think Blaze or Cueball will take care of you?"

I shook my head. "I won't let them."

"Stop being so stubborn, Rolling Stone. Please. I'll just worry and be at your place all the time, and honestly, Blaze scares me a little, so..."

All the arguing must have alerted Stix's mom because she opened the door with a big smile on her face. "Stop standing around out in the hall. It's cold out here since they never have the damn building heaters on. And lunch is almost ready."

She reached for my arm and helped me inside before I could protest. At that point, I didn't have the heart to say no as she led me to their living room and sat me down on the sofa bed she had all made up with sheets, a quilt, and several pillows propped up.

"I'll take this as my cue to leave. Feel better, Stone," Alpha said and left.

I sat down and rested my arms on my thighs as I gave in to the inevitability. With a heavy sigh, gentle fingers grabbed my chin and forced me to look up at eyes that looked like Stix's. "God, look at what they did to you, poor baby. We'll get you feeling better in no time. Now sit and relax, and I'll grab you some lunch. It's only a sandwich and some chips, but it's food."

As she walked away, Nova came barreling out of the room she shared with her brother. "Stone!" she squealed and rushed at me. Before she could jump on me, Stix grabbed her and swung her in the air.

"He's hurt, Nova."

"I know. I wanna make him feel better."

This was all too much. Too much attention on me. Too much kindness. "I can't do this," I whispered. When I stood, it was too fast, and I nearly passed out from the wave of dizziness before slumping back onto the bed.

Stix set Nova down and told her to go to the kitchen and eat, then sat next to me as she ran off and pressed a kiss to my cheek. "Get used to it, Stone. Not everyone is shit. And even you deserve to be mothered sometimes, asshole."

My eyes watered again as I looked at him. Life had been so confusing since the day I met Stix. I'd been a swirling mix of emotions that I couldn't figure out half the time. Before, life had been simple. Work, eat, sleep, rinse, and repeat. That had been my life for years after I left my abusers.

With a deep breath, I shoved back all my discomfort, confusion, and fears to let their kindness wash over me. What other choice did I have?

"It's hard for me... to accept this."

"I can tell. But you're also extra emotional after what you've just been through, and you're in pain. Just stay a few days, and let Mom baby you. I'll go to your place later and grab anything you need."

Before I could respond, his mother came out carrying a plate with a tuna salad sandwich on it, some chips, and a can of soda. "Sit back and just set the plate on your lap."

"I can feed him, Mom," Stix said, winking at me. Smartass.

I scowled as I eased onto the bed and rested my back against the pillows. "Don't you fu... Don't you dare."

"Behave, Nico. That mouth of yours will get you in trouble one day," his mom scolded.

She left us alone to do whatever, and I took a bite of the sandwich, which was pretty good.

"I'm going to grab your shit." He rubbed his hands together like some greedy mad scientist. "Ooo, I get to dig through Stone's room. What secrets hide in there that I can discover?"

I snorted a laugh that hurt a little. "Nothing. I'm boring."

"There's nothing boring about you. Okay, I'm off. Let's hope your roommates don't kill me. If you don't hear from me in twenty minutes, call the cops."

I rolled my eyes as he grabbed my keys and walked off, leaving me alone with my sandwich.

Stix stopped, turned to face me at the open door, and snapped his fingers. "Oh! I almost forgot to tell you. According to the hospital, you and I are married now."

Before I could bitch or kill him, he ran off laughing.

"Asshole," I scoffed.

CHAPTER 18
Stix

STONE AND I SAT in his temporary bed, watching TV and playing with each other's fingers while some show was on. I couldn't say what it was about being too distracted by his presence and his touch, as simple as it was, but I did it with him, knowing he enjoyed little touches. He looked like hell with a swollen and bruised face, especially his nose. I ached for him, wishing I'd reached him sooner. Then maybe he wouldn't have gotten so hurt.

I had to help him get undressed tonight because he wanted a shower, and my gut twisted seeing all the bruises along his body while trying to avoid what he looked like underneath all those clothes. He also had several scars I didn't want to think about but couldn't get out of my mind. Shit, some looked like someone put out their cigarettes on him. What happened to him? Who had hurt him enough to leave scars? But I kept my questions to myself. Stone was so closed off, so if I asked, he'd shut down. Hopefully, he'd trust me enough to tell me his story someday.

Despite my efforts not to stare at his body, his tattoos drew me in. I had a couple, but not like Stone. He had several along his arms and hands and a few on his chest. None of which were enough to hide his scars, but I wondered if that was his ultimate goal. After his shower, I had to bandage his chest again.

"I'm tired," he said.

"Oh, sure. I'll let you get some sleep."

I turned off the TV with the remote, but he grabbed my wrist as I got out of bed. "Stay."

My stomach did one of those roller coaster ride dips, not from fear but the thrill of the ride that went through me. "Okay." He watched me as I removed my T-shirt and jeans, suddenly feeling conscientious of my much thinner body. He was so fit and broad, and I had a first-hand look at it earlier.

"Do you need help to remove your shirt?" I asked.

"Yeah."

His face winced as I helped him sit up, gently pulled the shirt over his head, and tossed it over the side of the couch. I helped him lie down and crawled under the covers with him.

Stone turned onto his side, stifling a groan, then got settled. I rolled onto my side, facing him, and stared at his puffy and bruised hazels.

"Thanks," he said.

"It's cool, Rolling Stone."

I wasn't sure what I expected. A kiss? Holding hands? But it wasn't him just passing right out, which was stupid since he'd only gotten out of the hospital today, and he was on pain meds.

I watched him sleep, grateful he decided to stay here, if only for a few days. He needed someone to dote on him. His roommates certainly wouldn't do that. Once you got past his brooding silence and masked anger, you could see all his pain, the physical type. It was clear as day now that I'd gotten to know him.

When I went to his apartment earlier to grab some of his things, his roommates were in there playing video games. I had Stone text them that I was coming, so I didn't surprise them when I showed up. It was awkward as hell, though. Blaze just glared at me, and I couldn't tell you what the hell Cueball's blank face meant.

They made no demands or asked any questions, so either they didn't care, or Stone had told them what had happened and that he was fine. Knowing him, he probably told them to fuck off and not bother seeing him. He was surly like that.

Whatever. I came back with his things unharmed.

I lay there closer to him, listening to his steady breathing, and grabbed one of his hands before I finally fell asleep with him.

I was in that state between dreaming and wakefulness to where I couldn't quite tell what was real or not. Electricity filled me and traveled along my skin, leaving goosebumps in its wake. The familiarity of it had me waking up further to tentative and explorative touches. I glanced at the clock on the wall, showing that it was past six in the morning, which meant Mom and Nova were still asleep.

Stone's face nuzzled into my chest, inhaling my skin and trailing fingers over my torso. His touches, warmth, and closeness made my dick quickly grow hard. I closed my eyes, willing the swelling to go away, but it refused as Stone nuzzled into me. I steadied my breathing and tried to calm my heart rate, so he didn't know I had woken up because I didn't want him to stop. Knowing him, he'd get flustered and shove me away.

Have you ever pretended to sleep with someone next to you? It was because your body knew you were awake, so it tried to force you to take deeper and faster breaths, despite your best efforts to calm them.

Then he pressed his lips to my sensitive, pierced nipple, and that was it. I was done for. That was my favorite on-switch. I bit the inside of my cheek to keep from groaning. Stone wasn't up for anything remotely sexual until he recovered, so I grabbed his arm, touching me, and wrapped it around my torso to my back to show him that he could hold me. But he seriously needed to stop playing with my nipples unless he wanted me to do naughty things to him. Instead of the expected withdrawal, he moved closer. There was no way he couldn't feel my rock-hard dick pressed right against his torso. It didn't matter that I was a prostitute. My face and ears burned, anyway.

"Can I touch you?" he asked without looking at me, assuming he was talking about more than what he already did. I loved that he quickly grew more comfortable exploring this thing between us.

"Sure." Shit, was that my voice? It turned deeper and raspier. At least I didn't squeak like I was thirteen again.

I had expected him to keep touching me as he had been or exploring more, not cupping my fucking aching cock and nuts, pulling a gasp out of me, which then turned into a groan. His thumb traced the outline of my dick through my underwear, and beads of pre-come leaked through the thin cotton fabric. Could he feel how wet he made me already? There was something intoxicating and arousing as he grew more bold with his explorations. This was someone who'd hated me and internalized that hatred in himself. Now, he was open and free. Freer than before, anyway, and I was eating it up.

"It's so hard."

I coughed and nervously chuckled. "Well, you *are* touching it. It tends to do that."

"I've never touched a dick before that wasn't my own. Any desire for boys or men was snuffed out of me as a kid. So much so that any urges I have, bring anger, hatred, and fear, mostly at myself for giving into them, which you've already witnessed. I just hadn't recognized it until recently. I'm not angry anymore, but the fear is still there, like a toxic cloud that hovers over your head, and if it gets any lower, you'll suffer painfully. And I'm so fucking tired of being afraid and angry. How did I live that way for so long and not want to end it all?"

I swallowed, now feeling inappropriate with my hard-on, which he hadn't stopped touching. Being filled with arousal and empathy at the same time was a confusing sensation. Not to mention a slight fear at his hint of suicide. I wasn't sure what to say to that.

"If I didn't play boyish enough, I got a beating. If I dared look at a boy the wrong way, I got a beating. Hell, I got beat for simply breathing. It's why it scares the hell out of me when I lash out violently. No, it terrifies me. To have so little control and hatred to lash out like that. What made it worse was when I punched Blaze over you and... I felt no remorse. There's something wrong with me. I don't want to be like my parents."

"You're not. No way." Despite his earlier issues with me, he always seemed to hold back.

He ignored me as if he hadn't heard a word I'd said. "There was this boy I really liked. His name was Alec. No, I loved him or thought I did. God, I'd barely thought of him until recently, pushing him so far deep into my mind. I wanted him so much that all the beatings I'd received until then turned into mere swats in my brain. The pain was forgotten as this need overwhelmed everything else. I had wanted to kiss him so badly. Bad enough to push away my fears. And I did. He was a neighbor of ours at the trailer park we lived in, and we had become amazingly close friends. Best friends. One day, he came over to hang out with me. My parents grew excited that I was making guy friends until Mom walked in on us. Because why would I ever catch a break? She had been late for fucking everything, from after-school programs to activities, picking me up from friends' houses. Yet, of course, she walked in at that moment, right when our lips touched."

God, I didn't know if I wanted to hear this, but I would for him. How many knew of his story? Probably no one, and honestly, I wasn't sure why he trusted me now with it, but I wouldn't stop him, no matter how painful it was to listen to. I'd hold it close to me and never utter a word to anyone else about it unless he wanted me to.

"She sent Alec home with a strange calmness that was worse than her anger, though her tone had been biting. But once he left, the beast came out. She grabbed me by my hair and dragged me out of the room and right into the kitchen, yanking out a chunk of hair. She pulled out one of those metal spatulas and beat me with it. In between my hits, she told me how disgusting I was. That I was unnatural and no son of hers, and it's how I got some of my scars on my back. Others were from Dad's cigarettes and using my skin as an ashtray. He thought it was funny. Then again, he was always high as a kite. Once she finished with me, she dragged me back to my room to bleed and suffer until my dad got home. Then he beat me within an inch of my life."

I sniffed and wiped away some spilling tears because... fuck! The way he told his story was so ordinary, like he was telling a story of going to school or skating with his friends. "Why in the hell would they do that to you? How evil are they? I'm not ignorant. I realize some parents are horrible to their kids. Hell, my own dad left me because of it. Still, he never beat me. I just don't understand it."

He shrugged as his index finger traveled up my abs, to my chest, then down my arm. "I like touching you. It doesn't feel wrong. It feels good. Good. It's been so long since I had anything remotely good in my life."

"Because it fucking isn't!"

"My parents were either drunk or high most of the time, which only made them worse. They hadn't always been bad... before the drugs and drinking. Anyway, I woke up a couple of days later, broken, battered, and covered in stitches. I remember waking up to my mother crying while a doctor checked my injuries. Apparently, they claimed someone had attacked me on my way home from school. Her tears made it all believable, and I wouldn't dare contradict her. Hell, maybe they were real from her guilt once she sobered up, which wasn't unusual. She'd wake up to find me bruised and bloody, and I'd get rushed to the hospital, but only for wounds she couldn't fix herself, and never at the same clinic or hospital. Then she'd beg me to forgive her. I never did."

No wonder Stone had internalized homophobia all this time. I'd often wondered why he'd been so angry. He hated himself for being attracted to me and was in denial, blaming me for things that had nothing to do with his real problems. According to his parents, they made him so that he blamed himself for wanting things he shouldn't.

"I am so sorry, Rolling Stone. I wish I could give you some words of wisdom or... fuck. I wish I could hurt them back. Dammit!"

He finally looked up at me from his lower position on the bed. Just seeing his face had me in a new sort of rage, knowing he'd looked like that often growing up.

"I left them as soon as I made enough money. I saved every penny to do it working jobs here and there, from bagging groceries to mowing yards. It made it easier after Dad got arrested for dealing fentanyl, and a lot of it, so they gave him ten years, but he's already served half. I'm sure in a couple of years, they'll let him out. They have no idea where I am, and I intend to keep it that way."

"Well, they sure as fuck won't find out from me."

I finally got the balls to touch him back, hoping he wouldn't run or resist. My instincts were correct that it all had to be on his terms. He needed to be comfortable with the idea of being with me or a guy in general. After hearing his story, I felt even more guilty about that night I'd touched him as he jacked off, which was also my fault.

I gently combed my fingers through his silky hair, which was growing out a bit, and kissed his head.

"You know, you sure are strong for someone who's been hurt all his life."

He barked a laugh, then groaned, hurting himself. "Not at all. I've just been living day to day. No, not living, but surviving. There's joy in living. I have no joy. Sometimes I ask myself why I even bother."

There it was again. Those hints that he'd thought about ending it all. "Don't talk like that. You're strong as fuck. You could've taken the easy way out, but you chose to live, work through your pain, and make a life for yourself. Is it perfect? No. But you're here, and you have friends.

You have me, so you're not alone. Even better? You're away from those monsters."

I couldn't read his face when he looked up at me again. "If you say so."

"You're not giving in that easily to me now, are you?"

He cracked a small smile, then winced.

"Do you need pain meds?"

He shook his head. "I'll be fine. I'm used to the pain."

"Jesus, fuck, no one should be used to pain."

"How else are we to survive?"

"Good point."

His hand trailed down my torso again and cupped my now flaccid dick, which quickly thickened to his touch. "I think it's just you."

"What do you mean?"

"I haven't been interested in anyone. I liked my friend a lot when I was younger. He was really cool and nice. He had felt... special until I wasn't allowed to see him anymore. It took me a long time to forget him, and my parents helped with that, of course. I had tried my hand at women, but nothing stuck. At first, I wondered if it was my parent's influence that I had no interest in anyone, but then you came along. No matter how hard I fought you, the more I got to know you, the more I wanted. I just hadn't recognized it until recently. I'm rarely into anyone sexually. And one-night stands had, for the most part, been failures. I just kind of gave up dating altogether."

"Huh. Do you think maybe you're demisexual?"

"I'm not sure what that is."

"It's on the asexual spectrum, but to sum it up, you need like a bond with someone to be sexually attracted to them. It might explain your general lack of interest in sex with people you're not connected to, except with your friend when you were younger. And not to toot my own horn, but perhaps me, too."

"Interesting. Maybe? But we didn't have a bond. I hated you for a while. You made me so angry. I realize now that it wasn't really you, but..."

"That doesn't mean we don't have a bond, Rolling Stone. Why did you hate me in particular above all others? Why were you also so angry with me? I mean... What started it all? And why me in particular? Was it an instant hate, or did you slowly resent me more the more we got to know each other?"

"I'm not sure. Something drew me to you, and god, I fought it. I understand that now. My attraction to you made me so angry. But as time went on, the angrier I got. Then that first time you came out of Brie's... I was in such a rage. Shit, I sound so fucked up. I'm a mess, Stix."

"Whatever it was, something drew you to me. I'd like to think we have a bond, as messed up as it is. Yes, you're a bit of a mess, but so am I. So are all our friends. And who could blame you after all you've gone through?"

I loved that he was so open to me now. Like whatever had been crushing him, lifted away once he decided he wanted something and that maybe it wasn't so wrong.

"Thank you for trusting me with your story," I said, kissing his head again.

"Thank you for seeing past my walls."

CHAPTER 19
Stone

I'D BEEN STAYING AT Stix's apartment for five days, and now, I had to move on. I'd overstayed my welcome, taking up space and eating their food. Money would be scarce for a while since I couldn't work at the fish market, but I only took off days I'd saved up, which was seven. By next week, I'd return to work, whether or not the doctor allowed me to. I couldn't just not work. Regardless, I'd try to leave Stix's mom some money in return for eating up all their food.

At least my ribs and head didn't hurt as much, but the pain was still there like a dull ache that never went away, and shifting in the bed sent sharp pains through my chest, making it hard to breathe. But I managed to sit up and look at Stix, still sleeping. He hadn't left my side since that first night. I never asked again, but he'd stayed each night, always seeming to understand what I needed. How did he do that? It was like he could see through me and know exactly what was going on.

But what made everything worse was that he hadn't been working at all during the day. Maybe it was a good thing. Hell, I didn't fucking know. But he stopped doing his prostitution, or whatever he called it. So, while I felt guilty enough staying here, it grew worse since Stix hadn't been bringing in the extra money they needed because of me. I didn't deserve him, or anyone for that matter, but I couldn't bring myself to pull away from him. He helped me quickly grow used to living in my own skin. Hell, I became comfortable enough around him that I told him my story. And that happened so fast once I let go of my irrational hatred toward him. This was so much better. The fears lingered, but the pressure was infinitely less.

While I felt guilty that he hadn't been working, I was grateful for it, too. His being with other men renewed my rage and jealousy, but telling him to stop wasn't my place. We weren't really a 'thing.' Or were we? Fuck, if I knew. I'd never been part of a 'thing.'

Stix sensed my movement because he woke up, rubbing his eyes and yawning. When he stretched, the sheet he'd been using slipped off, and the outline of his morning wood punched through his underwear, making me grow hard. I'd been itching to try some things with him now that I'd come to terms with whatever the fuck I was. It didn't matter. I liked Stix. I didn't give a shit about the label. It was too confusing to wrap my head around, anyway. But I hadn't done more than touch him since that first night. To be fair, I'd been in pain, so doing anything strenuous like sex probably wasn't the best idea.

A groan slipped out of me as he slipped a hand inside his boxer briefs and rubbed himself. He was half asleep, so he probably didn't realize what he was doing.

He yawned again, and his eyes fluttered open, landing directly on me, staring at him as he stroked himself. His smile turned sheepish as he slipped his hand out. "Oops."

"Don't stop," I blurted.

His mom and sister had already left, which had woken me up, so he was free to do whatever. And seeing him jack off would be hot as hell. It was all I could currently think about.

Stix smirked and sat up, leaning against the back of the couch. "You want me to rub one off?"

"Yes."

"Only if you do it with me."

My dick bounced and throbbed, clearly liking the idea.

"Okay."

He lifted his ass off the bed, slipped off his underwear, and was now entirely naked. He was a lot leaner than me, but he had tight muscles throughout his body and very little body hair, except on his legs and his happy trail. I checked out a couple of his tattoos. One was of a small sword that looked like it pierced his left nipple, but he also had barbell piercings in his nipples, which I found fucking hot. And, of course, he tattooed a pair of drumsticks on his right pec. His using the tips of his fingers to move up and down his hard length pulled me away from my visual exploration to focus solely on what he was doing.

It was the second time I'd seen his dick, and my bodily response to him only confirmed how much he turned me on. His strokes were languid as he watched me watching him. It was perfect. Like if you imagined a perfect dick, it was his. Smooth, cut, looking soft as velvet, with veins, and a nice head that turned arousal red. He wasn't massive. Massive would fucking hurt. No, he was just right in length and width to where you would enjoy it inside of you. I'd never had anal sex before or even thought about it until now, but I'd heard from women who'd done it that it could hurt.

"You like what you see?" he asked, always the smartass.

I wasn't going to lie. "Yes. Stroke more."

"Not until you pull yours out."

I huffed, but I slipped my boxer briefs down to my thighs.

"You've got a nice cock yourself, Rolling Stone. Damn."

Stix scooted close enough to me to where we touched our shoulders. My face burned red, so I was grateful the bruising masked it. I hated to be vulnerable, and this was pretty vulnerable, but it was strangely hot, too.

His long fingers wrapped around his length, slowly stroking and slightly twisting as he slid upward before he swiped his thumb and fingers over his pre-cum to use it for a smoother glide. His breathing picked up as he got into it, which increased my breathing as I stroked in rhythm to his.

A groan slipped from him, making me leak. Fuck. I wasn't sure how he did that. It was a low and deep sound, but not loud like it came from deep within his core.

"This is kinda hot, Rolling Stone."

All I could do was nod, getting completely lost in what he was doing to himself. His sounds, the heat coming from his body, and those long fingers I imagined wrapped around my cock turned me the fuck on. It *was* hot. If this didn't prove I wasn't into him, nothing would. At that moment, I wanted nothing else in life other than Stix. All that anger and hatred vanished, replaced by want, need, and lust.

My heart beat so fast from rubbing one off together, and not only from the arousal. Some of the heart-pounding was from the residual fear of what my parents had done to me, like they could walk in at any moment, catch me, and, this time, they'd kill me. But the arousal kept me going, stroking, wanting to come with him. Hell, all I cared about was watching him come apart, not giving a shit about my own release. To see his wrecked face as he let it all go.

It soon occurred to me that I wanted to be the one to make him come apart. To have power over his orgasm. I slapped his hand away and grabbed his dick, which burned in my hand and was slick with pre-cum. Fuck, it felt perfect in my hand.

"Yes," he breathed, nuzzling my neck and up my jaw toward my mouth for a deep kiss. He thrust his tongue inside, and I suckled it briefly before we resumed kissing.

"Can I?" he asked when we came up for air.

I assumed he meant he wanted to stroke me, too, so I nodded.

"Fuck, Stone... your dick is sexy as hell."

That elicited a groan from me as I stroked him faster. I didn't know what the hell I was doing, only knowing what I liked, but he didn't seem to mind, and in fact, he repeatedly thrust into my hand.

"Mmm, yes, like that, baby," he said.

His calling me baby had my balls drawn up tight, and his stroking sped up. Soon, pants, slapping noises, and groans as we sucked our faces off could be heard in the room. Our kisses became as sloppy as our movements, making them almost dirty, which was sexy as hell. Never had I reacted like this to anything remotely sexual. Ever. And we were just giving each other hand jobs. It almost scared me to imagine what blow jobs or sex would be like. It might fucking destroy me if a simple hand job was this good.

"I'm going to come." God, was that my voice? Did I really sound as desperate to him as I did to my own ears?

"Yes, baby... come for me."

As soon as he uttered those words, my body froze as I pumped out spurt after spurt. The pressure was almost unbearable, and my body was desperate to finish yet to keep going, so it could feel this forever and ever. Stix milked me for all I was worth until I was empty, and my body shuddered with aftershocks.

"God, Stone... look at all that cum. So yummy."

Jesus. His words were going to get me hard again.

My body grew numb, but I didn't succumb to it to finish stroking him. His dick swelled in my hand and grew so fucking hot. Suddenly, he threw back his head and slammed his eyes shut as his body froze like mine did a second ago. His shooting cum surprised me for a second, which was stupid because I had expected it, but I'd also never made a dude come before or even seen a guy come other than me.

His mouth went slack and slightly open, and he looked utterly blissed out of his mind. He was so beautiful at that moment. It was raw and honest. No hiding behind smiles and sarcasm. Coming in front of someone was the most real you could be without having to say anything.

My movements slowed as I pulled the rest of his cum out of him, and his body relaxed.

"God, that was so fucking sexy, Rolling Stone. Watching you get wrecked and let loose? I want to see that over and over."

The feeling was mutual.

"I want that, too," I finally said. "I want you as mine."

He looked over at me with hooded eyes and a crooked smile. "Good, because I have plans."

I couldn't help but smile as I grabbed my T-shirt lying on the floor and cleaned us both up.

Once my heart was calm enough to not feel like it was about to explode, I pulled my underwear back on and threw on a clean T-shirt over my head. Stix got dressed, too, then sat on the edge of the bed and grabbed my hand. "I have to head in to work tonight at Alpha's."

"I figured."

"As much as I'd like to stay and keep you company, I've taken off enough time from work."

"It's cool. I think I'm going to head back to my apartment today. I feel better. But you definitely need to get back to work. Don't go broke on my account. Please. But…"

"But what?"

"You haven't been doing your other job, which is a big loss of money just for me. I can't ask you to do that anymore."

He looked down at my hand as he played with my fingers. "You don't care if I keep making money off men?"

I hated it more than anything. Hated Stix needed to sell himself to make money and survive. And as much as I wanted him to quit, I wasn't sure I had the right to. But I wanted that right. "I definitely care. You're mine now and mine alone. I really have no say in the matter, but it doesn't mean I don't want to fucking kill anyone who has touched you or wants to touch you. I hate Brie and Tony more than is healthy because they got to have you. At the same time, I can't ask you to give up your money for me. I don't deserve that sort of sacrifice."

To my surprise, and Stix was fucking good at surprising me, he bounced on the bed closer to me with a massive smile on his face. What did that mean?

"I didn't stop my day job for you. Well, I did, but not because you're injured. I haven't done it because it doesn't feel right. It's one thing doing it while single." He leaned in and pressed his lips to mine. It was soft and tender and more intimate than our sloppy kiss earlier. "I always thought if I found a boyfriend or something, he needed to be cool with what I did for a living. But now that I've found you, I no longer want this job in my life anymore. It feels... ick."

"But... you need the money."

He shrugged. "A real, legit job it is, then."

"Really?"

"Yep, and I find I'm okay with that. You *are* worth it. So, stop saying you fucking aren't, or else I'll punch you in the ribs where it hurts the most."

I gave him a shy smile, looking at him under my lashes. "Okay."

"Good, because I like you smiling. It makes you even hotter."

He pressed a kiss to my still-bruised cheek and ran off to get ready for work.

My body was still tender as hell, but I needed to return to my life. I'd been here longer than intended. Five days was too fucking long. It was hard to let go of the delicious meals, and though it wasn't like they made food from scratch, it was better than what I usually ate. Food always tastes better when someone else cooks. Not only that, but the affection from Stix's mom was even more addicting. And I'd miss sleeping next to him. I'd never slept so well, despite the pain. We were connected, and I felt safe with him so close to me. What a strange turn of events.

I was shoving my meager belongings into my bag when Stix's mom came home with Nova in tow. She stopped and watched me pack.

"Are you sure you want to leave? You're more than welcome to stay, Damien."

I gave her a small smile. "Thank you, but I've taken up enough of your time and eaten enough of your food. I'll pay you back soon, Ms. Jamieson."

She raised a brow and folded her arms. "How often do I need to tell you to call me Grace?"

I huffed a laugh. "Sorry, I'll try."

"Please stay longer, Stone!" Nova said with begging hands.

I ruffled her hair. "I can't, kiddo, but I'll visit a lot. Besides, I'm only two doors down."

"Fine!" she yelled, pouting and running off to her room.

"She's already a damn teen at five."

"She's sweet."

"Are you sure you don't want to stay for one more meal?"

"I'm fine. Really. Thank you."

I zipped up my bag and was about to leave before she stopped me. "Nico talks a lot about you. I've never seen him care for someone before, not like how he does with you. It's been hard on him since his dad left, always blaming himself for his leaving. His dad and I weren't getting along, anyway, and he probably would've left eventually. Nico's coming out was only a catalyst, I think."

I nodded. "That's what I told him, though I don't know your story."

"Just..." she sighed and wrung her hands. "I don't want to be one of those mothers, but while Nico may seem strong outwardly, he has his moments of struggles. He tries to hide under smiles and jokes, but he still hurts. His guilt runs deep, no matter what I say. Just... be gentle with him. I know you two seem to like each other, and I won't presume you all will work out or be together forever, but be gentle about it if it doesn't."

I simply blurted my truth. "Shit, I was horrible to him for a long time. Afraid of what it meant to be... into men. No, I was terrified. He's a first for me, and my fear runs as deep as his guilt. There's a reason for it that I don't want to get into, but once I recognized what I felt for him and accepted it... I'm finally happy. That was all Nico. He saw something in me I couldn't see for myself." I shook my head. "I'm not sure why I'm telling you this. You should probably tell me to fuck off for how I treated him. But... I'm already in deep, and it scares the hell out of me."

Grace placed a gentle hand on my cheek. "Nico was right. You're a good soul. He didn't tell me what happened, and I won't ask for the details. What matters is now, at this moment in time. If you made mistakes, the key is not to make them again. To learn from them and grow. Whatever you did or feel you did, it's clear Nico forgave you."

"I'll do my best to do right by him."

She pulled me into a gentle hug, careful not to hurt me. "You come over any time you like, okay?"

"Okay. Thank you for everything."

I fumbled my way into my apartment to find Blaze and Cueball in the kitchen making packaged Ramen noodles. Blaze was picking at his nails while sitting on the counter while Cueball stirred the pot of noodles. They both looked at me when I walked in, but I couldn't tell what was on their faces.

"Well, you look like shit," Blaze said.

"Thanks, Captain Obvious."

Cueball walked over to me and inspected my face. "They find the guys who did it?"

I shook my head, then walked off to my bedroom to rest for a few more days before returning to the fish market on Monday.

"That's it?" Blaze snapped.

I turned around. "What?"

"What the fuck do you mean 'what?' You get beaten, sent to the hospital, you text us what happened, and that you didn't want to talk about it, but you were recovering next door. The next thing we know, your bane of existence, or so I thought, comes waltzing into our apartment like he fucking owns the place to pack a bag for you. Again, what the fuck?"

Cueball shrugged. "It's obvious."

Blaze scoffed. "Not to me."

"It's a long story, and I'm tired."

Blaze pointed a spoon at me that Cueball had been using to stir the soup. "Tough shit. Speak. Because I thought you hated that asshole."

"I did... or I thought I did. It's a long story." I sighed and ran a hand through my hair that I needed to cut, hating it long because my parents used to pull on it to hurt me. "I like him."

Blaze's face was blank as Cueball nodded. He'd had it all figured out early on, but apparently, he didn't enlighten Blaze, which was pretty cool, I guess, leaving me to come out on my own to Blaze if I wanted.

I sighed again since Blaze's face was blank and clueless. "I *like* him... like him."

"Wait, you're gay, man?"

"Fuck! Does it matter?"

Cueball shook his head. "No, it doesn't."

And that was someone else who kept surprising me at every turn. Cueball.

Blaze tossed his hands in the air. "Whatever, man."

"Just be fucking nice to him or ignore him. No more hurting him."

He huffed. "Well, that explains why you fucking punched me. Whatever, I don't give a fuck. But a heads up would be nice before I think you hate someone."

"We cool?" I asked him.

"Yeah, we're cool."

Two days later, I got a call from one of the detectives who'd been working on my case. Honestly, I thought the cops wouldn't have given a shit. I was a nobody. He informed me they'd found four of the six guys. They'd been in hiding and couldn't be found, but apparently, they weren't too bright. They eventually headed home, thinking the danger was over, and the police had been waiting.

The detective had me come in and point them out as a witness. Then they'd also called Stix, the twins, Nacho, and Pippin to come in since they were there that night when the pricks had been harassing Stix. But it was Stix as the extra witness that had the men put in jail. Hopefully, they'd find the other two. Eventually, there'd be a trial, I guess. Whatever, they probably wouldn't bother us again.

CHAPTER 20
Stix

I STARED IN THE mirror, admiring my candy corn sweatshirt that said, 'Halloween Makes Me Corny,' then I put on the rubber mask from the movie Halloween and crept out of my room while sneaking around into the kitchen. Mom was getting Nova ready for trick or treating when I popped out. "Boo!"

"Jesus, Nico!" Mom rested her hand over her heart, and Nova squealed and ran away, giggling as I chased her.

When I caught her, I tossed her over my shoulder. "Let's go get Stone."

"Yay!"

"Later, Mom!"

"I want her back in two hours, Nico."

"Yes, ma'am."

I set Nova down, and we headed toward Stone's place. She ran first, knocked on the door, and stood back when Stone answered it, wearing a zombie costume with makeup. He looked pretty awesome. His white T-shirt underneath his jacket was torn up and made to look bloody.

He still wasn't one hundred percent after his attack, but he wasn't all bruised up anymore, and his ribs were better, so I'd asked him if he wanted to go with me to the Hampden Halloween Fest, which had trick-or-treating that was safe for little kids, unlike this neighborhood. Even better, it wasn't too far away.

When we got Nova back home later, there was a Halloween party down by the Old Town Mall, where we skated. The abandoned building we skated in would be decked out with lights and spooky decorations, with music and drinking. There would probably be drugs, too, but I stayed away from that shit unless it was weed. Not that Alpha let us do drugs. Weed was the only thing he permitted. Everyone would be dressed up and skating in costumes, and then most of us would sleep overnight there. It was always an epic party.

Alpha closed up the bar on Halloween night. I didn't know how he could afford the loss of income since it would make tons, but he loved Halloween and wanted to party. I couldn't blame him since he worked every single day for most of the year.

Hopefully, Stone would be comfortable enough to hang around me and my friends. He hadn't been open to telling people about us yet, except for his two roommates, which was fine. I could wait him out, though I desperately wanted to share him with those closest to me, especially to show them the genuine Stone, not the one who had hated me or the one who hid behind angry walls. God, it was just fucking nice to get to know him as he opened up more and more. He still resisted talking about his family too much, but I didn't really mind not hearing how much he suffered. It made me stabby.

"Do you like my costume, Stone!" Nova yelled. She had two volumes—really quiet for school or super loud, mostly because Stone was tall.

"You're in costume?" he teased.

She huffed. "Yes, I'm Wednesday."

"How can you be a day of the week?" He looked up at me and winked. Fuck, I loved a playful Stone. That was a first. I was beginning to think he had no sense of humor whatsoever.

"Wednesday from the Addams Family... duh."

"Oh, *that* Wednesday. Well, you look epic, Nova."

She twirled her black dress. "Thank you!"

He looked at me. "And what the hell are you supposed to be?"'

I shrugged. "I'm just Michael Myers, who likes ironic T-shirts."

"Nerd," he chuckled.

It took only fifteen minutes to skate toward Hampden Park. Nova piggybacked Stone on our way there, so it'd be faster. I had no idea how he did it with his cracked ribs, but I guess they were feeling better now since it had been a few weeks.

Once we arrived, he set her down.

"Don't run off, Nova. You stay close to us. There are stands and shops that you go into for candy. Don't take any from a random person on the street," I said.

"Okay!"

The place was fucking packed with people. It was a popular Halloween destination and a perfect place for families, while the shops and restaurants made tons of money. There were also crafts, games, and a costume competition, but we were just here so my little sis could get candy.

"I've never been here before," Stone said as we followed behind Nova, letting her run the show as long as we didn't lose sight of her.

"Yeah, I came here last year to take Nova. It was her first time trick or treating."

Stone rarely talked much, so the conversation quickly died, though I didn't mind. It wasn't awkward. Simply being around him felt good.

As we walked, I tested the waters by being close to him and touching his fingers now and again to see if he'd take the hint that I wanted to hold his hand. He finally did after like the tenth damn try by grabbing my hand and treading our fingers together. I smiled up at him, and while he didn't smile back, he looked pretty chill and comfortable. That was a good sign he warmed up to this boyfriend thing or whatever we had going on.

"Thanks for coming with me," I said.

"Nova's pretty demanding when you sic her on me."

I barked out a laugh. "Yeah, but how can you resist that face?"

"I can't, which is why I'm here."

Feigning a pout, I looked away. "And here I thought it was me you found irresistible."

"That, too."

The night grew colder, so I snuggled deeper into Stone as we walked in and out of shops, enjoying our company while keeping a close eye on Nova.

"This is pretty nice. Almost like a date," he said, surprising me.

"It is."

"I've never had a date before. Not a real one, anyway."

"I guess we'll just have to fix that."

Who knew what we could do for a date, considering we didn't have much money? And I wasn't selling myself for blow jobs anymore, making money tight.

Before we knew it, time was up, and I had to get Nova home. As much as I had fun with Stone and Nova, I was ready to party.

Stone hauled Nova on his back again, and I carried her fifty pounds of candy. Okay, it wasn't that much, but it was more than a five-year-old could eat in a year. Mom would probably dive into it periodically, too. I tried to stay away from as much sugar as I could.

After we got home, I grabbed my sleeping bag and a thicker jacket because it was getting cold out.

Once I finished getting ready, I knocked on Stone's door, who was also grabbing shit for tonight. When it opened, I was confronted by Blaze, dressed as Captain Sparrow from Pirates of the Caribbean. After what he did to me, I still hated the asshole, but at least he was cool with Stone when he came out to them. I had to give him credit where it was due. Tonight would be the big test for Stone in his comfort with his new self and around me. I haven't told my friends shit because it wasn't my story to tell, only with Stone's permission, which he hadn't given yet.

"Blaze," I said as a greeting.

"Stix."

He stepped aside to let me in, and I walked back to Stone's room. Blaze and I still didn't like each other, but at least he hadn't tried to hurt me again. When I entered Stone's room, I found him hunched over his bed, throwing some thin-ass blanket into a bag.

"Dude, that won't keep you warm."

"Well, I don't have a sleeping bag," he huffed.

"Then you can share mine."

He raised a brow. "You and I won't fit."

"You don't know me so well. I'm *very* agile."

He smirked and shook his head, but then it fell from his face. "Uhm... would you mind going on ahead without me? I'll go with Blaze and Cueball and... meet you there."

I tried to be patient with him. It had been weeks since we started this weird thing between us, but we hadn't branched out further than kissing and jacking each other off. Then again, he'd been too hurt to do much else. But I wanted fucking more, dammit. I thought, finally, we could admit to my friends we were together and move forward. Now, he was backing out. Again. This wasn't the first time he'd done this. And don't even get me started on how he acted at work. I wanted him to go at his own pace, but fuck, I had a pace, too, and it moved forward faster than Stone.

Patience, Stix. Be patient.

I sighed and turned away because I didn't want him to see my disappointment or to make him feel bad. As much as I wanted to go with him, this was still his show. "Yeah, ah, sure. That's cool. I'll, uhm, see you there."

Before I walked off, a gentle hand grabbed my arm and forced me to turn around. "Wait. No, I'll... go with you."

I gnawed on my bottom lip, still avoiding his face. "It's cool, Rolling Stone. We agreed to go at your own pace."

"No, this isn't just about me. Not anymore. I'm sorry, it's... this residual shit from my parents. Whenever I'm forced to face something that scares me, I want to run or ignore it, but I also really want to stop fucking running. It's a weird back-and-forth thing if that makes any sense."

When I finally looked at him, I melted when he cupped my face and kissed me. It was slow and full of tongue. When he pulled away, my eyes slowly opened.

"I'm sorry. We had a perfect day, and I'm ruining it. Let's go have fun, and I'll try not to be such a fucking baby about things. It's time I really got to know your friends. I've worked with them long enough without really doing so. And you can tell them about us."

A surge of excitement hit, making me bounce on my toes. "Really?"

He nodded, but his eyes were uncertain. "Yeah, let's do it."

"We can wait." But I really didn't want to.

"No more waiting."

My smile grew large, and I stood on my toes to kiss him again. "Does this mean we finally get to bone?"

Stone burst out in a deep laugh, showing off those cute crooked bottom teeth. It was the best sound in the fucking world. He seriously needed to do it more often. "Bone? What are you? Twelve?"

"Maybe."

"We can talk about *boning* later."

Stone finished shoving shit in his bag, grabbed his board, and we met Cueball and Blaze in the living room, who both had their shit for an overnight stay, too. God, I'd also have to hang around these two asses. Cueball wasn't so bad, except I couldn't tell if he liked me or wanted to kill me. At least, with Blaze, you knew where you stood with him.

"Let's fucking party!" Blaze yelled, pulled out a bottle of whiskey I didn't know he was holding, and took a shot straight from the bottle. He wiped his mouth off with the back of his hand and handed me the bottle. Was this some sort of truce? Or a 'welcome to the gang' moment?

"You didn't poison it, did you?"

Blaze barked out a laugh. "Wouldn't you like to know?"

"Blaze..." Stone reprimanded.

"What? I'm just teasing the little dude."

"Who are you calling little? I'm bigger than you are by several inches, asshat." I ignored his huff and took a long pull from the bottle before handing it off to Stone. His sip was shorter, and he gave it to Cueball, who also took a sip. Now that I thought about it, I'd never seen Stone drunk. Sure, he drank once in a while, but it was never a lot. I wondered how much that had to do with his parents.

"Ready to party?" Blaze yelled again.

"Let's do it!" I said.

CHAPTER 21
Stix

I WALKED INTO THE building first, with Stone and his roommates behind me. My jaw dropped at how epic the place looked. While the building was gutted and only had skateboard ramps, the place was decorated with neon paint, and black lights made it all glow, creating eerie and strange murals all over the walls. Rap music blared and bounced off those colorful walls, and there were carved pumpkins, skulls, candles, and more dotting every dark corner. Even better was a table covered in bottles of liquor and snacks. I knew for a fact that Alpha contributed to a lot of it.

We were totally trespassing, but no one ever came here except us and a few homeless people.

My friends were huddled over in a corner of the building, drinking, and laughing. None of them were skating yet, but I was itching to. As I headed in their direction, I removed my mask, and Ajax stood, towering over everyone and looking absolutely ridiculous as Ace Ventura, Pet Detective, with a fake parrot on his shoulder. Despite how silly he looked, he came bounding over to us, looking dangerous as hell. With unusually rapid reflexes for such a big guy, he grabbed Blaze by the front of his shirt and lifted him off his feet.

"What the fuck is he doing here?" he asked me without taking his eyes off the smaller man.

"Let me go, you fucking yeti."

I rested my hand on Ajax's arm to get his attention. "They're always here, man."

"Not with us, they're not. Not with them hanging around you."

Soon, we were drawing in a crowd with eager faces, ready to see a fight, while the rest of my friends came to stand behind Ajax with their arms folded. Cueball grew tense, who was as big as Ajax, so I worried for my friend. I needed to diffuse this as quickly as possible, needing all of us to get along. If Stone and I were to work out, my friends had to get on board with that and at least be tolerant of his friends.

"You better put me down, Sasquatch, or I'll cut you."

Ajax scoffed. "I'd like to see you try, you fucking midget."

"Enough!" Alpha yelled, running over here, looking like a badass biker for a costume. "Ajax, put him down. Now."

Of course, Blaze had to fuel the fire, the goddamn emotional arsonist. "You better do as your daddy says, little boy," he said with a smirk on his face. The prick was fearless. It could've been an act, though.

Cueball grabbed Blaze by the scruff of his shirt from the back and ripped him away from Ajax. "Enough, Blaze."

Ajax made a move toward them, but I stood in front and rested my hand on his chest. "Stop. They're with me. If I can forgive, so can you."

He paced back and forth, ruining his hair that was sticking straight up for his character. "I don't fucking get it. He hurt you. And that one..." He pointed at Stone. "I don't care if we have to work together. He's never liked you. What the fuck, man."

"If you calm the fuck down, I'll tell you."

Before I could explain anything, Stone stepped beside me and took my hand, threading our fingers together. Okay, I was stupidly happy and smiling like a loon right then. And while I thought he was adorable with his shaking and clammy hands, I also felt bad, understanding that this was scary as fuck for him.

"We're together," he said. "Stix and I... we're seeing each other."

All my friends were quiet, with eyes bouncing back and forth at us until Alpha barked out a laugh. "It's about fucking time!"

"You knew about this?" Jazz asked, pointing a thumb in my direction. "I'm so confused. I thought they hated each other."

I did a double-take, looking at the twins. They actually looked fucking awesome. Jazz was dressed as a dead high school football player, while her brother was dressed as a dead cheerleader. I loved it.

Then Blondie did a little cheer, making me laugh. "You two are so fucking adorable!"

"I didn't know for sure, but I had a good idea." Alpha waved a dismissive hand at Stone. "This one here was too pissy to see how interested he was in Stix. Glad to see he finally came around. Now, Stone is family, and he's with Stix, so I suggest you all suck it up and deal. That goes for his friends. I'm sure Blaze here is remorseful for what he did to Stix."

I scoffed because Blaze didn't have an ounce of empathy, as far as I could tell.

He bowed dramatically. "Of course, I'm sorry. I will forever be regretful for my actions."

I rolled my eyes and gripped Stone's hand tighter as I stood on my toes to reach his ear. "That went better than expected. Let's go get some drinks."

My friends had plenty of liquor to share, and I was sure Pippin had some weed, too, but I wanted to pull Stone out of there to let him breathe a bit. When I tried to let go of his hand, he held on tighter.

"Now I know why Ajax is also a bouncer despite his size. He's downright scary," he said.

"Ajax is all over the place. He has his good days and bad days, but he's super protective over his friends."

"I can tell."

There was some weird green punch, so I filled two red Solo cups with it. No doubt, it had five to six different alcohols in it and a splash of juice. I handed a cup to Stone, and we made our way back to my friends. Blaze and Cueball were there but sitting some distance away, talking to each other. At least no one was killing each other.

I rolled out my sleeping bag and sat on one end, expecting Stone to sit on the other side. Instead, he sat and pulled me over to sit between his legs. Damn, he really made a show of pushing past his fears and being open. I melted a little more for him each time he did something like this. Fuck, I'd also been dying for some sex. It didn't help that his dick was pointed directly at my ass now.

I hadn't been working, with my savings slowly dwindling, so I'd have to find a job soon, but for now, I was just trying to enjoy Stone and watch him open like some fucking flower after the last thaw of the year. Now, I wanted to take him and show him how good sex could be.

He rested his chin on my shoulder as he wrapped an arm around the front of me. Yes. This was where I belonged. Where *we* belonged. I fit perfectly inside him like this. Ignoring the weird looks from my friends, I took a big sip of the punch and coughed from the burn. "Holy shit, that's strong."

As predicted, Pippin lit a blunt and passed it first to Nacho. I rolled my eyes at Pippin for not noticing the stars in Nacho's eyes or how he grazed Pippin's fingers when he took it. Fuck, how blind could you be? Honestly, one of us would've smacked some sense into Pippin had Nacho not begged us to keep quiet and deal with it on his own time.

Nacho handed the weed off to Ajax, who took a drag as Blaze held out his hand. Ajax narrowed his eyes at him, debating whether to hand it off or punch him in the face.

"Pass it before it goes out," Pippin yelled, so Ajax finally handed it to Blaze.

Finally, it was my turn. I took the narrow blunt and put it to my lips before taking a long pull from it. I held the smoke in my lungs and brought it to Stone's mouth, but he shook his head, so I passed it on. Shit, I needed to remember he preferred to be sober.

By now, I was feeling good with a weed high and an alcohol buzz. I felt totally fucking chill, resting my head back onto Stone's shoulder as my friends chit-chatted and laughed. Usually, I argued or laughed along with them, but I liked just sitting here quietly, feeling Stone pressed against me, feeling toasty next to him despite the cool air. I smiled with my eyes closed as his fingers slipped underneath my sweatshirt and played with my skin, sending chills through my body. He was talking to Alpha about his health or something, and his deep voice vibrated against my back. Yep, this felt like being home, and I fucking loved that he was so relaxed now, being out in the open with me, despite being doubtful earlier tonight. I could get used to this.

No matter how relaxed I was, I wanted to skate more. I pulled away from Stone, and his hand slipped out of my sweatshirt before I turned and quickly kissed him to test the waters. He didn't freak out. So far, so good.

"I'm gonna skate."

I grabbed my board and lit a smoke. Then Stone followed me with his board.

The ramps were busy, so we both practiced our flat-ground tricks until space was available. I'd been practicing my triple heel flip, which had taken me forever to learn. I wasn't the best at skating, but I wasn't the worst. All that mattered was to just fucking have fun. With a cig in my mouth, I skated as I pressed the back of my board with my foot, lifting the front truck from the ground, then popped it to spin three times as I jumped, but every time I landed, I slipped from the board, sometimes falling on my ass. Dammit. I thought I had this down.

Stone grabbed my board before I made another attempt and pointed at the side of it. "Kick the side of your board with your heel right here as you lift to flip faster."

I did as he said, and sure enough, I landed almost smoothly on my board.

Finally, there was a break in one of the ramps, so Stone and I took one and worked on our moves. We both used the ramp, but in opposite directions, and I loved seeing him meet me halfway with a slight smile, popping that dimple and lifting those gorgeous cheekbones.

I picked up speed coming down, crouched as I approached the quarter pipe, then kicked off the lip, catching air before twisting my body and coming down to do it again on the other side, seeing how high I could get.

After a while, I took a break. I grabbed another drink and a smoke, sitting back down with my friends. Stone continued to skate, but my ass was sore from falling so much doing my flat-ground tricks.

I slapped hands with Alpha and Pippin as I sat on my sleeping bag. And since Stone wasn't here, I expected the inevitable questions, but there were none, and what made my family fucking awesome. Once you were in, you were family, and Stone became a part of our family. I wasn't sure about his roommates, but judging by the death glares aimed at Blaze from Ajax, I thought not.

Alpha sat beside me and slapped a hand on my back as I tapped a beat on the concrete with my sticks. It was something I'd been working on. Fuck, I wish I could actually write music. Maybe one day.

"That sounds awesome. Good beat."

"Thanks."

"How's saving for drums?"

I shrugged. There was no point in answering. If I finally had drums, everyone would know about it.

"You like Stone, okay?" he asked.

"I do. Like a lot. He's so stoic and shit, but he's really opening up."

Alpha looked behind him, assuming he was looking over at Stone. "He's watching you. Always watching you. You're good for him, I can tell."

"I guess. He's good for me, too. At first, I couldn't tell how he'd be, but yeah, it's been cool. I've never had a relationship before, if that's what this is."

"You should talk about it with him."

"Maybe. I've been just kinda letting Stone go at his own pace."

Alpha gripped my shoulder and shook me a little. "This is about you, too."

"I know."

He looked up and moved away from me as Stone sat down behind me again and pulled me into a protective embrace that was a little too tight, like showing my friends he owned me or some shit. I loved it.

It was about three in the morning, and we crashed for the night. Well, for the rest of the morning until whenever we woke up. At least tomorrow was Saturday, so we didn't have to go to any day jobs. Well, I didn't have a day job, but Stone did.

We were both tucked inside my unzipped sleeping bag, with his threadbare blanket over us. He was wrapped around me, spooning me with his warm body, and an arm slung over me as I used his other arm as a pillow. My lower back ached a little from my disease, but I was also comfortable with him around me, and it was surprisingly warm.

Our friends were all passed out, but Stone and I lay there awake while I enjoyed his lazy kisses on my neck, listening to the sounds of others around us fucking in their sleeping bags. It was turning me the hell on, making my dick grow hard.

I squirmed and wiggled around to face him, which wasn't easy in our little confined space. "Hey, you tired?"

"A little."

"How little is little? Like 'I'm going to pass out any minute,' little? Or 'I think I can stay awake for the right price' little?"

"Hmm, what are you offering?"

I fumbled to find his hand under the sleeping bag. When I grabbed it, I placed it on my growing bulge. "Isn't that enough?"

The place was dark, so I couldn't see if he was smiling or looking at me like I was an idiot. When it came to Stone, who knew?

"It's a pretty enticing cock," he said.

"Good. Let's go out to the building next door and have a little fun."

"Won't someone... catch us?" His voice sounded nervous, but I really wanted this. I needed him, and I was tired of fantasizing about him in my fucking bathroom I shared with my sister and mother.

"Nah, most people are asleep or fucking themselves, and there may be some about, but it'll be dark. No one will see us or care. Besides, putting on a show for others is kinda hot."

He groaned, but didn't complain, as I climbed out of the bag and stood, wincing at my tweaking back. I really hoped I wasn't about to have a flare-up soon. I reached for him, and he grabbed my hand so I could help him stand. We put on our jackets and headed outside to a blast of cold air.

"Are you sure about this? We're going to freeze our nuts off," he groused.

"Where's your sense of adventure, Rolling Stone? Besides, once we're into it, we'll be all nice and toasty."

"If you say so."

CHAPTER 22
Stone

TONIGHT HAD GONE BETTER than expected. Sure, I was nervous, but being around Stix helped, who was always so cool, casual, and laid back. It helped that I wanted him. Like, *really* wanted him. As in, if we didn't work out, I didn't know what I'd do. He was it for me. Who knew this would happen before we sorted out all our shit? *My* shit. I'd been so deep in the closet that I didn't even know I was in a closet. Now, I was ready to experiment with him. I wanted to earlier, but I'd been injured, and recovery took too fucking long. But that wasn't the only reason I held back, confused about how to approach sex with Stix. I'd never been that direct in asking for what I wanted sexually, which included women.

Sex had just never been at the forefront of my mind, and that included rubbing one off. Now, it was all I could think about, which said a lot about Stix and how I felt about him. And whenever Stix and I weren't together jacking each other off, I did it alone in my room or the shower. He'd fucking awakened something in me that had been dormant since that boy so long ago.

He took my hand and led us to the next building over. It was boarded up, but you could tell people had been inside since the boards simply leaned against the windows. We removed them, and climbed inside, then put them back into place. The large space was dark as fuck, except for one streetlight shining in through the cracks of the slightly boarded-up windows. Stix pulled out a small pocket flashlight I didn't know he had, grabbed my hand, and led us to an even darker corner.

Once he set it on the ground, lighting around our feet in an eerie glow, he lunged at me and slammed my back against the wall.

"Oof..." He smothered my complaint with a kiss, thrusting his tongue in my mouth. I melted under him, still asking myself every fucking day why I'd been such a dumbshit in not claiming him sooner. And I had no idea how he easily pushed through all my fears. I was just fucking comfortable around him once I let it all go. His hands around my neck slid up into my hair as he deepened our kiss, while my hands slipped under his jacket and fisted the back of his stupid Halloween sweatshirt.

He used his entire body to kiss me, sucking on my lips and tongue and thrusting into me with his groin. I felt his stiff cock hit me, and my mind went off the deep end, imagining him facing forward against the wall and me fucking the hell out of him as his cries echoed off the walls. His hands moved down while his fingers clawed at me under my jacket as if trying to get into my skin.

"I've been dying to have you..." he panted when we came up for air. His lips hovered over mine, refusing to completely separate.

"I... want you, too."

"How do you want me?"

My face burned, not used to dirty talk, or even telling people exactly what I wanted sexually. Thank fuck, it was dark in here. "Ugh, you're going to make me say it?"

He snorted a laugh, and I loved how he never got offended. "No, but I can tell you what I want you to do to me... if you prefer."

I nodded. "Yes."

"I want to taste you, Rolling Stone. I want to suck you down while you control my head, using me. Would you like that?"

Again, I nodded dumbly.

"I can't hear your nod."

"Yes."

Was this the prostitute talking, or Stix?

"Do you... normally talk like this to..." I couldn't bring myself to finish, not wanting to seem ungrateful to be here with him. But I couldn't help the doubts. They were as loud as my fears, though they were getting better.

He cupped my face. "No, Rolling Stone. This talk is only for you. I never said much during those times, wanting to get it over with."

I breathed easier, and the tension left me. "Sorry, I..."

"I get it. It's understandable. I prostituted myself, but that didn't mean I enjoyed it all that much."

"Sorry to ruin the moment. Can we get back to... you telling me how it's going to go? I like hearing it from you."

"You got it."

I hated being so insecure about this shit. Then again, I'd only been going through the movements of life, not really living. It was Stix who turned my life completely on its head, and I didn't hate it. For the first time in my sorry excuse for a life, I had hope.

He leaned in close and pressed his mouth close to my ear. "But I'm not going to suck you dry."

"You're not?"

"Nope. You're going to finish inside me if you want."

I caught my breath and swallowed. He wanted me to have sex? With me inside him? Tonight? I'd only had sex a handful of times, which had been a disaster for half of them, and unable to get it up sometimes.

"Again, only if you want. No pressure." His warm hand cupped my dick and balls through my black chino skate pants. "It's just... when I worked, it was only me doing it. No one was doing it to me... well, except for once. I've only been a bottom twice, and I loved it. I want that again with someone real. Someone I care about. Unless you... prefer to have me inside?"

"I don't know what I want or like yet."

"Yet? Does that mean you want to explore more?"

"I... yes. What do I need to do?"

"First, you need to lean back and enjoy the moment. But if you really want to try for sex, we need to prep me. It's been a while since I've taken a dick, and you're not exactly small."

While I wasn't very confident in the sex department, I liked that Stix was, and he didn't care that I currently had so little to offer.

He pushed me until I was flushed against the wall and dropped to his knees on the hard concrete. Long fingers wrestled with my belt buckle before opening it and unbuttoning my pants. He slowly slid down the zipper, which was agonizing because I was desperate for his mouth, something we hadn't done, either. His close proximity made me hard as a rock, and he hadn't even done anything yet. Fuck, no one ever got me as hard as Stix. He could just look at my dick, and I'd practically come.

My pants were wrapped around my ankles before he gripped the elastic waistband of my boxer briefs, pulling them down with my pants. My legs and cock were hit with frigid air, but Stix pressed his face between my groin and dick while gripping my length. He took a deep breath of me. "Mmm, you smell so good. Like musk, arousal, and whatever body wash you use."

He pulled out his wallet and grabbed a condom. "I'm going to wrap you, but you and I are going to get tested, so we can do away with condoms because I want to taste you and feel you inside... bare. I get tested regularly because of what I did for a living, though I was always careful. We're going to go together."

"Okay."

Once he rolled on the condom much too slowly, he gripped my length and stroked me. On instinct, my hands threaded through his coarse hair. It wasn't silky since he cut it and bleached it himself, but he still looked hot. My fingers tightened on the thick strands, and I boldly tugged his head toward where I needed his mouth.

He looked up at me. "I like this side of you, Rolling Stone. Take control. Use me."

I liked it, too. All my life, I've felt out of control with no power. Stix gave it all back to me in mere minutes. I looked down at him, shoved aside his hand, and gripped my cock. "Open," I ordered, finding a part of me I finally liked.

"Fuck, yes."

His hands rested on his lap as I guided my dick in his mouth. God, this was the boldest I'd ever been, and I liked it, a *lot*, making me feel like

I had a say over my life for the first time, and Stix was willing to sit back and enjoy the ride. I think he also liked giving up some of the control. Or maybe he was just happy to relinquish some to me.

I eased it in and shuttered my eyes at his warm mouth. I wish I didn't have to wear a condom to feel his hot, wet mouth wrapped around me, but I understood the need to be safe.

Stix tightened his mouth and shoved closer to the root as he swallowed me down. Fuck me. He barely gagged, despite my length. The sounds of his breathing filled the quiet and musty air, and I was pretty sure I whimpered a couple of times.

He popped off me, and I grunted a complaint. "Fuck my mouth, Stone. I can take it."

"Jesus..."

I swallowed, ready to blow, but not yet. I needed more. My thrusts were shallow, testing the waters, not wanting to choke him, despite his request, but I guess it wasn't enough for him because Stix gripped my ass with his hands and pulled me forward, forcing me deeper and faster in his mouth.

His noises were sloppy and full of slurps, grunts, and gasps, turning me the hell on. There were a couple of gags, and his throat constricted around me, and I almost blew right then.

"Oh, god... You have an amazing mouth." And he did. He was a fucking pro.

My dick swelled, and I fucking leaked all inside the condom as my nuts pulled up tight. Stix must have sensed I was about to come, so he popped off again. "Not yet, Rolling Stone."

"No!" My yell bounced off the walls of the empty building as my potential orgasm vanished, making him chuckle.

"Trust me, it'll be worth it."

Stix stood and pulled out a small packet of what I assumed to be lube. After dropping his pants and underwear, he opened it and poured some into his hand.

"We need to open me up enough to take you."

I nodded a little too eagerly as my breath hitched. "Show me."

He dropped back down to his knees and turned around so that his ass was facing me, glowing brightly from the flashlight on the floor. My breath caught again at seeing him so eager to be vulnerable like this. I wasn't sure I could do that, but it was sexy to watch.

"Grab the flashlight and point it at my ass. Watch how I open myself. Next time, you'll know exactly what to do and can do it yourself. It's even hotter for me when you do it. I'd love to feel your fingers inside me."

I grabbed the light off the ground and aimed it at him. His hole moved like a hungry mouth, and it was pretty pink. I wasn't sure how I'd feel about this, but I certainly didn't expect it to be even harder than I already was. If I had doubts about what turned me on or what I wanted, they fled with the sight of Stix with his bare ass in the air, begging to be fucked.

I squatted down closer, with one hand shining a light on his hole and the other hand stroking my cock. Soon, long, glistening fingers slipped through between his legs, and one finger inserted right into his hole. It just gobbled it up, and I shuddered, imagining it was my dick.

The building was filthy as Stix made raunchy noises along with the 'squelch' of wet fingers plunging in and out of him. I could see as his hole opened more and more, allowing for more fingers. I panted, watching him, needing to touch him or do something other than watch.

My hand let go of my dick and slid along the curve of his smooth, bubbly ass.

"Fuck, yes... touch me," he mumbled.

That spurred me to explore more. My hand glided down closer to his hole over his greasy skin from the lube as my thumb trailed along the crease of his spread cheeks, inching closer to where I really wanted to be. As his fingers thrust in and out, I swirl my thumb around his tight pucker. My heart and breathing stopped as my cock leaked inside the condom I still wore. Fuck, this was the hottest thing I'd ever seen or done. Nothing I'd ever been through compared, and I hadn't even fucked him yet.

His moan was guttural, going straight to my nuts. Fuck, I needed him. Like now.

"Please tell me you're ready."

"I don't know... I like you touching me like this. Who knew you'd be so dirty." His tone was teasing, but his panting gave away his arousal. "Do you want me?"

"Yes," I breathed. "So much."

"Then have me."

He stood, and my recent fantasies came true as he faced the wall and planted his hands against it while bending slightly to give me access. "Take me, baby. Show me how much you want this. Own me because, god, I want you so much and to feel you into the next day whenever I sit down."

Chills traveled along my skin with his words, even though I was no longer cold. He was right. My body filled with a fire I'd never felt before. I fucking burned for him.

I grabbed my cock and aimed at his hole, which was now bigger than before, just waiting for me. After I nudged my tip in, I held it there to check to make sure he was okay, not wanting to hurt him. Instead, he simply pushed back on me as his ass swallowed my dick right to the root. My head fell back as his ass sucked me in and blanketed me in heat. All the nerves around my cock fired off, and I knew right then I wouldn't last long. I also knew I'd want this again and again.

"Fuck me, baby. Just go. Hard and fast... make me feel it... feel you."

I didn't know when I dropped the flashlight as I grabbed his hips, pulled out, and slammed back home.

"Hell, yes. More."

Yes, I needed more.

More, more, more.

My hand moved toward the front of Stix's lean body and landed on his throat, which I gripped lightly and lifted him to stand as my cock sunk deeper into him. Bent at the knees, I thrust into him as much as possible. It was awkward, but I had to have him closer to me, to have him be a part of my body, sharing this moment as one. He swallowed under my tightening fingers as his hand reached for the back of my head and held on.

The world could be on fire right at this moment, and I would've been entirely oblivious to it.

My balls drew up tight, and my body tingled with electricity and pressure as I bit into his shoulder hard enough to leave a mark, but not enough to draw blood.

"Fuck yeah... Bite me. Claim me. Mark me."

The pressure was too much before I finally blew load after load into the condom, biting his shoulder again, and growling into his flesh. As I came down from my high, Stix's movements were rapid as he stroked himself to completion and finally spilled on the dirty concrete floor.

"Holy shit," he rasped. "So. Fucking. Hot."

When I slipped out of him, he turned to face me as I caught my breath. We both probably looked ridiculous with our pants wrapped around our ankles. My brain was in a fog as I got lost in the aftershocks of sex. But it wasn't only the diminishing arousal that had me gasping, but the loss of something I'd never had. Something that'd always been denied to me, thanks to my parents. But it was Stix who returned it to me like a gift.

He cupped my face with his non-lubed hand. "Look at me, Rolling Stone." I did, though I couldn't see him all that well. "You okay? I can't tell."

I nodded, grabbed his face in return, and smashed my mouth against his. His arms dropped behind him as I leaned into the kiss, deepening it and forcing him to arch his back. When I pulled away, I rested my forehead on his.

"More than okay, Nico."

His breath hitched. "I like you saying my name when you're high on sex. Say it again."

I smiled and gave him a small kiss. "Nico," I whispered.

CHAPTER 23
Stone

BECAUSE OF EVERYTHING STIX had done for me, from taking care of me when I got hurt to helping me see myself more clearly, I wanted to do something for him, but I had no idea what. Instead of beating myself up for it, I went to Cueball. He seemed to know what was better than me.

I found him lying on the couch, reading a book. Blaze was at work, thank fuck. I didn't need his teases and torments as I tried to wrap my mind around what to do. Life was confusing enough without getting Blaze involved.

"Hey, Cue," I said.

He put down his book and looked at me with those wide amber eyes that said absolutely nothing.

I shoved my hands in my jeans pockets and stared at my feet. "Can I ask you something?"

"Yep."

"So, like, I want to do something for Stix after all he's done for me, but I've never been with anyone before. I'm not sure what to do for him in return. I feel like I contribute to shit."

"Date."

"Huh?"

He sighed and lifted his book back up to his face. "Take him on a date."

Ugh. So fucking obvious now that he'd said it. "Thanks, man."

He returned to reading as I headed back to my room to plan.

Me: Can you take off work Saturday night?

Stix replied right away. I smiled, imagining him eagerly waiting for my text, which was completely juvenile, but I liked the idea.

Stix: Sure. I'll talk to Alpha. What's up?

Me: I want to take you out on a date.

Stix: OMG Sounds fun!

Me: Meet me over here at 2 on Saturday.

Stix: Please tell me we'll see each other before then. That's like four days away.

I rolled my eyes but laughed.

Me: Of course.

We hadn't had sex again since that night, just him giving me blow jobs and me giving him hand jobs because I kept wimping out. This time, my plan wasn't just to have a date, but to push my boundaries when it came to sex. We'd already gotten tested together and were clean as of yesterday, so no more condoms. Now, I wanted to try my hand at giving him a blow job and stop being a fucking pussy about it. I just hoped I didn't suck too badly at it, which was the main thing holding me back. But fuck, I really wanted to please him. It was time to stop being a fucking baby.

My heart hammered when Stix knocked on the door five minutes before two in the afternoon. It wasn't like something special, and I couldn't afford much, but still, I hoped he'd have a good time.

He came in wearing his army jacket, and underneath, he wore another weird T-shirt that said 'My Pen is Bigger than Yours' with a large print of a pen. His hair was freshly bleached and not a dark root to be seen.

He stepped up to me and planted a fat kiss on my lips. "Does this date mean you *like*, like me?"

I shook my head and smiled shyly. "It does."

Twenty minutes later, we were holding hands as we walked through the Baltimore National Aquarium at Harborplace, exploring through the reef exhibits. I had lived here for several years and never once came here. It didn't seem interesting to do it alone.

Stix had the excitement and energy of a toddler, as if I did something more than take him to see fucking fish, making me smile like an idiot. Fine, it was a pretty nice aquarium, not that I'd ever been to any before.

He dragged me to a section where you could actually touch some of the sea creatures. There were horseshoe crabs, baby rays, conches, and more.

"Shit, I've never even been here before. It's like if you live in a city, it's against the rules to visit all the touristy places, but now that I'm here, I'm bummed I haven't been. I'm so going to have to take Nova here."

"We can both take her."

He beamed at me with such a massive smile, lighting up his face as always, that made my heart beat a little faster. I liked doing that and being the cause of his happiness. Such a big change from giving him so much grief for so fucking long. This was way fucking better.

Our last stop at the aquarium was to check out the old World War II submarine, which was pretty cool, and we took a few selfies together inside.

By the time we wrapped it up, we headed to a bar and grill restaurant at Harborplace within walking distance to have some dinner and drinks. This date wasn't exactly cheap, not when you factored in how little I made, and while we couldn't do something like this all the time, it was nice to do something for Stix, and he looked like he had a great time. It made it all worth it.

The place was crowded, but we managed to squeeze in at the bar to eat and drink.

Apparently, Stix had been here before, as he shook hands and chatted with the bartender. The jealousy flared, making my skin hot and my heart beat too hard. I hated having these negative feelings. Was the bartender someone he'd sucked off? God, did I want to know? Stix did what he had to, so I didn't blame him or judge him, but fuck, I hated that he'd been with other men. It was irrational, but I was still new to this whole dating thing.

I must have been making a pissed-off face or something because he grabbed my hand. "I know what you're thinking, and you're right. But I don't do that anymore. Okay? It's just you and me now."

I nodded. "Yeah... sorry. I just get... jealous."

"It's cool, Rolling Stone. It's kind of hot, too. I've never been wanted by someone so much they got jealous." He winked at me, making my eyes roll, which was a common theme between us since the beginning.

He picked up the menu and frowned. "Shit, this place is kind of expensive."

"Get what you want. Don't worry about the cost."

"Stone, you don't have to spend so much on me."

"I know, but I want to. You don't fucking understand. You've done so much for me, and you don't even realize it. This date is nothing in comparison."

His face softened with one of his beautiful smiles. "Can I kiss you? Here?"

I swallowed and nodded, needing to get used to PDA with a man. Shit, not just a man, but anyone.

Stix leaned in, staring right at my lips with those dark, soulful eyes of his. Then he looked up to meet my eyes as he pressed his lips to mine. My eyes fluttered shut from the much too-short kiss. I nearly chased his lips when he pulled away. And as soon as we did, the bartender took our order as we sipped our beers.

"So, what do you dream about, Rolling Stone?"

Did nightmares count? I shrugged. "Nothing."

"No hopes? No dreams?"

Nothing. Not until him. Being with him was the first time I'd actually been living and not only surviving. Was I pathetic to tell him that? Did that make me look like a loser?

"Nothing," I said again, unable to come up with anything else.

He looked sad and pensive. I didn't want him that way. It was simply the truth, not meant for pity. "Nico... it's just my life. It's the way it is. I've come to accept that I don't have many opportunities for me beyond what I already have. My parents beat any sort of motivation out of me, and my grades sucked throughout school, barely graduating, so any chance of college was impossible. What are your dreams?" I asked, trying to turn the tables back to him. He was more interesting anyway.

He sighed and took another sip of his beer. "We need to get you some dreams, man. Anyway, god, I have so many. Too many. And all so fucking out of reach. First, I want to get out of that apartment and buy a little house. There are some super cheap townhomes in Baltimore, but they need some TLC. There's one in particular I've had my eye on that's been for sale for a while, and I keep thinking the place is simply waiting for me to snatch it up. I'd been saving for it, but... well, I need to find another job. And before you get all mopey and guilty, this is my choice to leave what I'd been doing."

The bartender returned and set our plates in front of us on the bar. I ordered an ahi sandwich, while Stix ordered crab cakes. I took a bite of my sandwich as he finished his story with his mouth full.

"Then there's my disease—"

My heart stopped. I had no idea he had health issues. Fuck, I hoped it wasn't something too serious. "Wait... what?"

He shrugged. "Just something I was born with. It's an arthritic autoimmune thing. Ankylosing Spondylitis. It's fine for the most part, unless I'm flaring up, which can be quite incapacitating. I need some injections for that to keep the flare-ups under control, but... it's fucking expensive if you don't have health insurance, which we don't. Like fifteen thousand a year expensive."

"Fuck... are you going to be okay, or..."

"I'm fine for the most part. The flare-ups aren't frequent, but they cause tons of damage to my joints and bones. Anyway, I don't want to talk about it. Things could be worse, trust me."

"If you say so."

I didn't want to think about my Stix in pain like that. This world was fucked up to hurt someone like that and not give him the means to treat it. Our country had the worst healthcare for those who couldn't afford it. Only the wealthy and those with steady jobs had the best healthcare. Some jobs force you to be part-time, so they don't have to pay for benefits.

"Then there's a drum set. I could probably buy one now, having some money saved, but..." he shrugged. "No place to play them. Not that I'll ever be in a band, anyway. It's a nice dream, but not really practical or reachable."

"Why?"

"Come on. I have no training whatsoever, and no one I know who's in a band is looking for a drummer. It's fine. It could be worse. I have a loving mother, a great sister, and we're happy. That's the most important."

I couldn't argue with him there. I'd always been jealous of his relationship with his mother. Something I'd always wanted with my parents, but they were too addicted to drugs and drinking to fucking care.

We finished our meals, talking about our friends and shit. I ordered us another beer and headed to the restroom to piss and wash my hands.

When I came out of the bathroom and headed to the bar, I froze, seeing an older man sitting next to Stix. He was fucking gorgeous, but he had to be in his forties. He wore an expensive, nice suit, and not a strand of black hair was out of place. I moved in closer to hear what he was saying to Stix without Stix knowing I was there. What was this man's game? The jealousy ripped through me, but I didn't want to jump the gun and be a nutjob if it was just something innocent.

"It's nice to see you again. I tried to reach you, but you never responded. Now here you are, like fate. As you can see, I'm back in town."

What the ever-loving fuck?

Shit, was this fancy dude a client? As much as I wanted to end their conversation right then and there, as the rage surged, wanting to beat this man for soliciting my boyfriend, something stopped me, especially when I heard the dollar amount.

"I'm not—" Stix started to say before the man interrupted him.

"I just need you for a month while I'm here in town for work, and I can pay you twenty thousand dollars for your time, but you need to be at my beck and call, night and day. I enjoyed our evening together last time and had hoped to meet with you again. You're exactly what I'm looking for. I'll also cover the rest of your expenses. Perhaps a new suit."

I couldn't see Stix's face, but I knew he was counting every dollar that would go toward his dreams.

My throat felt thick and dry as my hands fisted at my sides. It was my fault he'd given up so much money. This deal would be so good for him. He could put down money toward that house or get his meds for a fucking year. My eyes watered because I'd have to give up Stix if he wanted to pursue his dreams. His health was more important than my heart. While I understood I could still date him as he did this, I didn't want to. Knowing he'd be with another man... no. There was no way. What made it all worse was that I'd completely fallen for him. It was fast, hard, and heavy, but he was it for me. I was obsessed. I always had been.

The gentleman slid a card Stix's way over the bar. "Think about it. That's my direct number. Call me, but don't wait too long. This offer is for a limited time." He stood and returned to wherever he came from, but I only had eyes on Stix as he lifted the card and read it.

With a deep fucking breath, I walked back to him. "You should do it."

"What? Did you hear all that? Oh, no. I'm—"

"Do it. You can get your meds or that house. I'm... in the way. It's okay, Stix. Do it."

I pulled out a hundred dollars from my wallet and dropped it on the counter to cover the meal and drinks, then I turned and walked out, trying not to let the tears spill, unable to face him or else I would fucking break.

Not in public. Break when you get home.

CHAPTER 24
Stix

Oh, HE FUCKING DID not. Was he kidding me right now? He didn't even give me a chance to explain that I wasn't interested in that man's offer. Sure, it was a fucking ton of money, but I wasn't some selfish prick that I'd give up something good and special for a fuck and a buck.

"Eric," I yelled. "Money's on the counter... I'm assuming you're to keep the rest. I gotta run."

The bartender waved me off as I grabbed my board and ran after Stone. That bastard was not about to get all noble on me now with some self-sacrificing bullshit. No way.

I caught up with him on the street corner as he waited to cross traffic. "Hey!" I yelled none too kindly because I was fucking pissed. Sure, I understood about jealousy and irritation with what had happened, but this whole sacrificial shit was enough to make me want to punch him. I wanted Stone, not some rich douchebag that wouldn't last. And Stone deserved that, too, but first, he was going to get ripped a new asshole.

The crosswalk sign said to walk, but I reached him just in time to grab his arm. "Stop right now! Don't you dare walk off."

When he turned to face me, he looked down at his feet, but not before I saw the few tears on his face. All my anger washed away into guilt and understanding. He definitely didn't want to let me go.

Stone wiped his nose with the back of his hand and looked down the street. Anywhere but at my face. "I'm sorry. I... couldn't stay there. You should call him. It's so much money, Stix. It's... okay. I'm not mad... just..."

I angled my face and body to get him to look at me. "Dammit, Rolling Stone, I'm not taking it. You didn't give me a chance to tell you that."

His brows slammed down on his eyes and clenched his jaw. "Then, you're a fool. Twenty thousand dollars... Jesus. Are you nuts? Fucking take the money. You deserve it. Your family deserves it. Get your fucking house and meds. Buy yourself that drum set you've always wanted."

I pinched his chin between my fingers none too gently. "Shut. The. Fuck. Up. I'm not doing it."

"You're being an idiot! Take the fucking money."

"No! What the hell do you take me for?"

"I... What do you mean?"

I waved my hands in the air as I paced around him. "What the fuck do you think I mean? Do you really believe I would just toss you aside for some rich asshole? Yeah, it's a fuck ton of money, and if you weren't here in my life right now, I'd take it. But I won't because I fucking care about you. Deeply. Like... by a fucking lot. God, you're an idiot sometimes."

That stopped him, and he opened and closed his mouth like a damn fish, trying to come up with words. "You... what?"

Then I deflated and rubbed the back of my neck. I nearly told him I loved him. Did I? Maybe. I'd never been in love before, but I understood enough that it was way too soon, and I didn't want to freak him out. "Look, I like you a lot. I want something serious here with you, and I can't do that if I'm fucking around with others for money or not."

As his mouth did that fish thing again, I raised my hand to stop him. "You don't have to tell me you care about me, too. I'm not expecting you to feel the same or to say it. I'm just... tossing it out there, so you realize how important you're becoming to me."

I stood in front of him, looked up into his watering eyes, and rested my forehead on his.

"I don't deserve it," he muttered.

"God, you're so fucking stupid sometimes. Yeah, you do. More than anyone I know. You deserve someone to care about you and love you." Okay, maybe a little hint about how I was really feeling. And it wasn't a lie. He did deserve it. And seeing how he was with my little sister, Stone should never be afraid of turning into his parents. He's so sweet and caring—more than he realized.

"Why?" Fuck, he sounded so small and insecure. I hated it because it wasn't his fault. His fucking parents did this shit to him.

I pecked his lips. "Because once you get out of your head, you're sweet, kind, tender, thoughtful, and you have a gorgeous smile with an adorable dimple and cute crooked bottom teeth. In those rare moments when you do smile, I know you're feeling good. That everything is currently right in your world. It makes my heart beat a little faster seeing it."

"But I was such a dick to you."

"Yeah, you were, and I taunted you, too. But I think we're both way past that now, right?"

Stone dropped his board and rested his hands on my hips. "Are you sure about this? God, it kills me to see you give up so much money, but... I think it'd kill me more to see you with someone else. Walking away from you was one of the hardest things I'd ever done."

"Good. It better be painful because you're stuck with me, so don't you ever turn your back on me like that again."

"Your breath stinks like beer and crab," he said with a smirk. I knew it was a deflection from his growing emotions, and I was okay with that. My breath probably did stink, anyway.

I snorted a laugh. "Asshole. Now give me a kiss."

After a quick kiss, since Stone was still working up to this PDA thing, we skated home, holding hands like a couple of dorks. And I was a dork in love. Honestly, I hadn't even been sure it was love I'd been feeling. While those feelings were strong, I'd never been in fucking love before, so I had nothing to compare it to. Then, when he walked away, willing to let me go, so I could get money to make my family's life better, yeah, it hit me hard right then, despite how pissed I'd been. I didn't want him to walk away from me. All that I could think about was finding a way to keep him.

We made it back to our apartment building, and Stone took my hand and led me inside his place, bypassing his friends playing a video game without a glance, and dragged my ass into his bedroom.

"Get naked, Nico."

Seriously, I loved it when he used my name in that sexy, growly way of his, and ordering me about was even hotter.

I removed my jacket, tossed it on the bed, and removed the rest of my clothes as he ordered. Once I was naked and hard already, I sat on his bed and waited for him to strip down, but he didn't. Instead, he dropped to his knees between my legs, staring right at my dick that bounced a couple of times in excitement.

He looked up at me with wide hazel eyes and rested his hands on my thighs. "I want to... try. Tell me what to do."

"First, you need to get naked."

He shook his head. "No, I want this all about you. I don't want my own dick distracting me."

I spread my legs more, and he scooted in closer and took a handful of my cock, slowly stroking it. Just him touching it had it beading pre-cum because Stone did that to me with so little effort.

"Just do what you like, Rolling Stone."

"Please tell me."

"Your mouth will be perfect. You really can't do it wrong. And you know where we're most sensitive, so focus on that."

"Okay..."

I leaned back on my hands, acting more casual than I felt because, holy shit, Stone wanted to suck me off. He stroked me, which he'd done a few times already, as he hovered his mouth over my dick. His breath ghosted the sensitive head, forcing more pre-cum to leak. Stone looked up at me again before his tongue peeked out and swiped over the leaking beads, giving him a little taste of me. It was like that one simple taste pushed him forward and swallowed me down.

"Oh, fuck..." I threw my head back as his mouth engulfed my length, filling me with moist heat. Shit, thank fuck we did away with condoms.

My first experience with getting sucked off by Stone while wearing a condom would've ruined the moment. Now, I got to feel how good his mouth and tongue were.

He started out tentatively, trying different sucks and licks, seeing how I reacted or didn't react. Shit, he could do this all day, and I'd be happy as a fucking clam because this was Stone we were talking about.

"Is this okay?"

I groaned when he stopped to talk. "So fucking okay."

His mouth wrapped around me again, fisting the base of my length as he took me as deep as he could.

"Grab my balls," I muttered.

Stone tugged on them gently as he gagged around my head. Holy fuck... He was sloppy, clumsy, and drooling everywhere, but shit, it was amazing. The best, really. Mainly because here was a man who stood so deep in the closet that he hated himself and me. Now he opened up, experimenting with his new self in his new skin and actually liking it. That was what made this moment so fantastic. Yeah, the sex was fun and good over Halloween, but this? This was him giving in to everything he wanted and being unafraid. The last step would be to let me fuck him, but if he never wanted that, I'd still die happy.

He swirled his tongue under the ridge of my head and over my crown, which drew my balls up tight. "Shit... just like that..."

What the hell was I doing? I wasn't even watching the show; I was so immersed in the sensation of Stone's mouth. I sat up and watched him singularly focused on pleasing me, and it was game over. Just seeing him with his mouth full of my dick did me in.

"I'm going to come... Stop."

He shook his head.

"Stone, you may not..." I couldn't finish because he just doubled his efforts.

It was like my nuts exploded, pulsing over and over in his mouth. My eyes rolled in my head, and my toes curled as he tried to drink me down. Some cum leaked out of his mouth, but he tried to get it all. My body shuddered as he sucked the last drops out of me until I had nothing left to give.

"Oh, my fuck..." I groaned.

He looked up at me with questioning hazel, blown nearly black. His mouth turned red, and his lips swelled, while his face glistened with spit and cum. Fucking stunning.

"That's the sexiest thing I've ever fucking seen," I said as I leaned down and grabbed his face to give him a sloppy kiss, tasting myself on his tongue.

We pulled away, and I still held his beautiful face in my hands with eyes so earnest. "Was that okay?" he asked.

"Dude, that was more than okay. It was the best head I've ever had."

He looked at me dubiously. Who could blame him? But it wasn't a lie. "Really?" The question was more sarcastic than doubtful.

"Yes, really. Now, it's your turn. Get naked, Rolling Stone."

Despite our earlier hiccup, this was the best date ever.

CHAPTER 25
Stix

FUCK.

I really wished there was a stronger word than that. It was the following Friday after my date with Stone, and I had to be at work tonight, which was now out of the question. Not for a while until I got to see the eye doctor, which wouldn't be open until Monday. Why did my flareups always fucking happen on the weekend? I suppose I could go to the emergency clinic, but that shit was crazy expensive.

Even with sunglasses on and under my covers to knock out all the light, the pain in my eyes ached so much I could barely see. Any sort of light sent stabbing pain right through my eyes and straight to my fucking brain. Iritis was the worst out of all my symptoms. And with eye inflammation, it was only a matter of time before my back would go out on me. It was inevitable. All this meant I'd be out of work for at least a week.

If I had some Advil or something, that would help with the eye inflammation, but we ran out of it, and I didn't want to go outside to get any, not unless I wanted my brain to explode. Well, it wouldn't literally explode, but it would fucking seem like it. Or I'd want it to, just to end the torture once and for all.

Shit, I hated being not only in pain but helpless. Mom was at work, and Nova was with Mrs. Gordon. So, that left just me all alone with no help. I could've called Stone, but he hadn't come home from work yet. Everyone was at work.

My phone, which I had lying on the bed next to me, rang. Blindly, I reached for it and tried to unlock it using my face, but it was useless without opening my eyes. The longer the phone rang, the more frantic I got, until I finally slid my glasses down and opened my eyes enough for the phone to scan my face. The brightness of the screen stabbed my eyes like ice picks.

"This better be good," I groused, slamming my eyes closed again as they watered.

"How are you feeling, sweetie?" Mom asked. "I'm on my break and just wanted to check on you. I could take off the rest of my shift and come home."

"No. We already talked about it this morning. I'll live. Just... you can't afford to take time off, at least not until I can find another second job."

"Shit, I hate this. I hate that I can't even provide my kids with the most basic health care. If your damn father would pay what he should..."

Yeah, and Dad had the money for it, but he clearly didn't care about us at all.

"First, I'm an adult, so child support wouldn't be covered, anyway. Second, this is beyond basic health care. I'll be fine, Mom. Monday, I'll go see a doctor and get some drops."

She sighed on the phone, and though I couldn't see her, I knew she'd try not to bite her nails, as she was prone to when stressed.

"Go back to work. I'm okay. Really."

"Okay, honey. I'll see you tonight. It'll be late, but Nova will be with Mrs. Gordon. Love you."

God, I hated that Nova had to stay late. It would also mean more money spent.

"Love you, too."

I hadn't realized I'd fallen asleep until I heard the knife-stabbing pounding on my door, which went straight to my brain. Maybe they'd go away if I stayed super quiet.

"Stix, open the fucking door!"

Stone?

What time was it? Was he off work already?

Even though it was dark outside, and all the lights were off, any sort of light that hit my eyes was like acid on my retinas, but I still tried to get out of bed. And that was when it happened. My left lower back tweaked on me as I bent the wrong way. It was only a matter of time, but I thought I'd have more of it. I should've known this would be a bad one since both of my eyes were affected this time. Usually, it was just one.

I eased out of bed as gently as possible, but the pain brought tears to my eyes.

"Stix! Open the goddamn door!"

"I... can't. Give me a minute," I yelled as loud as I could, hoping he'd hear me.

It took about five minutes to reach the door as I literally inched my way through the apartment. Each step sent a sharp pain through the left side of my body, and my eyes were nearly blind, so I had to feel my way. Stone must have heard me because he either stopped pounding or he left.

I finally opened the door to the bright light of the hallway and nearly passed out, even with sunglasses on.

"Jesus... Stix. What the hell? Your Mom called and said you needed some Advil, so I stopped by the store, but I had no idea you were this bad off."

He quickly shut the door behind him and pulled me into a hug. With just his presence alone, and after being in pain all day, I sobbed like a fucking baby, more so from his presence.

"I need to sit. I... can barely walk."

Stone led me to the couch, and after I got settled, he rushed off, only to return with some water and pills. "Your mom said for you to take four."

"It'll help my eyes a little, but my back is fucked until it's run its course."

"That's it. I'm taking you to the overnight clinic."

"No! I can't afford it and don't want to delve into my meager savings."

Stone sat on the couch with me and pulled me close to him as carefully as he could. "We're going. We'll worry about the money later, but this is bad. Tell me, how long does it take for you to recover without any sort of treatment?"

Too fucking long.

"Stix," he prodded when I didn't answer.

"My eyes take about two weeks to get better without drops, and my back… at least a few days to where I can walk semi-normally after living on a heating pad day and night, but I have to be careful the entire time until the flare-up has passed."

"We're going. Let's worry about money later. I'll even pay for half. I had no idea you were in so much pain, baby."

My aching eyes watered again when he called me baby. That was it. That was my breaking point. I would give him my soul if he called me that forever. "Okay." I told Stone where I kept the money, and he grabbed whatever we would need, and we left.

Because I couldn't walk far, by the time we made it down the stairs of the apartment building, we just walked to the bus stop a block away, which would take us a few stops down before we reached the emergency clinic.

Stone had to fill out all my paperwork, but at least the Advil was starting to kick in, so my eyes didn't feel like they were about to melt off my face.

Two hours later, we were back with some steroid drops for my eyes and painkillers, minus over five hundred dollars. Fuck, that took a bite out of my savings.

Stone didn't drop me off at my place, but instead, brought me to his. "You're staying with me this time, and I'll take care of you."

"I'm fine, Rolling Stone. The meds will have me back on my feet in no time."

"I don't care. I want to. You did it for me; now I want to do it for you."

I eased down onto his bed and patted it. He sat next to me, and I cupped his face to pull him into a kiss. "How'd you get to be so sweet? Even after everything you've been through. I told you, you were special."

"I've never been sweet. Ever. And I'm not trying to downplay it. It's just... you. You're the one who's special. I want to be... better. For you."

"No, you're amazing. Get the fuck used to it," I said before stifling a yawn. Shit, I was tired, and those pain meds made me all woozy.

"Lay down, and I'll go grab some of your things and tell your mom you're okay if she's home."

"Okie dokie."

I had no idea when I'd fallen asleep, but when I woke up, it was morning. My eyes still twinged with pain, but nothing compared to yesterday. Shit, it'd been a long time since I hurt that badly. I wasn't all better, not for a while until the flare-up was gone, but for now, the meds would tide me over.

After a good yawn, I tested out a stretch. I hurt, but it wasn't enough that I couldn't walk. Thank fuck. While I was grateful that Stone had insisted on helping me, losing so much money still stung. I wasn't sure I'd ever be able to recoup it.

I gently rolled over to see Stone staring at me, filled with concern. His eyes were red with dark circles under them, and he looked exhausted.

"Didn't you sleep?"

"I'm fine."

"That's not what I asked."

He rolled onto his back and sighed as he rubbed his face. "You just... tossed and turned all night. It's cool. You're hurting and trying to get comfortable."

"Shit, I'm sorry."

His angry eyes snapped at me. "I said it's fine. Stop fucking apologizing."

"Well, someone's grumpy in the mornings."

"Asshole," he muttered, but the flicker of a smile said he didn't mean it.

He rolled over, tucked an arm under his head, and ran a hand through my hair. "How're you feeling?"

"Better. Broke, but better. There's still some pain, but I don't feel like I'm being stabbed all over anymore."

"We'll figure out the money thing."

"No, *I* will figure out the money thing. As soon as I feel better, I need to find a day job. I could wait tables, since I do that already at Alpha's. Tips would be decent, but honestly, being on my feet day and night makes me want to curl up into a blanket taco and never come out."

Stone leaned in and kissed my lips, then each of my eyes. Shit, and he said he wasn't sweet.

"I should probably get back home soon," I said.

"Stay with me. For a while, anyway. I like you in my bed."

"Well, it is better than sharing a room with my sister, as much as I love her. But that pink just clashes with my punk black."

"Dork."

Before we could banter anymore, his phone rang. Stone reached to the floor where he had it charging and answered it. "Hello?"

He was quiet as he listened to whoever was on the phone.

"Okay. Thanks for all your work. I'm glad it's finally over."

He looked at me and nodded. "I understand, but a trial seems like a big deal for this. Can't you just... toss them in jail?"

He sighed and ran a hand through his cropped hair. "Okay. Yeah, I get it. I just... it's hard to take off time from work and shit." There was more silence before he said, "I'll ask them. Thank you."

Stone hung up and tossed his phone back on the carpeted floor. "That was the detective on my case. He said the trial should be simple, and they would all stand trial simultaneously, but they needed you and me to come in. He'll reach out to you to make arrangements. Shit, I've already taken off enough work, but the detective claimed work should cover it. *Should*, being the operative word. Doesn't mean they will."

"Good, let's nail those pricks to the wall and send them to jail. It probably won't be too long. Maybe a couple of years, but hopefully, that will change their tune the next time they decide on hurting someone."

"It may be more. They're charging them with a hate crime, so..."

"Even better. Whatever happens, I'll be there."

"Thanks, baby."

CHAPTER 26
Stone

ONCE STIX FINALLY RECOVERED and had been staying with me so much, we hardly separated after that. He usually spent the night at my place since I had a private bedroom, and we were frequently getting caught by people at Alpha's for making out wherever we could. Pretty much the only time we didn't spend every moment together was when I needed to work at the fish market. Stix would use that time to search for a job. My job wasn't hiring at the moment, but I'd asked anyway.

It was Thursday, and tonight, Stix's mom invited me over for dinner. Afterward, I planned to have Stix stay the night again, but for different reasons than usual. Fuck, my hands grew clammy at the thought of it.

It wasn't only from nervousness but excitement. Maybe a little lingering fear. I wondered if that would ever go away.

But even more exciting and fucking scary was me falling so damn hard for him. We'd barely been together as boyfriends. Boyfriends sounded too adolescent. Partners? We've been dating for around a month and a half. While it may be weirdly fast, looking back on things, I'd fallen for him a long time ago. Once I got past barriers, walls, confusion, and other protective challenges, things started to clear, like after a good rain, and I wanted him. Stix was right. We shared a bond, as weird as it was, but it worked for us.

Now, I finally got the balls to really tell him how I felt. Why was it so scary after being so comfortable around him now? No, it wasn't about comfort around him. It was being comfortable in my own skin. Stix just made it easier for me.

I rubbed a hand through my fresh haircut, which the barber sheared extra short, just the way I liked it, while I looked in the mirror to make sure I was presentable, and my clothes didn't have too many wrinkles. I didn't want to appear like a complete loser when Grace, Stix's mom, invited me over.

When I knocked on their door a few minutes later, Nova answered it.

"Stone!" she yelled and raised her arms.

I lifted her in the air to her giggles and carried her inside. "What's up, dollface? How was school?"

"Good. We drew pictures today."

"Don't you draw pictures every day? Isn't that like a kindergarten thing?"

She giggled again. "Yes, silly. But this time, I drew you. Wanna see?"

"Sure."

I set her down, and after giving a quick wave to Stix and Grace, Nova tugged me to her room by my hand. Sitting on the dresser sat a drawing in crayon that she handed to me.

"See, that's Mommy, Nicky, me, and you. This is our building, and I drew a tree because we don't have trees and thought it was pretty. And I drew a rainbow, too!"

I took the drawing and scanned it. She gave us all rectangles for bodies, arms, and legs, but you could tell who was who. That Nova put me in the picture as part of their family rattled me to my core. I'd never felt like I had a home or family, even though I used to have those things. My life had been so horrible that I was often completely lost and alone. Now, this little family gave me hope that there was more to this pathetic life than I'd first believed.

I swallowed the lump in my throat and smiled at her. "What a stunning picture, Nova."

She jumped and clapped. "Yay! You can have it. It's for you."

"Oh, I don't want to take your gorgeous art."

"You have to. I made it for you."

Fuck, this kid was going to kill me with sweetness. "Thank you, dollface."

"You're welcome!" And just like that, she ran back into the kitchen, completely oblivious to my swelling heart and an overwhelming sense of belonging, making it hard to breathe for a moment, so I sat and looked at the picture again until I could collect myself.

Dinner was simple as always, but Grace cooked pretty well. Tonight was some cheesy Tex-Mex chicken casserole thing, which tasted better than anything I could've made.

"You're coming over for Thanksgiving, right?" she asked.

"Thanksgiving?"

I looked at Stix, wondering why he hadn't asked. He shrugged and smirked, which was his standard response to pretty much any question. "She wanted to be the one who asked."

Shit, when was the last time I celebrated Thanksgiving, or Christmas for that matter? My roommates and I would just watch football on TV, eat whatever crap we had in the kitchen, and then head out for drinks. On Christmas day, we'd exchange some stupid cheap-ass gift, but that was it. No decorating or anything. None of us had much of a home life growing up.

"Don't you dare tell me no, Damien Sloan," Grace said at my lack of an answer.

I huffed a laugh. She and Stix were so much alike.

"Yes, ma'am. I'd love to."

"It's not much, but the diner makes Thanksgiving meals for its employees to take home. It's enough to feed us all, and it's free."

"Sounds great. Thank you."

After dinner, Stix and I were in my room, eating each other's faces and touching our skin everywhere. And I loved touching him. Sometimes, it was even better than sex. I enjoyed the intimacy, which showed more love than sex could sometimes. It was healing.

His lean body was hard, but his skin was so smooth and soft. I still couldn't wrap my head around that he was mine, and that I was okay with it. His simple nearness always shut those negative voices down. Voices that sounded too much like my parents.

"Stix," I panted as we came up for air. "I... I'm falling for you." Shit, I couldn't say it. I wanted to, so much, but uttering words I'd only said once before was more complicated than expected, probably because of what had happened after I uttered those words the last time. Hopefully, he knew what I meant without me having to say them.

Stix smiled with swollen lips glistening from our kissing and rested a hand on my cheek. "Good, then we're on the same page."

"I'm ready for... I want you inside me. Tonight."

His dark eyes grew wide as he sat up in bed. "Wait, what?"

"Ugh, don't make me repeat that."

"Are you sure? I don't mind being your bottom." He winked at me, making me roll my eyes.

"I know you don't, but... if I want to be with you, I want to... experience all of it."

He raised a fist in the air. "Well, then... fuck yeah!"

I shook my head and snorted a laugh. It was so like Stix to fist pump this. "You're such a nerd."

"But a cool and adorable nerd, right?"

"You'll get no argument from me."

We grew silent as my hands grew clammy. "Does it... hurt?"

"Hmm, it can if you do it wrong. And there will be some burning and pressure. But, oh, when you hit that hot button deep inside? Chef's kiss. It's the best."

I reached into my banged-up nightstand and dug around in there, pulling out some lube I used for jacking off way too many times since Stix had come into my life. In fact, I shook it and looked inside to make sure I had enough, then handed it over to Stix.

"Get naked and on your stomach in bed, baby," he said while tossing the bottle onto the bed and stripping down himself.

Once we had our clothes removed, I rolled onto my stomach. My clammy hands gripped the sheets as my heart rate kicked up to a thousand beats. This was so fucking vulnerable for me, and I wasn't sure I liked it at all, but my need to do this and overcome my fear was greater.

"You okay, Rolling Stone? You're stiffer than normal, and I'm not talking about your gorgeous dick."

I huffed a laugh into the blanket. So weird that before, his smart mouth would've had me in a near rage. Now, it put me at ease. "Yeah."

He smacked my ass, but not hard enough to sting. "Booty up. We have to get you prepped."

God, was I ready for this? I needed to be. I lifted my ass in the air and squeezed my eyes shut as my face turned into flames.

Instead of shoving fingers inside me as he had done for himself over Halloween, he slid his hands gently over my ass. "Fuck, Rolling Stone. Seriously, no one has a right to have such a perfect ass. Shit, it's so smooth and bubbly."

I said nothing as he explored my skin that hadn't been touched by anyone before. Well, he did sort of touch it once on that strange night I'd jacked off in front of him, but this was completely different. Sensual.

Suddenly, his finger trailed along my crease before landing on my pucker, as if testing the waters to see my reaction. But I held still for him as my face burned even hotter. I shouldn't have been embarrassed. Stix just fingered the hell out of himself right in front of me before I fucked him. He didn't give a shit. But he was a lot more sexual than I was—a *lot* more.

Instead of the expected finger going inside me, something hot and wet glided across my hole. My rapidly beating heart suddenly stopped when Stix did it again. Fuck, why did that feel so good?

"Is this okay?" he asked.

"Uh, huh. What... is that your tongue?"

"Oh, yeah. You're gonna love this, and it helps open you up."

His long fingers spread me open more as his hot breath ghosted over my sensitive nerves, and then he swiped over my hole again with his tongue. Soon he was licking, probing, and nipping. My ass seemed to like it, shoving back for more. Groans, moans, and some weird high-pitched sound bounced off my bedroom walls until I realized those sounds came from me.

Before I begged for even more, because I was seriously about to, he pulled his mouth away. Fuck, that was pretty hot, and I didn't expect to be as turned on by rimming as I did. My dick leaking all over my sheets proved that.

The sound of the lube bottle opening had me tense, but I forced myself to fucking chill. This was what I wanted.

"You ready for this, baby?"

"Yeah."

A wet, oily finger nudged its way in or tried to, but my hole was saying, no fucking way.

"You need to relax. Try to breathe through the penetration and bear down, making it easier and less painful."

Once I forced myself to relax my muscles, his finger eased in with little resistance, which didn't hurt at all as he slid it in and out of me, then he shoved it deeper and wiggled his finger around until my body froze, and I saw flashes of light. My dick throbbed and leaked even more from him touching my prostate. That had to be the area he talked about earlier. I was definitely liking this so far.

"Are you still doing okay, baby?"

"Uh huh..." I couldn't form a coherent sentence, let alone a thought.

A few minutes later, a slight burn happened. Stix inserted a second finger, and while there wasn't much pain, it wasn't the most comfortable either, but the more he stretched me, the more I opened up for him and the less it burned.

I was practically panting and creating a puddle underneath me as his fingers kept hitting that hot button as he dug deeper and deeper. A sheen of sweat blanketed my skin from arousal despite the coolness of my room.

"Oh, dude... I wish you could see your gorgeous, pink hole all happy. It's just taking my fingers like a pro. Shit, you're going to suck my dick up like it was made for you."

Fuck. I hated and loved his dirty talk. I hated it because my face fucking burned with embarrassment. But I also loved it because not only was it hot, but he told me his words were only reserved for me.

"You ready for me, baby?"

"Yes."

"Turn over on your back. I want to see your face completely blissed out by the time I'm done with you."

CHAPTER 27
Stix

YEAH, I MAY HAVE sounded all casual and cool, but fuck, I turned into a nervous wreck inside. Sex had never made me feel this way. Well, except the first couple of times when I lost my virginity, but that shit didn't count. But seeing Stone so openly vulnerable for me swelled my heart. I understood him enough to know this was a big milestone for him, and it couldn't have been easy. So, that he trusted me this much? Yeah, it fucking had me melting. If I hadn't been in love before, this would've sealed the deal. And I was. He just didn't know it yet.

I also worried that it wouldn't be good enough for him or that I'd accidentally hurt him, and he'd never want it again.

Yep, I was a mess on the inside, but on the outside, I was all dirty talk and busy keeping him turned on.

He rolled onto his back with his arms spread out, exposing himself like a trusting dog with his cock so swollen and angry red while leaking all over his sexy abs. Good, he was turned on as much as me, and my dick almost fucking hurt; I was so hot for him.

I spread his long, thick legs and sat between them, allowing me to hover and kiss him. He hadn't shaved today, so his scruff burned my skin, and I loved it. It was one of my favorite parts of kissing a man. Kisses I rarely got because I hadn't dated forever and refused to kiss my clients.

My tongue slid in his mouth between two plump lips that I also nibbled on. When I pulled away, I tugged on his bottom lip with my teeth before letting go.

"So sexy, Rolling Stone."

His blush was fucking adorable, which he rubbed with his hands as if he could erase it.

I smirked as I grabbed his cock, so hot under my hand, and stroked him. "You ready?"

He nodded, looking down at my dick with wide eyes as if it offended him. "You sure that's going to fit?"

I snorted a laugh. "Yeah, it'll fit, baby. Remember, you're bigger than me."

Grabbing the lube, I oiled up my dick. "Pull your legs back," I said.

Stone grabbed behind his knees and pulled his legs far enough back to open himself up to me.

"Let me get in there, and then you can let go."

I slicked his hole up one more time and nudged the crown of my cock against him. God, he was so quiet; I worried he didn't want this, so

I had to ask him again. "You can back out, baby. No hard feelings. It's okay if you don't want this."

He shook his head. "No, I want it. I'm just... nervous."

"Well, tell me to stop if it's too much."

"Okay."

I nudged my tip in a little further until I met complete resistance. Stone scrunched his face up, so I reached for him and pressed my hand on his cheek. "Open up for me, baby. Relax and bear down."

He relaxed around me and took a deep breath as he pushed down, allowing my cock to slide in. It was only a little bit in, but it was a start. I sat there, allowing him to adjust before I inched further in. "Talk to me."

Stone's eyes were closed, and he was gripping my forearms. "I'm fine. Keep going."

Every time I inched inside, I would pull out and push back in a little more to get his body used to the friction and having me inside. And each time, he loosened up more and more. With one last push, he sucked me all the way in, and I was fully seated in him.

We both panted as he got used to me while I did everything fucking possible not to come yet.

"Shit, Rolling Stone. You feel so fucking amazing wrapped around me. I knew you'd suck me right in. Hell yeah, this ass was made for me."

He peeked his eyes open, and his smile was small but crooked. "You *are* an ass."

"So true," I sighed.

My hands rested on either side of him as I pulled out and slowly pushed back in. I needed to just pound the hell out of him, but that would've ruined the moment. Soon, he took me with complete ease as I slid in and out of him and picked up speed. His hands traveled up my arms and gripped my biceps, digging his fingers into me while arching his back. His moan made my dick jump inside him. Hell, yeah. I hit that sweet spot, so I did it again and again.

As Stone further relaxed, he got more into it. I leaned down and gave him a sloppy kiss with a lot of tongue as I thrust, popping my hips to keep hitting his prostate. Sweat glistened on his face, and his mouth was salty from it, so I licked his upper lip before swallowing his delicious tongue.

I smiled on his lips when he wrapped his legs around my hips and pulled me deeper into him. "More," he breathed. "Faster."

Each time I pulled out and slammed home, Stone grunted and arched his back. His fingers digging into my arms were hurting, but I kind of liked the pain. It was my way of knowing I was turning him so the fuck on that he had no idea what he was doing and losing his carefully constructed control.

Our panting could barely be heard over the slapping of our groins against each other. And I was doing everything possible to keep it together. I really needed Stone to come first. This was his moment.

"Come for me, baby. Grab your yummy cock and stroke. I need to feel you cinch around me until I blow."

His eyes were hooded, and his hazels were nearly black, looking up at me as his long fingers wrapped around his cock. He swiped his fingers over his cockhead for some pre-cum to use as lube, then stroked fast.

"Fuck. Fuck. Fuck," Stone chanted every time I hit his prostate hard.

I was quickly growing tired and sweaty, and before I thought I couldn't take it anymore and just gave in to the bliss, Stone froze as hot jets of cum shot out all over his abs and chest, and some even reached his chin.

"Holy shit," I rasped. "So fucking sexy. God, look at you covered in cum."

My eyes rolled up into my head, and my toes curled as his ass gripped the hell out of my dick. And that was all she wrote. I quickly followed him as I shot my load inside his warm walls.

"Jesus... Fuck, baby. So, good. So, good."

Once I was depleted, I fell on top of him, uncaring that I was lying on cold cum and sweat.

"That's it. Call the morgue. I'm dead."

His chuckle was deep, reverberating through my body. Then gentle fingers caressed my damp skin, making me entirely too sleepy. "Man, that was nice," I said. I looked up at him to see where his mind was at. He seemed to be into it, but I was familiar with the 'afters' when things became clearer. Sometimes, they turned quite awkward.

"It was surprisingly nice. I enjoyed having you inside me, which was way better than I expected."

"Yeah?"

He nodded. "Yeah."

I slipped out of him and reached between his legs, waiting for my cum to spill out. Soon, it leaked and swiped his tender hole. "My second most favorite part. Like I've marked you somehow."

"What's your first?"

"Coming, duh."

His face turned bright red, and he smiled shyly. "Yeah, that was pretty stupid of me."

"You're so fucking cute."

"I'm not cute."

"You are... one hundred percent."

I licked the clef in his chin, then climbed out of bed because we needed to get cleaned up. I reached out a hand to him, and he took it and sat up, wincing. "I'm going to feel that for a couple of days, aren't I?"

"Nah. Maybe a little tomorrow. Let's take a shower."

I started the water to allow it to get hot, which always took a while in this old place. Hopefully, his roommates wouldn't need the bathroom for a bit because I planned on worshiping Stone's body with soap.

Once the shower was warm, we stepped in together, and I wrapped my arms around him as the warmth washed over us. He held me back and rested his head on mine. I loved an affectionate Stone. It came in small doses, but I ate up whatever he offered. It was amazing he had anything to give, to be honest. Not after what he'd been through.

I pulled away from him, grabbed his woodsy body wash, and poured some into my hands. Once my hands were all lathered, I ran them across his body, touching the bumps and ridges of his scars. I tried not to let it upset me because I couldn't do much about his past suffering, but I also didn't want to upset him, since he was so relaxed and malleable under my care.

Stone's eyes fluttered closed as I lathered his hard lines and smooth skin. He swayed a little, getting sleepy.

"Have you ever been in love?" he asked.

Yes, you. "I have. Once." I didn't lie entirely, but he didn't need to know I meant him. At least, not yet.

"What's it like? I don't think I've ever loved someone or something."

God, that was so fucking sad, making my heart ache for him. He needed and deserved love. We all did. The world would be a better place if we had a lot more of it.

"Well, it's not like loving your mother or sister—"

"I don't have those types of love."

"I realize that, baby. I only mean it's different from loving a friend or parent. It's hard to describe, but the surge is overwhelming. Like you simply look at them, and that love surges throughout your body with this urge to take care of them and promise them the world. You want them happy, and every time they show it because of you, it sends this wave of pride through you. I don't know. I guess it sounds stupid. It's just an emotion that's so strong, yet feels perfect and perhaps a little scary."

He looked down at me with hard hazel eyes. Boy, when Stone got jealous, it penetrated you to your very core and straight to your soul. I loved his protective and jealous side. Maybe jealousy wasn't the healthiest emotion, but I loved being wanted and needed, even possessively so. "Who was he to you? If you loved him, why aren't you still together?"

Fuck, should I tell him? We'd only been together for two months. It was way too soon, right? But could he take it? Would he run from fear? Or would he embrace and accept it? Being able to tell which direction Stone would take wasn't easy. He was often hot and cold when trying to figure out who he really was. Even after accepting us in this relationship, he still struggled between feeling deserving and the fear that was so deeply rooted, thanks to his parents.

I sighed and bit the bullet. "We're still together."

His eyes grew wide, and he took a step back, assuming I was cheating or something. "Stone... think about what I just said."

I watched his eyes process my words, and then his brows furrowed as the answer finally settled in his brain. "Me?"

"Yes, you, dumbass. I'm fucking into you. Like a lot. You're the first person I've ever had something serious with, so maybe it's a little fast. What the fuck do I know? But it is what it is, and I'm not taking it back. You're the only one I've loved, Rolling Stone."

I waited him out while holding my breath for his reaction. Would he run? Stay? "I don't expect you to say it back. But yeah, this love thing is pretty new to me."

He grabbed my face with two hands and pulled me into a deep kiss, using his entire body, pressing against me and swallowing my tongue. I moaned in his mouth before he pulled away. "I feel the same. It's... hard for me to say the words since I've never said them. Why is it so scary? Like I'm going to be sick."

I huffed a laugh. "Because once you fall in love, you have so much more to lose."

CHAPTER 28
Stone

I STILL TRIED TO wrap my head around Stix and me, saying we loved each other. Well, I hadn't actually said the words, but he knew what I meant, I hoped. And it'd been two weeks now, worrying if I'd ever get the balls to say them. But fuck, thinking about him telling me those words still made my heart pound in complete love and mind-gripping fear.

I'd always wanted to be loved, and now he did, which was the most terrifying thing ever. What if I fucked things up, and he left me? God, I was so bad at this dating thing, or so it felt that way. I'd never had a boyfriend or a girlfriend before or had these sorts of emotions, with fears of disappointing him or losing him. I wouldn't be able to take it. It was too lucky. Too easy that I got Stix after all the shit I put him through. It all could be snatched away in a blink of a moment.

I had all these thoughts coursing through me as I cut and sliced the fish with shaking hands. Would this fear ever leave me? Would I ever be comfortable enough in our relationship not to have these worries anymore? The only thing keeping me from going over into the deep end was Stix telling me first he loved me. All his little reassurances and confidence kept me moderately sane, not to mention the cute texts he sent me all the time with weird emojis that left me guessing what the hell they meant.

When I wrapped up work for the day, staying later than normal, I scrubbed my hands and arms of fish as much as I could, then left to meet up with Stix at his new job he'd been working at for a few weeks now. It wasn't exactly on the way home, but I liked going home together whenever we got off close to the same time. And today was Friday, so we both worked at Alpha's tonight.

I skated the two miles toward FarmMart, the latest little bougie grocery chain that sold expensive as fuck organic food that no one could afford unless you had tons of money. It was out of the way because no one would shop there in the poorer sections of Baltimore. But it also meant Stix got paid more, which eased my guilt from him not working his prostitution thing because of me. Between FarmMart and Alpha's, Stix did really well money-wise. Better than me. I was so fucking proud of him.

The late November day was cold as hell. Tonight, the temperature would go down to freezing for the first time this fall. My jacket, scarf, and beanie did fine, keeping me warm, but my hands and face were cold as hell. My hands, especially after working with wet, cold fish all day. They were raw and chapped.

When I reached the swank grocery store, I skidded to a stop, popped my board up, and grabbed it as I walked inside. The place smelled of fresh bread and something cooking for those who preferred healthy, prepared meals.

There he was. Every time I saw Stix now, my heart stopped beating for a second. It was weird seeing him without all his earrings and chains around his neck as he worked the register as a cashier. When he looked up, his smile took my breath away. Yep, I was in love and had so much to fucking lose.

I made my way toward him and stood close as he rang up over five hundred dollars worth of groceries that filled only about three bags. Fucking crazy. Do you know how much food I could buy with five hundred dollars?

"Hey, baby," he said without looking at me as he packed groceries in brown paper bags. "I'm gonna be late at Alpha's tonight. Sorry, I forgot to call you, so you didn't have to come all this way. But we have a cashier who's gonna be late, and I need to stay until she shows up."

It was almost Thanksgiving, so Stix had been busy as hell as everyone got ready for the holiday. Even without waiting for an employee, he'd been working late here and there due to the store's popularity. "That's fine. I can wait."

He looked back at me and smiled. "Thanks, but just go on. I don't know how long I'm going to be."

"Okay."

"I love you," he said in front of all the customers. Getting used to his PDAs was hard, but I accepted them as gifts. Yet, I couldn't say it back. He knew I loved him, but I just couldn't say the actual words yet, like if I did, my bubble would pop, and this happy fantasy would be over.

Instead, I gave him a tentative kiss on his cheek as a consolation prize and quickly left to avoid any stares from the shoppers.

When I arrived at Alpha's, Stix hadn't come in yet, but he texted he'd be here soon. I was in the employee lounge, putting away my crap, when Alpha walked in.

"How's it hanging, Stone," he said.

"Hey."

"A man of many words as always."

I rolled my eyes. "You're as bad as Stix."

"Ha! Well, that's why we get along so well. How are you two doing?"

"I'm in love," I blurted before my face set on fire.

Alpha's smile spread wide across his face, and I ducked into my locker, pretending to rummage through something, so he didn't see my mortification.

I sensed him moving close to me, then saw him leaning against the locker next to me in my periphery. "That's a good thing, right?"

"I... think so."

"You mean, you don't know?"

I shook my head, still buried in my locker. "I wish I was confident like he is. The fear is... strong."

"What are you afraid of? Losing him?"

"Yeah."

"Look, man, I don't know what happened to you. Something bad, clearly, considering your fear of being with Stix, now this fear of losing him. I've been watching you, Stone. You don't talk much but say a lot without realizing it. I know why people call you Stone, but you're not a stone, are you?"

I shook my head.

"Have you thought about some therapy?"

I finally stood straight and met his kind blue eyes. "I can't afford it. My insurance only covers basic health shit."

"There are places you can go that are more affordable, and then there's group therapy. Some are even free."

"Really?" I hadn't even thought of that option, assuming seeing a therapist was only for those who could afford it. Maybe there was hope for me to overcome all these fears and insecurities. I'd been afraid of things most of my life, but I'd never been insecure about anything because I had no one in my life to be insecure about it until now. "How do you know all this?"

"I've been in therapy for years, dealing with my own shit. I still am because I find it really helpful on my bad days."

"You have bad days?"

Alpha gripped my shoulder and smiled. "We all have bad days some-times. Life isn't easy, man. I can give you a list of places to call, but only if you want. No pressure."

I nodded. "Okay. Thanks."

If I could afford it, I'd definitely do it. I wanted to stop being such a nutjob for Stix.

Despite all my fears and worries, he came in later like a whirlwind full of smiles, instantly easing my anxiety. Only he could do that. It was how I recognized how I felt about him. That he overwhelmed all my negativity, giving me light and goodness exactly how Alec used to. And if that ever went away, I'd die. I hadn't realized how starved I was for love until Stix gave it to me so freely.

It helped that he peppered me with kisses throughout the night whenever he got a second to breathe.

Before the end of the night, Stix came up to me and leaned into my ear. "I hope you're not too tired tonight."

"You always have sex on the brain, dude," I teased. I liked it when I relaxed enough to banter with him.

"Uhm, have you *seen* your body? Those tats? That adorable dimple? Or that sexy clef in your chin? Dude, looking at you gives me a perpetual chubby. So, yeah, my brain is always in hyperdrive, sex mode."

I rolled my eyes, but I flushed at the compliments, too. "Well, how can I say no to that?"

"Exactly! I knew you'd see it my way." Then he scampered off to take orders for the last call.

It was close to three in the morning by the time we got back to my place and naked in my bed. Stix had our cocks meshed together, rubbing and gliding easily from the lube and our pre-cum. My hand wrapped over his, so we could do it together. The sensation was unreal. Fucking him was the best, but rubbing our dicks together came in second. His velvet skin pulsed and heated on mine, making that now familiar tingling and pressure grow.

Stix's free hand gripped the nape of my neck as we pressed our foreheads together, panting and grunting as we got closer to toppling over the edge together. I was close. So close. But I wanted to wait for him, to chase him or come together.

"Fuck, Stone... your cock feels so fucking good next to mine."

I punched my hips on instinct for more friction.

"I've been waiting for you."

He looked at me in the eyes with a knowing smile before his eyes rolled up in his head. I loved that I didn't have to explain shit to him. He got me. He understood that I meant my failure in relationships and sex was because I'd been waiting my entire life for him. Stix was mine and mine alone. He may have sold himself, but he held back those moments that made it special for only us, like kisses, having sex facing each other, no condoms, and his dirty talk. It was all mine.

"I love you, Rolling Stone," he panted.

That was it and all I needed to send me to the brink. I moved my free hand toward his chest and tweaked one of his pierced nipples as I came over our hands and dicks. He cried out and thrust in our hands.

"Yes... so hot," he rasped and soon followed me.

Before my heart settled and my breathing calmed. Before I got up all in my head. And before I let the worries and doubts consume me, I told him. To finally get it out there. "I love you, too."

He bit his bottom lip, smiling, before he pressed his mouth to mine. Our kiss grew deep, slow, needy, and full of tongue.

"That was the hardest thing I've ever said," I admitted when we pulled away.

"I know, baby. But I'm happy you told me. You're so strong."

I didn't believe him, but I let him believe it. I didn't feel he lied to me, but he always tried to make me feel better.

"I want to be stronger."

"Fuck, I wish you saw what I did."

"How? I'm always nervous, embarrassed, or anxious. What if I fail at this? What if I do something wrong?"

He ran fingers through my hair and down my cheek. "Nothing worth doing is going to be easy. Will we have problems or struggles? Probably. All couples do. But that's okay. It doesn't mean you or I failed. We just dust ourselves off and keep trying to make this thing between us grow and grow. And before you tell me how insightful I am or some shit, that's all my mom. And she's right."

I took a deep breath and nodded. "You're right. I don't feel strong or anything, but I trust you."

After we cleaned up our mess and a mess it was, we snuggled into sleep. Well, he passed out. I stayed up for another thirty minutes thinking about what he'd said. I would do anything to protect this thing we had between us. It was the most important thing in my life. He was the most important person. And I never wanted to let it go.

CHAPTER 29
Stix

I WAS LOCKING MY apartment in the early morning before heading
to work when I stumbled into Brie, kissing a man goodbye in his
doorway. As the man walked off, Brie had a big smile on his face and
hearts in his eyes, watching him go, then his eyes landed on mine.
The man was tall, lean, and a little older, with salt and pepper hair.

I walked over to him, smiling back. "New boyfriend?"

He bit his lip and nodded. "Yes, we met last month."

"I knew you'd meet someone good for you. You deserve it, Brie."

"Thanks, it's been nice."

Nice to be wanted. The words were clear, though he didn't utter them.

"So, you and Stone, huh? That bad boy is dangerous."

I huffed a laugh. "Oh, once you get past all the barbed wire and electric fences, he's a softie."

"If you say so. You still... working for men?"

"Nah, I'm not doing that anymore. I recently got a job at that new FarmMart. Pays pretty well."

He reached for me with long fingers and brushed away fallen hair. "I'm proud of you. I miss you, but I'm proud of you."

"Thanks. Well, I've gotta go. Call me if you want to hang out or anything."

"I will."

When he headed back inside his apartment, I left for work.

It was nice to see him with someone. He needed love, not an indifferent fuck, for as long as he did with me. I should've stopped it earlier, but that money had been too good. Oh, well. Those days were over, and Stone was worth it.

I hated taking the bus, but it was faster than my board or the subway, and I didn't want to ever be late if I could help it, but I always had my board with me. Once I got there, I walked into the small grocery store. Well, it wasn't tiny, but smaller compared to the bigger chains. But the price of their groceries allowed them to pay me more. The money was pretty damn good.

The day had gone well, except for specific customers. I wasn't used to dealing with wealthier people. They weren't always pleasant and could be quite demanding. But I would always slap a smile on my face and push through their entitlement to help them as best as I could.

The late afternoon grew slow, so I spent my free time away from the register to stock some items when a man came in, carrying a grocery basket, looking up at the signs over each aisle for what he needed. It was then that I recognized him. My heart literally stopped beating, and my lungs stopped breathing. He fucking looked the same, even after three years, though now with some grays through his dark brown hair. Being only forty now, he still looked young.

Strange emotions filled me, from anger at being abandoned to fucking missing the hell out of him. We'd been so close when I was younger, or so I thought. Was it all a lie? Nova didn't even remember him, so she didn't care, but my father had been a part of my life for most of it.

I stood and watched him from where I was kneeling, putting away boxes of gluten-free pasta. He noticed me staring and looked at me with confusion. There was no recognition on his face, probably because of my bleached hair. It had been brown before. Then the clarity hit. I saw that moment when everything clicked into place. There was no joyous reunion or rushing to hug each other as much as my body wanted to. It was my rational brain keeping me glued to where I stood.

He swallowed and nodded his head. "Nico."

"Hi, Dad."

Did I have the right to call him that anymore? Did he even deserve that title?

"W-what are you doing here?"

My hands fisted as I finally took a step forward. "I work here."

He nodded and looked around at anywhere but me. "Ah... good."

"How... are you?"

Dad looked back at me and frowned. What was going on in his head? Did he regret coming in? Did he miss me at all?

"I'm good. Yeah. Things are good."

I nodded. "Yeah, me too." I rubbed my neck and took another step closer. "I... miss you," I blurted. He didn't deserve it, but it was the truth. Maybe if I could get him to remember how much he loved us, he'd come back into our lives. Not to live or anything, but perhaps he'd want to get to know me again or know his daughter.

Without even thinking, I rushed toward my father and wrapped my arms around him, pulling him into a hug. The grief of his loss hit me so fucking hard right then. He smelled just as I remembered, bringing back all those memories of him holding me, comforting me, and reading to me at night as a kid before bed. My eyes leaked and held on tighter. "I've missed you so much." He moved as if to hug me back, but instead, he gently pried my arms off him.

I looked up at him as the tears spilled, unable to control them if I tried. His jaw was clenched, and his eyes were filled with discomfort, uncertainty, and some annoyance, making me instantly regret my reaction to him.

I wiped my wet face. "Sorry. I... didn't expect to react to you like that."

"It's good to see you, Nico."

My heart was full of hope despite all the warning signs he was placating me and didn't really care. It was a desperate hope that this could all be fixed, and I could finally let go of all my guilt for being gay. "Yeah?"

He nodded and looked down at his feet. "Yeah... sure."

"I'm... so sorry I ruined things for you and Mom."

Fuck, the tears were welling again, but I did my best to hold them back.

He swallowed hard again and nodded. "It's... okay."

"Do you forgive me?"

"Yeah, son."

Son. Did that mean he really forgave me?

"I've got to go."

Before I could say anything else, he turned on his heels and rushed out the door, dropping the basket on the floor.

I rushed into the apartment to the scent of tacos. Awesome, I loved tacos. Mom was in the kitchen cooking while Nova was coloring, as she loved to do. I kissed my sister on the head and kissed my mother's cheek. Then I dug into the fridge for a beer. Cracking it open, I took a large swig.

"Good day?" she asked.

"Yeah... uhm, I ran into Dad."

Mom's back was to me, but her entire body stiffened. "And what did... Nova, please go to your room."

"Why? I'm drawing. I don't wanna."

"Now, young lady. I need to talk to your brother."

"Ugh, fine." Nova grabbed her crayons and coloring book and stomped off to our room. When the door was shut, Mom turned to face me.

"What did that piece of shit want?"

"It wasn't like that... he was good. He said he missed me."

She raised her brow and folded her arms. "Did he now?"

"I... told him I was sorry about ruining your marriage, and... he said he forgave me."

Mom visibly deflated, and her dark eyes grew sad. "Why would you do such a thing? It wasn't your fault. Your father made his own choices. You being yourself was not wrong. We've talked about this before, Nico."

"If I just... kept to myself—"

"Then what? Never find love? Never have Stone in your life?"

That stopped me. She was right. I loved having Stone in my life. He was one of the worst and best things to happen to me. "God, you're right."

She stepped up close to me and cupped my face with her hand. "Sweetheart, let your father go. Stop feeling guilty over this. It wasn't your fault. Life is fine. We aren't rich, but we're happy, right?"

I nodded. "I want to see him, Mom."

She stiffened again and went back to the simmering meat and onions. "Why would you want to torture yourself?"

"I only want to see if I can make things work. I miss him."

She dropped her head and took a deep breath without looking at me. "He doesn't want you. I know it's cruel, but he hasn't reached out to you once, honey."

"You don't know that! I saw him. He forgave me. He said he missed me! I want to see him and try."

She turned around and clenched the spatula with a tight fist as she frowned. "No, he's going to break you. I can't have that."

I wasn't to be dissuaded. It was a risk I was willing to take. "Tell me where he's living now. I want to visit him."

She turned back around to stir the meat again. "No."

I walked over to her and gently turned her around to see her tears. It broke my heart to see her hurting. I understood why, but she needed to trust me. "I know you're worried about me, but I need to do this and try."

"He's just going to hurt you even more."

"Yeah, he was all awkward today, but we hadn't seen each other in three years. Please, let me do this. If you don't tell me where he is, I'm going to find him, anyway. It will just take me longer."

She said nothing, walking over to an old desk, sitting in the living room, and opening a drawer. She pulled out a file and handed it to me. "Those are the divorce papers. His address is there. I can't promise you he's still living there."

I took the file and kissed her cheek. "Thanks, Mom."

"Well, know that I'll still be here when he breaks your heart again." With that, she left to finish dinner.

I wrapped my legs around Stone's waist as he thrust in and out, needing him deeper and harder. He held me close as we sweated on each other, and when he was close to coming, he sat up high to move faster.

"Stroke yourself, Nico," he demanded, only using my real name during sex, which turned me the fuck on. While Stone tended to be more insecure regarding our relationship, get him all hot and bothered, and he grew more controlling. I loved it and wish he'd do it more often.

I stroked as I was told, but I wasn't as into it as I usually was, being plagued with my mother's words and my need to bring my father back into my life. It was fucking distracting.

"Stroke!" he growled.

Fuck. I gripped myself harder and pumped my dick faster as Stone picked up speed, slamming in and out of me. His cock swelled, and he burned before he let loose.

"Fuck, fuck..." he grunted.

As he slowed down, I still hadn't come, but I was closer. I tried to shut out the noise in my head and focus on the moment, and finally, it quieted down enough for me to explode.

Stone pulled out of me and padded to the restroom, returning shortly with a warm washcloth to wipe up all the cum on my hand, stomach, and ass.

He tossed it on his floor and crawled back into bed with me. He laid on his back and rested a forearm over his eyes. "Did I do something wrong? You weren't into it at all."

Shit. I guess I could see how it'd look on the outside. Usually, I was full of dirty talk, and I'd been quiet all night.

I rolled over to face him and pulled his arm away from his face. "No, baby. It's not you—"

"You came over here, just took me to bed, and we fucked, but you're not yourself. Just be honest with me. What did I do?"

I grunted as I sat up and straddled his stomach. "Don't do that. I'm allowed to have bad days that have nothing to do with you." Regret hit me for snapping at him, and I closed my eyes. "I'm sorry. My mood right now is also not about you. I just..." I sat up straight and rubbed my face. "I saw Dad today for the first time in three years."

His eyes grew wide, and he raised himself to pull me into a hug. "Shit. Why didn't you tell me? Why go straight to sex if you needed to talk?"

I grabbed his face and gave him a quick and soft kiss. "Because I needed you. I just wanted to feel you. My mind is all over the place. I... miss him so much, and I didn't even realize how much so until I saw him in the store. Then I told Mom about it, and she got upset when I mentioned I wanted to see if I could fix things between him and me."

"Reasonably so, baby. He left you all without a word or a dime. Fuck him."

"You don't understand! He seems to miss me. I just have to try. If I don't, I'm going to regret it."

"And what if he turns his back on you again?"

God, I didn't want that to happen, and it would probably hurt like fuck. "I'll have to accept it."

He ran his long fingers through my messy hair, then gripped my face. "And then will it be over? If he turns you away, will you finally let go of this guilt and move on?"

I nodded but wasn't sure I could ever let go of the guilt. "Will you come with me?"

"Of course. Whatever you need, baby."

I rested my forehead on his. "Thanks."

CHAPTER 30
Stone

LATE SATURDAY MORNING, I held Stix's clammy hand and played with his fingers as we rode the subway train toward where his dad lived near Patterson Park. It was kind of far from where we lived, but close enough that his dad could've seen Stix and Nova at any time he wanted. Mostly, the wealthy lived around this area. There weren't tons of single-family homes in Baltimore, but you could buy a pretty nice townhome built in the 1900s and over five thousand square feet. If Stix's dad lived out here, he could've also afforded child support. It was illegal for him not to pay, but Grace never fought it, believing it was best to separate herself and the kids from their father. Not that she had the funds to fight it.

This was a bad idea, but Stix was determined, carrying way too much guilt and wanting to make amends with his father. Fuck, when he told me he apologized to his dad, I wanted to throttle Stix, but I didn't. For the first time since I'd met him, I saw where his insecurities lay. His mother had said Stix put on a good show of confidence and strength, but he wasn't always. I saw what she meant now. Regardless of whether I agree with him or not, I would support him as he's always supported me and held me up every time I felt like I was going to fall.

The train stopped near Upper Fells Point, where several blocks of high-end townhomes were built by a bygone era. All had been refurbished and expensive looking with beautiful trees and landscaping, except the trees were bare now. It was in the city with traffic and everything, but I knew inside the homes would be gorgeous.

We stepped off the train, still holding hands, as we walked several blocks over to his dad's house and stopped in front of it. It was red brick like the rest of them and about three stories tall, but it had a bright blue door.

"I hope he's home," Stix muttered.

I hoped he wasn't. Then again, that would mean we'd have to come back.

We stood there so long; I thought he'd changed his mind, but then he let go of my hand and lifted his shoulders straight. "Ready?"

I nodded and followed him up the small brick steps, standing behind him as he rang the doorbell.

Stix shoved his hands in his jeans pockets and waited.

I didn't know if my coming was such a good idea. If his father were some homophobe, he would hate me right off the bat, and he may not want to talk to Stix at all. But this was Stix's show. If he needed moral support, I would be that for him.

The door suddenly opened to a man about Stix's height with dark hair. Stix looked more like his mother, but I saw the resemblance, especially in the mouth and nose area.

The man looked right and left down the road before looking back at Stix. "Nico. What are you doing here?"

"Can I come in and talk for a minute? It's kind of cold out here."

His dad scanned the street again and nodded. "Just for a bit. I have to be somewhere soon." I recognized the lie for what it was. Why couldn't Stix?

"That's all I need. Thanks."

We entered a beautiful home that showed he had money and enough of it to afford this place. It was big and open, with hardwood floors, white walls, and decorated in creams and blues. Yeah, he could definitely afford child support, the prick.

After he closed the door behind us, he padded off barefoot. "Follow me."

He led us to a study with the walls covered in books, and in the middle sat an antique wooden desk. But he didn't sit behind it and instead chose the four club chairs in front of a roaring fireplace that snapped and popped. Stix and his sister might have had all this if their dad hadn't decided to be greedy. I hated him more and more as we sat down.

"Are you going to introduce me to your friend, Nico?" he asked.

"Oh, yeah, this is Damien Sloan, my boyfriend."

Honestly, I was shocked he admitted it so readily, but maybe I should've known better. He'd always been open about us and his sexuality. Then again, his dad left him over it.

The polite thing to do would be to reach for his hand and shake it, but he didn't deserve my politeness. I was here for Stix, not for this prick. He didn't exactly reach out his hand, either.

"I see."

Stix sat up straight and leaned forward, sitting directly across from his dad. "Look, I know you hate me being gay, but... It's who I am. While I feel terrible about coming out and shit that made you leave, I can't change myself. I'm so sorry I hurt you with it, but... I miss you so much. Seeing you at the store the other day, I want to fix things between us."

"Nico, why are you really here? Is it money?"

Stix tensed and furrowed his brows. "What? No! I can make my own money. I just thought... I want to see you again. And Nova... she's so sweet and getting so big. I—"

His dad sighed and raised his hand to stop Stix. "Son, I can't—"

"Please. I'm sorry I hurt you. We used to be so close. Let me try to fix this."

At least his dad had the decency to appear remorseful. "Son... I didn't leave because you came out as gay."

Stix's jaw dropped to the ground. "What?"

"I used it as an excuse."

I so wanted to fucking kill the fucker. I *knew* it.

"W-why would you do such a thing?"

Someone came into the house and shut the door. "Justin?" a woman called out.

"In here."

The woman had blond hair and a curvy figure, wearing expensive clothes, high-heeled shoes, and jewelry. But her biggest accessory was a child of about two years old on her hip. A little boy that looked like Stix's dad. Shit.

"What's going on? Who are these... men?" The distaste on her face was unmistakable. We were unwelcome.

"This is... Nico. My son," he said, pointing at Stix.

"I see. Can we talk for a moment? In private?"

His dad stood and left the room to chat with his wife or girlfriend in the hallway. "What does he want? Money? Tell him he can't have any. You have another family now. Do it, or I will." She loud-whispered, no doubt so that we could hear her.

"I'll take care of it."

I looked over at Stix, who picked at the loose strands from the hole in his jeans, so I couldn't see his face but read his body language. His fucking dad just crushed him with this news and his lie.

When his dad came back in, he sat down again.

"I'm not here for money," Stix snapped, but pain threaded through his agitation. "Why did you fucking lie?"

"I'm sorry. I... cheated on your mother and got Rebecca pregnant. Please understand that your mother and... we weren't getting along. We had been high school sweethearts, and then she got pregnant with you, making me get married before I wanted to. I was a teen, forced to be a grown adult, and it was fucking hard. Nova being born was a surprise and happened right when I was getting established in my job. I was stressed, we were fighting... Then Rebecca came along, and well, what's done is done."

"What's done is done? Are you fucking kidding me?" I snapped.

Stix rested a hand on my knee and shook his head, then looked back at his dad with disgust. "So you told us it was because of me, you left to cover up your cheating?"

His dad rested his elbows on his knees, leaning over as he combed his fingers together. "Yes. I'm sorry."

Stix stood up with fisted hands. "Sorry?! Sorry doesn't cut it! All this time, I'd harbored all this guilt for tearing up the family because of who I am and coming out to you. You let me believe all this time it was my fault! No! Sorry doesn't cut it! Fuck you! I hate you!"

Stix stormed out of the room and out of the house, slamming the door behind him. With a huff, I stood and scowled at the man, looking back to where Stix had left. "I've been feeling guilty about this, especially after seeing him again the other day, but I'm a coward."

I scoffed. "You got that right. You're definitely a coward. It's pathetic to let your family struggle financially, not even contributing to their care, while you've been playing house with a new child and a trophy wife. Nico is fucking better off without you. Despite what you've done to him, he's so strong. Everyone loves him. He's such a good soul, and not even you could fucking ruin that despite your best efforts. You fucking owe him."

With that, I let him stew on my words, not that he would give a shit, and walked out to find Stix.

He hadn't run off, thank fuck. He stayed and paced back and forth on the sidewalk, gripping the hell out of his hair. When I reached him, I stopped his pacing and pulled him into a hug. He gripped the back of my jacket and started to sob.

"I'm so sorry, Nico."

"You gonna tell me you told me so?"

"Fuck no. You should know me better than that by now."

"I'm sorry."

I held him tighter as I stared up at the man looking out the window. He quickly closed the curtain and hid like the coward he was. "Let's go home, baby."

After we got home, he told his mother what had happened, leaving out the cheating part, believing she didn't need to know that. It would only hurt her. I disagreed because she deserved the truth, but she wasn't my mother.

Then we ended up back at my place for a while, and I held him bundled up on the fire escape as we smoked cigarettes. We'd have to go to work soon at Alpha's, but sitting here in the cold, not speaking, taking in the sounds of the city was strangely calming while I tried to be his shield to the harsh world, even for a moment.

The day before Thanksgiving, Stix came storming into my bedroom madder than I'd ever seen him, waving around an envelope.

"He's got some fucking nerve!"

"What's going on?"

"Dad! The balls on him, considering what a fucking coward he is."

"What'd that fucker do now?"

Stix handed me the envelope, and I opened the unsealed flap, pulling out a slip of paper. I turned it around to see a check. My eyes bugged out of my head. I'd never seen that much money in one place before. "Holy shit."

"No letter. No apology. Only a big fat fucking check, and for what? Why now? His guilt? He'd been living in bliss for three damn years, and when I show up, he *suddenly* cares? Give me a break. I can't be bought! We're doing just fine without him!"

I sighed and let him rant until he calmed down, which would be soon because Stix never stayed mad for long. He finally sat down on my bed and deflated. I wrapped an arm around his shoulder and kissed his head. "Feel better?"

"No," he huffed. "Seriously, why? All those times he could've been helping out Mom..." He ran a hand through his hair, then fell back into my bed. "Whatever. Tear it up. I don't want his fucking money. I only wanted his love."

"Well, you're not going to get it."

"Ugh, great. Mr. Blunt Stone has arrived."

"It's the truth. Your dad's never going to give you what you want. You know this, baby. Just take his damn money, put it in a bank, and get yourself that damn house, your meds, and some goddamn drums. Treat you and your family for a change on his dime. You all deserve this."

He sat up, took the check out of my hand, and looked at it. "Shit, fifty thousand *is* a lot of money."

Fuck. His dad at least made up for some of his shit. It wasn't nearly enough, but it would help. "Yes, it is. It can pay off half of that house. Or get you a three-year supply of injections. This is the least your dad can do. This right here?" I pointed at the check in his hand. "That's the bare minimum."

"Shit, you're right."

"Use it, baby. Get that house for your Mom and Nova."

Stix suddenly lunged at me so hard it knocked us both off the bed, and I landed hard on my back on the floor. I let out an 'oof' as he laughed. "I love you, Rolling Stone. Thanks for knocking some sense into me."

"Uh, you're the one who knocked me down... literally."

CHAPTER 31
Stix

WHILE WE ENDED UP tangled on the floor after I knocked Stone down, it soon grew heated. The check drifted off on the floor when I let it go as our mouths consumed each other. Stone's hands slid up my back and into my hair, where he fisted it, pulling me into a deeper kiss. Yes, this was what I needed. I didn't want to make love or have things gentle. I wanted to get fucked and fucked hard. Stone was capable of delivering.

"Fuck me," I panted on his mouth when we came up for air.

"Okay."

"Don't be gentle. I want to feel you all over my skin and into the next day."

"I don't want to hurt you."

"Mmm, but I want you to. Mark me, claim me. Please, baby. You've gotten rough before, but I know you can do more. I love it and need it."

He sat up off the floor, taking me with him, while grabbing the hem of my pullover hoodie and yanking it off. Then he eased me off to stand while stripping naked and stroking himself to get hard. It didn't take long as I kneeled in front of him, watching him grow and glisten with beads of pre-cum.

"Get naked," he ordered.

I stood and removed my T-shirt that read, *'This is what an awesome boyfriend looks like.'* Stone took one look at it, rolled his eyes, and scoffed. "Seriously?"

"What? I'm not fucking amazing as a boyfriend? I'm hurt, Rolling Stone."

Before I could finish getting undressed, he stood toe to toe with me, fisted my hair from the top, and shoved me down to my knees. "We need to shut that mouth of yours up. Open."

I looked up at him and opened my mouth as he shoved his dick in as far as it would go. Yes. This was precisely what I needed.

"Gagging sounds are much better than that smart-ass mouth of yours."

His face was bright red, not used to talking dirty, but I fucking loved that he did it just for me, willing to break through his insecurities.

He shoved his cock in my mouth, deep enough for me to gag. His body shuddered, and his eyes closed from the sensation. "Yes... fuck. Gag all over me." When he let me finally come up for air, he slipped out of my mouth, leaving behind a trail of saliva. "Why do I think that's so hot?"

"It feels powerful, right?"

He simply nodded.

I sucked on him some more, slurping and drooling as he tested my gag reflex over and over. This was what I wanted, next to being fucked. To be used like my body was made just for Stone to do with as he pleased.

Suddenly, he growled and yanked me away from his dick. "Fuck, I'm going to come. Not yet."

Stone pinched the tip of his dick, panting. "Remove the rest of your clothes and get in the bed." His voice was so deep and husky that it made my nuts tight.

I scrambled out of my clothes and into the bed. "How do you want me?"

"On your back. I want to see your face destroyed from coming."

"Now you're speaking my love language, baby."

His smile was crooked, and I fucking loved that he was opening up to this, looking more confident by the minute. Once on my back, he climbed on top of me and straddled my thighs before bending down and biting the barbell piercing on my nipple. He tugged on it with his teeth hard enough to sting and forced me to arch my back for more and for less.

"Shit... harder. Bite it."

And he did. His bite sent a sharp pain that went straight through my nipple and to my back. Who knew why I liked it, but I did. Maybe because this was the type of pain that had pleasure behind it, plus, it was Stone controlling me, doing whatever he wanted to me. I fucking loved giving in to him because I'd been the one to do all the work when it came to sex while I'd been prostituting myself.

He licked away the sting, only to bite me again on my other nipple. Both of them ached now as he nipped and bit along my skin, making his way down to my leaking and swollen cock. It bounced around, desperate for something to fuck. It could complain all it wanted, but I wanted to hold off.

Just when I thought Stone would swallow me down, he didn't. He simply ghosted his breath over the sensitive skin as a tease. "This is mine," he grumbled.

"Yes... all yours. My entire body is yours to do with as you want. Do anything to me."

His hand traveled up my abs to my chest and landed on my throat, gripping it. "Like this?"

I nodded, getting lost in my growing arousal. Forgetting all my pain from my father. "Tighter."

He gripped it tight enough on the sides of my throat to where it was uncomfortable, but not where I couldn't breathe before he leaned down and swallowed my moans with his mouth, sucking my lips and tongue. I could tell he was really opening up to this. It had always been in him. He'd given away enough hints. But now, he was finally letting go and accepting this role I desperately wanted. It also gave him a sense of power and control, things he'd never had.

"Fuck me. Now."

He let go of my throat, reached over me to his old nightstand, and pulled out some lube, pouring a little into his hands. He slathered our dicks in it, and then he swiped some over my hole.

"Don't prep me."

"Nico..."

"No. I'll be fine. My body knows you by now. I can take it. But I need the burn." I rubbed his chest with my hand as he looked at me dubiously. "I like it rough sometimes."

"Is this a way to distract you from your dad?"

"And what if it is? I'll still enjoy it."

He seemed to accept that and nodded. "Okay."

I grabbed my legs to spread myself as he lined himself up and then shoved himself all the way in. He threw back his head, and I panted from the burn and stretch. Once we adapted, he placed his hands on the backs of my thighs and sandwiched my body as he thrust hard and deep, piling into me. We both quickly started to sweat, especially him, as his muscles drew taut and his veins protruded from the effort of slamming hard into me. Fuck, the veins in his corded neck popped as the sweat glistened on his skin. So fucking sexy. Shit. How could this man be so damn gorgeous? And he was all mine.

I grabbed my ankles to give him more of my ass and take his cock hard and deep. I was going to feel it for days, and exactly what I wanted.

"I-I've... got my legs," I panted between his hard thrusts and his groin slapping against my ass. Stone took the hint, gripped my throat again with one hand, and twisted my nipple piercing with the other. The combination of the pain as he pegged my prostate sent wave after wave of euphoria throughout my body. It singed in this strange combination of sensations.

It was quickly taking its toll on his body, and with each thrust and slap, he grunted louder and louder as I whimpered.

"F-fuck... Nico. My Nico... You feel... fucking amazing."

He was getting close. His cock swelled and burned inside me as he kept pumping, watching me with furrowed brows and a slack mouth. I wanted to chase him, so I grabbed my dick, but he slapped my hand away. "That's fucking mine."

Holy shit, that growling demand with the pressure on my prostate nearly had me exploding right then and there, but I held back to give him my cum.

"Yes... all yours."

His body suddenly froze as the first hot spurts shot out. Then his thrusts grew sporadic as he squeezed the last drops out. Once he finished, he leaned down on his trembling arms and gave me a sweaty kiss before pulling out of me and working his way down to my cock, which he swallowed whole.

"God, this is gonna be quick. I've barely held it all in."

He grunted around my dick as the sound vibrated through me. Only a few deep sucks had me finally exploding into his mouth, and he swallowed all of it like a pro.

Licking his lips clean, he shoved my legs back again while my dick still pulsed to watch his cum leak out of me. He swiped some with his fingers and swirled it around my pucker, and then his eyes pinned me down with his intense hazel gaze. "Fuck, Nico... what do you do to me? I'm a fucking monster around you when it comes to sex."

I waggled my brows despite my exhaustion now. "A sexy beast, you mean."

He huffed a tired laugh and fell next to me in bed. "If you say so."

"I'm always right."

He rolled his eyes and pulled me on top of him. I leaned down and kissed the tip of his nose. "Thanks for that. It was exactly what I needed."

"I loved it, too. You bring out this thing in me I didn't know I even had. It's... freeing."

"Good. I want you to feel free, Rolling Stone."

"Now that you're feeling better, you're taking that check lying on my floor, depositing it, and when it clears, you're going to make a down payment on that house."

"Still bossy, I see."

"You know I'm right."

"You gonna help me christen the house when I get it?"

"With your mom right there?"

"Uh, no. It's gonna be a surprise because after I buy it, I need you and my friends to help me fix it up, and make it nice for her. Mostly just painting because it needs it."

He brushed away my sweaty bangs and took a deep breath. "Anything you need, baby."

CHAPTER 32
Stone

I JUMPED OFF THE lip of the half pipe at the skate park, making good air, and pushed off with my hand while grabbing my board with the other. The thrill of making a trick land perfectly always sent waves of exciting knots through my stomach.

The day after Thanksgiving, my friends and I, along with Stix and his friends, were at the park, skating, and finally all getting along. Even Blaze chilled out, except around Ajax. Both of them constantly snipped and circled each other like rabid dogs. Regardless, we had a good day.

Dinner at Stix's apartment had been really nice, too, like I was part of something special. A real family filled with love and good conversation.

Grace and Nova pulled me into their little family and treated me like one of their own. God, I still felt like I didn't deserve it, but I welcomed it, not about to turn my back on a good thing.

No one had to work today, so we all headed out to skate. It was colder than hell, but the parks tended to be less crowded during the late fall and winter months.

After skating for a while, I took a break to grab some water. Stix came running over to grab his board for his turn, but before he ran off, he gave me a quick kiss. It took a while to get used to his love of PDA, but I learned to enjoy it, showing the world that he belonged to me.

Jazz suddenly fell, ripping her jeans at the knees and bleeding everywhere. She limped, madder than a hornet, as her brother, Blondie, and Nacho tried to help her sit down. She shoved them off, bitching at them, but they were undeterred. Blondie grabbed a whiskey bottle, sitting on the ground they'd been sipping from, and poured some onto her wounds. She growled and shoved him off again. Damn, she was tough when angry. Usually, she was pretty smirky and chill.

I pulled my eyes away from them to watch Stix skate. He was so lithe and smooth when he skated and did his tricks. He wasn't perfect, but he was pretty damn good. And he was pretty fucking amazing as a person. I loved everything about him, even the things I previously thought I hated. Thank fuck, I got my head out of my ass and finally recognized our bond. Good thing Stix at least recognized it. Once I let go of all my fears, I realized I'd been waiting for him my entire life. That one person who was so important to me, like my friend Alec, that I'd lost thanks to my parents.

Deep down, I didn't think it was a gay thing. Stix was more than simply an attraction to men. After dating him for a while and recognizing I wasn't so straight, there was no interest in men in general. No one. Just him. Well, Alec had been a dude, but it wasn't about that. Just who he was. How close we were. Who knew? Maybe it was my love for him that kept me solely focused. In the end, I quit caring because I had no plans to ever be with anyone else. My sexuality ceased to be important.

My phone buzzing in my ass yanked my attention away from Stix. I pulled it out and answered it.

"Hello?"

"I'm looking for Damien Sloan."

"This is he."

"Hi, this is Officer Johnston at FPD in Fredericksburg. I'm giving you a courtesy call to inform you that your father, Jimmy Sloan, has been released on parole."

My hands started to tremble and grow clammy as the world washed away and replaced with dark memories of being beaten and burned during his drugged-out rampages.

"Are you still there, Mr. Sloan?"

"Uhm, yes... Thank you."

I hung up, unable to talk anymore or process that my father was out of prison before his time. They warned me it was a possibility. Not just releasing him for good behavior but due to overcrowding in the prisons.

Suddenly, Stix squatted in front of me, looking up with dark, concerned eyes. "Baby, what's happened? Talk to me."

"It's... fine. It's okay. Dad can't find me. He doesn't know where I am." At least, I tried to convince myself of that. The only ones who had my number were the police, obviously.

"Who? Your father?"

I nodded as he grabbed my cold fingers and kissed them on both hands. "Talk to me," he said again.

"He's been released on parole. He's... out."

"Fuck. What do you want to do? Maybe... we can go to the police and show them your scars. Tell them they abused you, and he needs to serve more time?"

I shook my head. "No, there's a statute of limitations. Besides, at the time of his arrest, I'd still been too afraid to come forward. Now, it's too late. And I can't prove that he or my mother caused all these scars."

Pulling away from Stix, I stood and paced, running a hand through my cropped hair. "Fuck. No. No. It's fine. They can't find me. I'm safe."

He stood in front of me to keep me from pacing, then grabbed my shoulders. "Damn right, you're safe. Even if they could find you, you have a big family watching your back. None of us will let them get to you."

"Can... we go home now? I'm not up for... skating."

"Sure, baby. Anything."

Later that night, I was curled up against Stix's naked body. He'd been sleeping over every night now, and I loved it. I loved feeling his lean, hard body pressed against me, filled with warmth and the scent of sleep, along with all things Stix. I nuzzled the back of his neck as we spooned, taking a deep breath of him as my mind drifted to my parents.

While I was safe or had convinced myself of that, I wasn't as afraid as I had been earlier. In fact, I started to think about Stix's bravery in confronting his dad. Sure, it was out of a desperate need to be accepted and end this abandonment thing, but once he realized what a piece of shit his father was, he stood up to him and told him how he felt and how bad his father made him feel. I admired him for it. I'd lived my life in fear. Afraid of my parents and afraid of life. They'd beaten me down so much that I simply breathed, worked, and ate. That was it. That wasn't a life. But now that Stix was in my life, along with his friends and family. I felt wanted and loved. It made me feel strong and want to be a better person. To have something to look forward to as I got older.

Then an idea formed in my mind because I was so fucking tired of being afraid. It was getting better, but today's call reminded me I'd never be free until I faced them. Like Stix, I think I needed closure to move on. To finally let go of the pain, and then I could do what Alpha suggested and find some therapy. Stix was worth it. He deserved the best parts of me. Not just broken ones.

"Stix?" I whispered.

He mumbled and scooted his ass back into me, hitting my dick, which quickly hardened. While I loved being turned on by him more than anyone else had in my life, now wasn't the time.

"Nico..."

"Hmm, wha' babe..."

"Wake up."

Stix stretched and rolled over. "What's wrong?"

"I... want to see my parents."

His eyes blinked open in the filtering light from the city through my blinded window. "Why? They don't deserve to see you."

"I want what you got. Closure from my parents... like you did with your dad."

"You sure?"

"Yeah. Will you come with me?"

"Fuck yeah, I'll be there."

"Okay, I'll get us train tickets for tomorrow morning."

He scooted closer to me and pressed his nose against my chest while draping half of his body over mine like a protective barrier, making me feel loved and safe. "Sounds good, baby."

We left early in the morning, finally on our way to Fredericksburg on an Amtrak train. Stix was lying down and resting his head on my lap, sleeping. I had no idea how he contorted his body to be a small ball in the seat.

My fingers gently played with his hair as I stared out at the Virginia woods and countryside. The sky was gray and ominous, reflecting my mood, and all the trees were bare of leaves. It was still pretty, though I never really appreciated it as a kid, with my life filled with so much ugliness.

I expected to be more afraid than I currently was. Maybe because I wasn't running anymore, ready to face my tormentors, or perhaps because Stix was by my side, making me stronger. Whatever the reason, I was grateful I wasn't a trembling wreck, ready to flee at the first sign of danger.

The train ride was only two and a half hours from Baltimore. It had seemed so far when I first left this place, but it wasn't. Stix and I stepped out of the train station, hand-in-hand, and searched for the Uber I'd already set up for when we arrived. I hated spending the money on my parents, but it needed to be done.

"How are you feeling?" Stix asked when we got into the car and drove off as I stared out the window. The town was pretty and quaint. Not so much where my parents lived, but the town proper was nice. Nicer than Baltimore, anyway.

"I'm alright."

He rested his head on my shoulder, leaving me to my thoughts as we drove the fifteen minutes it took to get to my parent's mobile home park. My roots that I never talked about before. Stix was the first person to see where I came from. Shit, he was the only person who knew what I'd gone through.

The car stopped, and we climbed out before it took off. I stood there, taking in the shitty neighborhood full of rundown trailer homes. Why have something nicer when you could buy drugs? I had no idea what my parents did for money to pay for their habits or pay for anything, really. Mom used to be a nurse, of all things. You'd never know it now. They could've had a happy and decent life were it not for the drinking and drugs. What a fucking waste.

We walked on the dirt road filled with weeds with my hands shoved in my jeans pocket. While I needed his touch, I couldn't bring myself to hold his hand here. I didn't trust the people not to do something horrible. The neighbors we had at the time, if they were still living here, heard my screams and cries. No one came to help.

Dead shrubs, which struggled to make the place look nice and failed, littered the neighborhood. There was garbage in the yards, along with whatever shit they collected and left it out to rot, from cars to washer machines. The place was a hoarder's nightmare.

My parents' house was a rundown doublewide. It had seen better days, which had worsened since I'd left with shutters around the windows falling off or hanging by a thread. There were two rusted metal chairs sitting in a pile of cigarette butts and empty beer cans. I walked up the shaky wooden steps, opened the screen door with a torn screen, and knocked before I second-guessed myself. My stomach twisted in a painful knot, but I tried to ignore it. Now that I was here, that residual pain my parents inflicted was like a ghost across my skin. My body remembered as much as my mind.

I couldn't hear any sound on the other side of the door, so I had no idea if they were home or not. A beat-up Ford Escort was parked out front, but I sensed no movement inside the house.

"Fuck it." I stooped down, reached under the wooden steps, turned over the small, upside-down planter, and pulled out the key, which had always been there in case they lost their keys or got too high to let me in the house.

With shaking hands, I unlocked the door. Only Stix's hand pressed on my back gave me the strength to walk the rest of the way in.

The first thing that hit me was the stench, like garbage, stale cigarette smoke, and body odor, but they hadn't entirely trashed the place. Surprising. Mom used to clean and pick up whenever she was sober.

"Hello?" I called out to silence. "God, this place is such a shithole."

"It's fine, Rolling Stone."

"It's not fine. There's nothing wrong with being poor, but they brought this shit on themselves. Assholes."

I stepped through the living room filled with worn furniture that had been around forever and walked past my old bedroom, completely ignoring it. Only bad memories existed there. Then I stopped in front of a closed door that led to my parents' bedroom and knocked on it.

They still didn't answer, so I just fucking opened it and braced myself for what was inside. My parents could be dead for all I knew, and I found myself not giving a shit if they were. If that made me a bad person, so be it.

The stench of body odor, alcohol, sleep, and stale air was even stronger here. Both of my parents were lying in bed, wrapped around each other, sleeping, or passed out—probably the latter since they didn't wake up to my pounding.

My breath kicked up, and my eyes watered at the sight. If I didn't know better, they looked like two peaceful lovers who'd missed each other. And maybe they were. It was a love I'd never received from them, except before, when they hadn't been stoned out of their gourds.

I stepped inside and touched their throats to make sure they still lived because I must have cared a little. Then, with a deep breath, I walked out, closed their door, and rushed out of the house with Stix close to my heels.

"Hey! Stop, Rolling Stone. Talk to me."

I turned to face him, gathered him in my arms, and buried my face in my neck as the grief hit me. Memories of pain consumed me, but this was my moment of letting go of them and letting go of my past. I hadn't needed to tell them how I felt after all this time. Seeing them there, still passed out, I realized they would never care or understand. It was beyond their drug-induced minds. There would never be any closure from them, so I needed to make my own closure and let them go. My past was over. Now, I only had my future to look forward to—one with the love of my life in it.

Stix slid his arms underneath my jacket and shirt and rubbed his calloused hands across my skin, saying nothing and letting me get it all out. I never appreciated or loved him more than at this moment. His moment of silence to let me handle things as I needed to, without doling out advice and placating me with words.

Once I calmed down, I pulled away and wiped my face with my T-shirt under my jacket. "Ready to go home?" I asked.

He gave me a brief smile before stepping up to me and giving me a small kiss. And right then, I didn't give a shit if it was in front of all these people I had always hated. "Anytime you are, baby."

Fuck, I was even more grateful he didn't question me leaving before I said my piece to my parents and the entire reason for being here. I loved that he understood me. He always had.

We walked off hand-in-hand until we reached the end of the neighborhood before I called an Uber to take us back to the train station.

CHAPTER 33
Stix

As SOON AS I signed on the dotted line... Well, several lines; I rushed out of the realtor's office, gripping a file full of paperwork with Stone close on my heels. My heart was about to burst. He stopped me and turned me to face him.

"You did it, baby," he said. "I'm so fucking proud of you."

I pulled him into a tight hug and swallowed back the happy tears. It was hard to hate my dad after sending me all that money, allowing me to reach at least one of my dreams.

"I can't believe the house is fucking mine."

He said nothing as he kissed my head and rubbed his cold hands under my shirt and jacket.

After learning how to buy a house, I was honestly surprised they still sold it to me despite the hefty amount of money I put down on it. I had little to no credit. However, the owners were desperate to sell, and no other people were interested in the place since it required so much work. The instant thirty thousand down helped a lot, and I had to finance the remaining seventy thousand.

It was a week before Christmas, and while I wanted the house as a present to my mother and sister, it wouldn't be ready on time. The place barely passed inspection, and I still had to set up electricity and running water. Everything seemed to be in working order, so I didn't have to purchase any expensive things. There were only window units to keep the place cool in the summer and radiators to keep the place warm.

Once Christmas was over, all my friends and I would start working on getting the house presentable during our free time, which would take a while, so it probably wouldn't be ready to be lived in until February at best.

"Do you know what you should do now?" Stone asked.

I shook my head, still holding onto him as the emotions calmed the fuck down.

"Let's go buy you some drums you've always wanted. We can store them in the house, and you can play them whenever you have some free time."

God, I wish, but it wasn't going to happen. I didn't need a drum set to tempt me or remind me that not all dreams were meant to come true.

"No. I can't, Rolling Stone."

"Why not? It's what you've always wanted, and you can afford them now."

"Let's be real. I'm never going to be a drummer. Why bother?"

He removed his hands from my back and cupped my face. "Who says that will never happen?"

"I say. The chances are minimal at best. Come on, Stone. We need to be realists. It's a pipe dream. While I'd love to be a drummer and live my life with an awesome band, I'm also happy. I don't have to fulfill all my dreams. Now, I have a house, my wonderful family, and you. My jobs are pretty cool, and I'm making decent money. Not all of us are meant to do great things, and I'm okay with that."

"I won't fight you on that. It's your life, not mine, but I would still like you to get a set of drums. You love creating music. At least play because you love it. Give yourself something."

I guess it couldn't hurt to buy a set and play as a hobby. "Okay. I'll think about it. Wanna see the house?"

"I'd love to."

I hadn't shown Stone the place yet. While I'd shown a couple of friends, my dreams were becoming more elusive, and I needed to stop getting my hopes up. Now that I owned the place, I felt free to show it off.

The ride on our boards took us about twenty minutes to get there. We stopped and stood in front of the townhome, crying and desperate for love, and I would be the one to do that. I really needed to learn how to do most repairs and fix things up myself, but for now, all I needed was to make the home liveable—my home. With time and saving money, I could fix it up nicer.

Instead of climbing in through the window as I had last time, I slipped my key into the door and, with a deep breath, turned it. The lock stuck for a moment, and my gut twisted, worried that I'd wake up from a dream and none of this was real. But then it opened.

Stone kissed my neck with his cold lips as we stepped inside.

"Fuck, I can't believe this is all mine." My voice echoed against the empty rooms and walls, but soon, they would be filled with our things and love. Soon, every inch of this house would be all about happy memories.

I grabbed Stone's hand and pulled him into the kitchen. "It needs new flooring, but I'll worry about that later. And maybe the cabinets need some sanding and staining, but they're functional. But this place is so much bigger than what we have at the apartment."

I opened the refrigerator door, which needed serious cleaning, and once the electricity was turned on, it would hopefully be running. If not, I was sure I could get a used one—same thing with the stove and oven.

Stone ran his hands against the countertops. "These are cool, like butcher's block. You can clean and sand them, and they'll look amazing. No need for new fancy counters."

"Yes! This house has got character, right?"

"Definitely."

I grabbed his hand again and tugged him toward the upstairs and straight into the master bedroom. A room I had initially planned to give Mom, but honestly, I wanted it to be Stone's and my room. Would he move in with me? While we hadn't been together longer than three months, the house wouldn't be ready any time soon, so we had more time to figure things out. We kind of rushed things, but we fell into each other naturally. Besides, he was it for me.

"Look how big this fucking room is," I said. "And it even has its own bathroom. No more fucking sharing between the three of us." I pointed at the ceiling. "And see that molding? Isn't it pretty? The whole house has it, which needs some mending, but it's gorgeous. Damn, maybe I should learn to fix up houses for a job, not that I have any idea if I'd be good at it or not."

"You'll be amazing at it because you're smart as fuck. And your mom is going to love this room. She's going to be so proud of you, baby."

I wrapped my arms around him and looked up into his hazel gems. "I want this room to be ours. The other rooms are bigger, too. More than enough room for Mom and Nova. But this place? I want it as ours."

"Me?"

I nodded. "Yep. Will you move in with me when we're done? I know it's all soon and shit, but I love you, and you love me. We're our forever persons, right?"

"Definitely."

"So, what do you say? Will you be a part of my family?"

Stone frowned and swallowed hard. It wasn't that he was upset. That was his 'uncertain' and 'feeling unworthy' look. I was growing quite familiar with all facets of Stone.

"I mean... what if I screw this up?"

I pressed a quick kiss to his lips. "There's no way."

"Come on, Stix. You said you wanted to be realistic and shit."

"And we've talked about this already. Sure, we could have fights and crap. All couples do, but I'm not dumping your ass over a fight. Just because we disagree on things doesn't make you unworthy or some shit."

He swallowed hard again and nodded. "Okay."

I smiled at him and bit my bottom lip. "Yeah?"

"Yeah."

"Awesome, because the first thing we're going to do is christening it."

"Right now?"

I feigned a pout. "You don't want me? I thought you were perpetually hot for me."

He rolled his eyes, and his smile was crooked. Instead of making a joke back, he turned into controlling Rolling Stone and stood toe-to-toe with me while fisting my hair from behind. "You want me to warm up your cold ass?"

"Yes, please." My voice was breathy, and I was instantly hard for him.

"Drop your pants and put your hands against the wall."

My stomach dipped in anticipation as I undid my pants and slid them down, along with my underwear. I braced myself on the wall that needed a serious painting and pushed my ass out.

"You got lube?" he asked.

"Wallet."

He dug in my pants, pulled out a packet of lube, and opened it. Soon, the first wet finger slipped inside me. Fuck, I loved it when he prepped me. Or just anything, really. Even if we simply lay in bed, holding each other and kissing. I was beyond proud of him for pushing past his fears and insecurities. It didn't take long for Stone to open up and finally be comfortable in his own skin. Sure, he had his moments of doubts, and they would be there for a long time, thanks to the damage inflicted on him by his parents. But for now, he was doing amazingly well, despite his internalized homophobia.

By the second finger, I stopped him. "I'm ready. Just give me your big, gorgeous cock, baby. Let's make this room ours. Let's give this place its first happy memory."

"You got it," he growled, shoving himself in with one hard thrust.

It burned for a moment as he filled and stretched me, but we'd already established that I loved it. It made me feel alive and reminded me of how much I wanted Stone.

"No, I need to see you," he suddenly said.

He quickly pulled out, leaving my ass in hungry and desperate need, before spinning me to face him. He dropped to his knees and pulled off my shoes, pants, and underwear.

I always knew Stone was strong, but not how strong when he lifted me and slammed my back against the wall.

"Wrap your legs around me, Nico," he said in his deep, raspy voice when he was completely turned on.

I did as I was told, and while it was awkward at first, he slipped back inside me. "Hang on for the ride, baby. I want to see your face as you get wrecked."

My legs and arms clung tightly to his hard body as he thrust into me, shoving me harder against the wall each time. My fingers dug into his muscles as his face pressed close to mine. I met him halfway as we panted and grunted through our kisses. Soon, I stopped feeling the cold of the place as I was enveloped by Stone's heat, inside and out. His body burned as he scorched my ass with his hot cum.

I quickly let go of him, lifted my sweatshirt, and jerked myself off while he was still in me. I'd nearly forgotten to get myself off, being so in tune with Stone and his climax.

He adjusted us, but stayed inside as he watched me come all over the fucking place. My head fell back, hitting the wall, as my body was ravaged by wave after wave of pressure, pumping out every last drop on my abs and hand.

Stone finally slipped out of me and set me down while we panted for breath, leaving a cloud of warmth in the cold air. He zipped himself up, and since we had nothing to clean up with, he took my hand and cleaned it with his mouth, and I nearly busted again, watching him lick and suck my fingers. Next went my abs and cock, sitting on his knees, cleaning off the cold cum.

"Fuck, Rolling Stone. How'd you get so hot and sexy?"

He licked his lips as he stood back up. "You bring it out of me, I guess."

I kissed his lips, covered in my bitter essence. "It's always been there, baby."

CHAPTER 34
Stone

IT WAS JUST AFTER Christmas and a couple of days before New Year's Eve. I had never really celebrated Christmas except for the small thing I did with Cueball and Blaze. But this year, I first spent the day with Stix and his family. My first real Christmas since I could remember. I even helped them put together the fake Christmas tree in the living room corner on Christmas Eve, hanging lights and ornaments. Grace also made us a nice ham dinner with mashed potatoes and green beans.

I had sat on the couch with Stix on Christmas day as we exchanged presents. It was weird for me, and I was a little uncomfortable and uncertain about the gifts I picked out for them, not used to this family thing. But Stix told me to get the fuck over it. That his family loved me and to love them back. Presents didn't matter. I had to admit I loved Stix's tough love since I sometimes needed a swift kick in the ass to see things clearly.

I'd gotten Stix a new set of drumsticks that were nicer than his and a little pricier, but his old ones were all banged up, and he needed a new set. I also got him a new keychain for his house key that was also a pair of drumsticks. While he got me one of those weird T-shirts he loved so much. It was in black and said 'Like a Rolling Stone.' Of course, I had to roll my eyes as I put it on. And it wouldn't have been Stix had he not given me the most ridiculous gift of all, which was a pet rock with googly eyes. I named him 'Rock Hudson,' which made Stix laugh.

I got Grace a coffee mug from the aquarium and some fresh fish I cut myself, which we had for Christmas dinner. And for Nova, I got her one of those nightlights that shone on the ceiling, reflecting the Milky Way, which she loved.

Then that afternoon, we spent it celebrating with our friends and skating.

It was the best Christmas ever.

Now, a few days later, I was on the fire escape smoking and freezing my ass off when Stix came climbing out of my window and sat next to me as he plucked the cig from my hand and took a drag before handing it back.

"By all means, smoke mine," I grumbled, but I wasn't really upset with him.

"Don't mind if I do."

He leaned in and gave me a quick kiss. Small kisses, long kisses, dirty kisses, or sensual kisses. They were all equally special when it came to Stix.

"Guess what?"

"What?"

"You're supposed to guess, Rolling Stone."

I grunted and thought about it. "Hmm, you found a new stupid T-shirt."

He snorted a laugh and playfully punched my shoulder. "No, shithead and love of my life. I went to see a real doctor today. A specialist. He cost some money with no health insurance. I'll get some soon as the store is upping my hours to full-time. Thank fuck. Anyway, he's a rheumatologist and said that the company that makes those injections has a program for those who don't have health insurance or a lot of money. They're offering me the injections for cheap once I complete all the proper paperwork. Thank god! Now I can start feeling better and not worry about flare-ups."

My eyes bugged out. "No shit?"

"No shit!"

"Finally!" I wrapped an arm around him, pulled him against me, and kissed his blond head. "You deserve this, baby. Thank fuck, you're going to be feeling good soon. But why didn't you tell me you were going to the doctor? I would've gone with you."

He took my cig and puffed again before handing it back. "Nah, I wanted it to be a surprise. Plus, you were working. Don't lose pay on my account."

"I would quit all my jobs for you, Nico."

"I love you, too, but don't ever fucking do that."

The day was cold as fuck being early January, as we all piled out of Alpha's and Pippin's cars, carrying gallons of paint, brushes, rollers, and more. Shit, even Blaze and Cueball were here to help.

"The place should be warm inside. Once the utilities were turned on, I put on the radiators, so it should be toasty. I do not want to paint while freezing my nuts off."

"Lovely image, Stix," Alpha said, carrying two bags of supplies toward the front door.

"Who doesn't like images of nuts?" he quipped.

Jazz raised her hand. "Yeah, nuts are hairy and wrinkly. No, thanks. Give me a girl's vag any day."

Stix feigned a gag and shuddered. "Girls are gross."

"And you're fucking ten years old," she retorted.

He stuck his tongue out at her and unlocked the front door.

Once we walked inside, Alpha put two fingers into his mouth and blew a loud whistle. "Alright, everyone. Let's get organized. Pippin and Nacho, take the salmon-colored paint, head to the first bedroom on the right, and start painting there. That's going to be Nova's room. Jazz and Blondie will paint the room Grace will stay in. That's the green mist-colored paint."

Blaze raised his hand. "Where do you want me and Cue?"

I raised a brow at his eagerness. He sure was chilling, though he was still a dick now and then. "You're actually going to be with Ajax—"

Ajax looked wide-eyed between Alpha and Blaze and started pacing the empty living room. "No fucking way."

"Yes, fucking way, dude. You and Blaze need to learn to work together."

Ajax huffed and folded his arms, while Blaze looked ready to torment Ajax with a smirk and a comment that would probably result in paint being dumped over Blaze's head. Cueball shook his head at his friend to shut him up before Blaze opened his mouth.

"Cueball, you're with me. We'll be working on stripping wallpaper down here and smoothing out the walls so that we can paint."

Cueball simply nodded and went to work, gathering materials.

"Twins, you all take the second bathroom with the navy blue paint."

Jazz raised her hand. "You sure you want us to paint? It's not exactly something they teach in foster care."

"You'll figure it out, but I'll be in there to guide you."

"Your funeral," she grumbled.

"Of course, Stix and Stone, you all hit the room that will be your bedroom. And no sex."

"You really are a fucking party pooper, Alpha," Stix huffed to his laugh.

"Well, maybe this will make you feel better. When we're done painting, I've hired a cleaning crew to do a deep clean in the house as my gift to your new home."

Stix jumped Alpha and hugged him, saying my thanks as quickly as possible before I yanked him off the other man, growling. Yeah, my jealous tendencies weren't going anywhere anytime soon, but I felt better about them when Stix looked at me with stars in his dark eyes made just for me.

It was evening by the time we stopped painting. I could tell Stix's back was fucking killing him as he grimaced and shifted around until he got comfortable. He took his first injection a week ago, with another injection ready for next week. By then, the doctor said he should start feeling the effects. For now, he had to suffer.

I grabbed two beers and handed one to Stix before I sat down on the dirty wood floors next to him. All our friends were gathered with us, drinking and smoking weed to relax after a hard day. We weren't finished, but we made a big dent in the place. It was already looking better. Once we moved in, Stix would start saving my money to buy some used furniture to fill up the place and fix it up even more, and I planned to help him with that.

I looked over at him as he smiled with a faraway look on his face. "What are you smiling about?" I asked, pressing a kiss to his cheek, speckled in dried pine green paint.

He shrugged. "All the things I want to do to this place to make it our own. Maybe I could even learn to put in some plants out in the tiny front and back yards."

"And we'll be here to help," said Alpha.

Every once in a while, a profound sense of appreciation and love for this strange new family hit me. They had stuck it out with me, despite being such a cold asshole in the beginning. Now, I couldn't imagine a life without them. They'd do anything for each other, always watching their backs and being there when they needed each other. We may have been poor most of our lives, struggling with the losses of family members and friends and being rejected by too many people in society, but together we could survive it.

The house took longer than expected to fix up. God, it was so fucking hard to keep things a secret from Grace, especially for Stix, while we died to move into the new place, but we managed.

It was mid-March, as we took the Uber to the house to finally introduce his mom and sister to their new home. Stix had a blindfold on his mom and Nova to really build the suspense and surprise.

"Nico, where are you taking us that requires a blindfold?"

"Well, if I told you, it'll ruin the surprise. Think of this as an early birthday present."

"Sweetheart, that's not until April."

"I can't wait that long. Stop nagging, woman. We'll get there when we get there!"

She snorted a laugh and tried to smack him, which resulted in her smacking me instead. "Hey, what'd I do? I thought you liked me?"

"Oh, crap... Sorry, Damien. That was meant for Nico."

"I don't like this blindfold on," Nova whined.

"We'll be there in just a minute, munchkin. You're like the worst at keeping secrets."

The car finally pulled up in front of the house, looking infinitely better than the rest of the houses. Well, the place still needed work, and there weren't any plants yet since the weather was too cold out, but it looked so much better than before.

Stix and I helped Grace and Nova out of the car before it drove off, and he finally removed their blindfolds. Nova looked confused, while Grace blinked her eyes and looked right at the old brick townhouse we painted in white.

"What is this place? Who lives here, Nico?"

"I think you know the answer to that, Grace," I said.

She looked right at me, then back at Stix as her eyes watered. "This is ours? How? Where'd you get the money for this place?"

"We get our own house?" Nova yelled.

He laughed and picked her up. "Yep, it's all ours, munchkin."

"Nico... really, where did you get the money for this?"

"Let's go inside first, Mom. Then we can talk there."

As we showed Nova and Grace where their bedrooms were and explored the rest of the house that looked so much better than before, Stix told his Mom how he came into the money from his dad, using it to put money down on the house. She also had no idea he was finally on his injections.

She grew so overwhelmed she ended up sobbing. Stix folded her into his arms as he looked at me with concern in his eyes, which asked if we fucked up somehow.

"Mom, you're supposed to be happy."

"I am, and I'm not. Jesus, I'm supposed to take care of you, but all you've done is take care of me and Nova. I feel... like a horrible parent."

"You're the best parent, Grace," I said. I swallowed as I gave her a quick rundown of my story and what my parents did to me. "So you see? You're amazing. Look at what a wonderful son you've raised."

"I wanted to do this, Mom."

I knew she heard me because she nodded, but then she took Stix's face in her hands. "I know, honey, but this isn't your guilt talking, right?"

"Not anymore. Dad proved it wasn't my fault, but I needed to do something for you and Nova. I want this for all of us. Now, before you get too grateful, and I *am* amazing," Grace rolled her eyes as Stix always used humor and sarcasm to push away uncomfortable moments, "but Stone and I get the master bedroom."

"I wouldn't have it any other way. And I insist on helping with the house payments."

With the three of us contributing, it would be an amazing home full of love. I looked forward to what was in store for Stix and me.

CHAPTER 35
Stone

FIVE YEARS AGO

I pulled back the old, ugly brown and yellow kitchen window curtain, watching as my mother fell to the ground, crying as the police hauled away my father. I was twisted with doubt, disgust, and hope. The disgust came from my pathetic fucking mother, who cared for nothing but herself. The police were hauling away the one man who kept her drugged up and drunk. But the hope was something new. A little wisp of light in so much darkness. With him gone, maybe things would start to change. Mom could get off the drugs, and life could grow to something resembling normalcy.

But the doubt rang the loudest in my mind. Doubt that he'd stay in prison. Doubt Mom would change. And doubt that my life would ever improve. Years of being beaten down left little room for things like hope or happiness.

The noise that grew the loudest was that Dad would be gone at least for a while, and I wouldn't have to suffer his blows, cigarette burns, and belittling words.

The cops interviewed me that night, asking about the drugs, but I couldn't give them any answers. All I knew was that my parents did them, not how they got them or where my dad sold them. Then they asked about my face covered in bruises. As usual, I lied. I shouldn't have, looking back on it, but I was still too afraid and used to lying. They spilled out of my mouth as easily as breathing. The police didn't believe me, but there was little they could do with me being an eighteen-year-old adult.

When they left, everything grew quiet except for Mom's fucking sobbing. The rage filled me, wanting to beat her, too, for it. I fisted my hands, watching her curled up on our beat-up sofa as she wailed. But I held back my clenched hands, not daring to mark her. I refused to turn into my parents, as much as I wanted to hurt her.

"You're fucking pathetic," I said and walked off to my room, where I turned on my ancient CD player, cranking it up to some punk rock loud enough to tune out her crying before I fucking hit something. Those were words I'd never dare say before for fear of my father. Now that he was gone, I had a sense of new found strength.

My door slammed open, and Mom came at me with her spatula from hell. My instinct was to drop to my knees and beg her not to hurt me. But with Dad gone, I held onto my anger instead. The fear was there, but I refused to back down. I was fucking over this life.

"How dare you! Take off your shirt!"

"No!"

"Take it off!"

"Fuck you!"

My entire body trembled in terror and rage. It was an odd combination, but I relished in the anger. Bathed in it. It was so much better than the fear. It made me feel strong and powerful. Like I could do anything.

She took her spatula and smashed my CD player with it, and I didn't stop her. The quiet rang in my ears louder than the music and her yelling.

"Take off your fucking shirt and get on your knees."

"Fuck. You." God, was that my voice? It was eerily calm. I sounded... dangerous.

She must have sensed it, too, because her eyes grew wide and held fear before it morphed into anger, and she lunged at me. I gripped her arm and twisted it enough for her to drop the metal spatula. She cried out as I bent it back further behind her, and then I shoved her out my bedroom door. Mom tumbled to her hands and knees with confusion on her face when she looked back at me, saying nothing.

"You will never touch me again, or I'll fucking kill you."

I slammed my bedroom door, locked it, and fell onto my bed. For the rest of the night, everything was quiet. Mom quit sobbing and didn't come after me again, taking my threat as truth. But it wouldn't last long. She'd eventually cave. Beating me was just another form of addiction for her. Nothing would change.

I climbed out of bed, dug into my tiny closet, and pulled out a duffle bag, tossing some clothes and toiletries inside. At the bottom of my closet, under the floor, I created a cubbyhole where I stashed any money I'd earned into it and grabbed it all. It wasn't much, but it was enough to get me fucking out of here once and for all. I didn't own anything of sentimental value, so I zipped up the bag, snuck out of my room, and grabbed a couple of sodas and snacks.

I quietly left the old mobile home, closing the door behind me and careful not to wake her up. After walking a few feet, I turned to look at the old place. There was nothing there. No emotions that kept me longing for the place. No sense of home or love. Only pain and suffering. I turned around and walked off, never looking back again.

Good fucking riddance.

Present Day

Stix and I walked into the elementary school on Saturday, where the group therapy session was being held. Alpha found me one that specifically talked to those who came from abuse, whether from abusive parents like me or a spouse and others. He said that talking to people like me would help me not feel so alone and that together, we could heal.

I'd been doing much better with my confidence and being more open about my sexuality, but I couldn't deny I had moments where I couldn't breathe. When the fear gripped me so tightly, I felt like I would choke to death. They didn't last long, but the anxiety was enough for Stix to convince me that while I was doing better, I needed more help than what he could provide me.

As we reached the closed doors to the gymnasium, I looked through the glass to see about twelve people sitting in a circle on uncomfortable metal chairs. There was a man in his forties holding a clipboard, I assumed was the therapist. He didn't look as awkward as the others. The whole vibe felt depressing as the doubts threatened to consume me.

Stix tugged on my clammy hand he'd been holding. "Hey, you can do this, Rolling Stone. Once you get to talking and opening up, you'll see that there are others just like you. It's a good way to make new friends, too."

"I don't need any more friends. I have enough."

He smiled, always patient and understanding with me. God, I wasn't sure I would've even come this far had Stix not been this way. "These friends will be more relatable. I get that you're introverted, but I bet they are, too. And we've talked about this. You said you wanted the help, but if it's too much, that's okay. We can come back when you feel you're ready."

See? Understanding as fuck. I loved how he didn't pressure me. With a deep breath, I let it out and nodded. "No, I'm ready. I need to do this... for us."

"No, baby. For you. I love you just as you are." Stix cupped my face, pulled me down into a soft, lingering kiss, and then pressed our foreheads together. "I believe in you."

"I love you," I whispered and pulled away before I stepped through the doors alone. My heart pounded against my chest, and I clenched my fists as I walked over toward the group who all watched me. Fuck.

"Hello, you must be Damien. We wanted to wait for you before we started. I'm Dr. McKenna." He waved his hand toward an empty chair between a hugely pregnant woman and an older man of about sixty.

I sat down, clenching and unclenching my hands to hide how much they were shaking as I looked back at the doors where I had left Stix. He was standing there and gave me a thumbs-up. He promised he wouldn't leave, and I trusted him, but I needed to see him to give me strength.

"You're the newest member of our little group, Damien. I'm glad you're here. Everyone here is just like you, who has suffered at the hands of others. Do you want to tell us a little bit about yourself and why you're here today?"

My throat closed up, and I struggled to breathe, staring back and forth between my feet and Stix. The sweat prickled my back and pits as my leg started to bounce. I couldn't do this. It was too intimate—too many people. Only three people knew my story. Not even my closest friends were aware of what had happened to me. If I couldn't tell my friends, how could I tell people I didn't even know?

"I... uhm..."

Fuck.

God, and the therapist was so patient as he waited for me to speak, but everyone else stared at me. They probably thought I was a nutjob. I bet they had no problems talking and telling their stories openly.

The therapist must have noticed that I kept looking back at the door because he said, "If you want your friend to come in and sit with you, that's fine if it makes you more comfortable. As long as it's fine with the rest of the group."

Everyone murmured their assent.

"Okay," I whispered.

The doctor waved Stix inside. "I think Damien would appreciate you here. There's an extra chair leaning against the wall," he said when Stix walked in.

Stix grabbed the chair, walked over to me, unfolded it, and sat down, taking my hand. I could instantly breathe better. He was fucking magic, I swear.

"Hey, everyone. I'm Nico, Damien's best boyfriend ever."

The group chuckled, and it instantly put me at ease.

"Welcome, Nico," the therapist said.

"Hey, since I'm here, I mean, I've got my own issues I can share if you want."

The therapist nodded at him as I played with Stix's fingers, watching him with a surge of love. His brown eyes twinkled with humor and kindness, and his blond hair flopped in his face, forcing him to finger it back. "Well, apparently, my dad left when I was nineteen after I came out as gay. For years, he made me believe it was my fault for his leaving, wishing I'd never come out because it ruined the family. But recently, when I tried to make amends, he finally admitted he left because he had cheated on my mother and used me as an excuse to hide that fact. Fucks you up, ya know? I mean, he didn't abuse me or anything, but it still fucking hurt."

"Abuse comes in many forms, Nico. Sometimes words and actions are worse than fists," Dr. McKenna said.

Stix's smile dropped, and he swallowed. I know he felt that. I squeezed his hand to show that I was there for him, too, though he was a fucking lot better at it than I was.

"Damien, do you feel more comfortable sharing your story now? It's up to you. There's no deadline to talk. Only when you're ready."

I looked at Stix again as if I could somehow absorb his strength.

"You can do it, Rolling Stone," he whispered, squeezing my hand.

I nodded. "My home life hadn't always been terrible. Not until my parents started taking drugs..."

CHAPTER 36
Stix
Epilogue

EIGHT MONTHS LATER

"Let's celebrate!" I announced to Stone, who was on the computer, signing up for community college courses. He wanted to get certified as a home remodeler after he'd grown interested in it since we'd been working on our house, but it required licensing. This way, we could start our own business together, working on other homes. That was the plan, anyway. I'd already been taking a few courses, but convincing Stone was another story. While his therapy had gone really well, he still struggled with insecurity and worthiness sometimes, though not nearly as often.

"What are we celebrating?"

I rolled my eyes. "The first day you scowled at me, duh. It's been a year, Rolling Stone. How could you possibly forget?"

He rolled his eyes in return. "I'm trying to, but you won't let me."

"Well, if you hadn't scowled at me, we wouldn't be where we are today, now would we? It's a cause for celebration."

"You're so weird. You know that, right?"

I smiled and pecked his cheek with a kiss. "But that's what you love about me."

"Unfortunately."

I snorted a laugh and tugged him up to stand. "Come on. I have a present for you."

"I've already seen your dick."

"Boy, you sure are snarky today. I love it! Seriously, though, we're celebrating those asshats finally going to jail after what they did to you. Sure, they only get five years and deserve more, but now it's one less thing we have to worry about."

"I liked celebrating your first idea more."

"Ugh, make up your mind, Rolling Stone. Hot and cold, I tell ya."

"And *that's* what you love about me."

"I love everything about you," I said before I kissed his nose.

We grabbed our boards and headed outside. The day was fucking hot and humid. I hated wearing shorts because my legs were scrawny as hell, but I'd die from the heat if I didn't. Stone called them chicken legs but said they were sexy chicken legs. I constantly questioned his ability to determine what was sexy or not.

Stone followed me as he banked around corners, hopped off curbs, careful not to get run the fuck over by cars, and did tricks. He looked sexy doing them, and he had gorgeous legs, unlike me. They were full of muscles, and he had tanned skin.

Twenty minutes later, we stopped in front of a tattoo shop.

"Shit, are we getting tats?" he asked with wide eyes and a smirk. I knew how much he loved tats.

"Yep. I've been saving up for this, and you'll get what I tell you to get."

He raised a brow. "Please don't tell me I'm getting one of your quirky sayings or your name on my ass."

I pretended to think about it, rubbing my chin. "You know, an ass tattoo sounds pretty good. I could stare at it as I'm—"

Stone smothered my mouth with his hand. "Trouble. That's what you are. But I'm all up for a tat, just not on my ass, baby."

"Do you trust me?"

"It's not that I don't trust you, sweetheart. I just... question your taste."

"Ugh, you're so mean today."

He quickly kissed my cheek. "Whatever you want."

"Now we're talkin'."

Two hours later, we stepped out of the shop with new tattoos. Stone got a pair of drumsticks, but they were cooler and more ornate than what I had, while I got a tattoo of a rock that looked like it was rolling away. Hey, it was better than tattooing our names.

"Your tattoo is terrible," Stone said, inspecting my bicep where I had it done.

I huffed, feigning being hurt. "Well, *I* love it. It's as exciting as you are, apparently."

He snorted a laugh and bumped me with his hip. "I love mine, though. That was a good idea."

"See! I can come up with cool things sometimes."

Before we skated on, Stone grabbed me by the throat and slammed my back against the brick facade of the building. "I can think of some cool things, too, like what I want to do to you when we get home."

I swallowed under his hand, quickly getting hard. "Yeah, and what's that?"

He leaned close to my ear and bit my lobe until it stung. "Let's just say you won't be able to sit for a week."

"Fuuuck, yeah. Take me home, Stone. Now."

"Good thing Grace and Nova aren't home because I'm going to make you scream."

"You always know my love language, baby."

"Because you know mine."

The End

Afterword

Thank you for reading Stix & Stone. I hope you enjoyed the journey my boys had gone through. This book was important for me to show Stone's struggle. I really tried to convey his confusion and lack of understanding of his feelings and how sometimes internal hatred can be projected outward to those around us. This was especially important with Stix since Stone was completely drawn to him from the beginning and didn't understand why. While Stix could see deeper into Stone than anyone else could. I also did my best to show how he was demisexual without realizing what it was, assuming that something was wrong with him or he was broken, somehow. He clearly wasn't, but he was in his head. He'd been through hell and back. Fear is very good at masking the obvious that sits right in front of us sometimes. I didn't outright say this, but it's implied that he avoided labeling himself because it was labels that harmed him the most. Labels by his parents resulted in pain. It was easier to just *be* rather than apply a name to it.

I wrote Stone a little bit all over the place intentionally, and I hope I didn't annoy my lovely readers too much. You were supposed to find him a bit frustrating. All his confusion and frustration morphed into bullying toward that one person he was drawn to the most. While Stone struggled, I wanted to give him Stix. His balance. The one person who was so much like his Alec from his teen years. The light. The sun. Stone needed Stix's light to finally see what was in front of him, no longer blinded by his internal struggles and self-hatred. He also needed Stix's ultimate patience. While Stone gave Stix, in a strange way, normalcy, removing himself from prostitution while Stone doled out tough truths.

While Stix was the sunshine to Stone's grumpiness, Stix had his own issues from his desperation to be loved by his father, who had abandoned him. You all probably wanted to throttle him when he tried to apologize to his father and make amends. We all know looking in from the outside, things appear quite different, but to Stix, he had blamed himself for his father's abandonment. But what I loved most was when Stix sat with Stone in group therapy and admitted what had happened to his father, realizing his father's abandonment wasn't the worst of it. That gaslighting can sometimes be just as harmful to a young person.

The money Stix received may have been a little far-fetched, but I wanted him to finally achieve at least one of his dreams. Besides, his father owed him, dammit! But a part of me also wanted it realistic. That while we have hopes and dreams, we don't always achieve them or aren't able to. Stix was a realist in this regard, knowing he'd never become a drummer despite how much he loved it.

I would also like to note that I suffer from the same disease Stix does and something that I've had since I was a young teenager. His experience was similar to mine. Others may have different experiences with Ankylosing Spondylitis. This was just my personal experience put into the story.

This book nearly killed me as much as A Home in You. So many changes, and the characters just weren't working out with my outlines I had planned for them, but in the end, I'm happy with them. Next stop... Pippin and Nacho. Will Nacho finally get his man, who is completely oblivious? Some may want Ajax and Blaze next, but they will have to wait. I don't want to do two enemies to lovers, back to back.

FREE - All the Ways I Hate You

https://BookHip.com/JJCRDLB

Acknowledgements

I'm not sure where I would be without the continued support system I've had since my debut novel. I have an amazing team of alpha readers and beta readers, my ARC team, who have no problems giving me their honest opinions, and my Street Team, who push the promotions to really get me noticed and help me succeed as an MM romance author. I love them for it.

Thank you to my husband, Hao, who humors me in all my creative endeavors (which are a lot) while he read my debut novel. Despite my best efforts, I just couldn't get him to read a male/male romance, though he thoroughly respects the genres. But he's always willing to help me make my creations a reality and support me through my overworking.

I also want to give a special thank you to my growing list of author friends, especially Joelle Lynne, and all their amazing support. I love how people can lift each other up. We need more of this.

About the Author

Thank you for reading *Stix & Stone*.

Courtney W. Dixon loves to write steamy romance books, but in each story, she gives her characters challenges and struggles. She writes her characters as having flaws, imperfections, and who don't always do the right thing. Humans are never perfect and make a lot of mistakes in their lives. In the end, she tries to help them grow to be better as they achieve their HEAs.

You can find Courtney working in Central Texas with her husband, two boys, and two crazy dogs, none of whom know how to knock on a door while she's working.

You can also send feedback via email at <u>courtneywdixonauthor@gmail</u> <u>.com</u>

Printed in Great Britain
by Amazon